1700 Grant Street

by KC Decker

Cover Design by Larch Gallagher
Copyright 2018 By KC DECKER

ISBN-10: 0-9993334-3-7
ISBN-13: 978-0-9993334-3-3

His mind is filled with beautiful things,

Past revelations and future sins.

He takes me to places that I've never been,

To the edge of light

Where darkness begins.

—Christy Ann Martine

Chapter One

Forward

Have you ever been at a crossroads in your life? A legitimate, gut-wrenching diverging of your once steady path? A position where no matter which choice you make—you are destroyed, yet…triumphant?

It's one thing to deviate here and there, stumble—if you will. Or perhaps dally with *what could* happen, but I'm talking about the life-altering, affect the rest of your days, kind of decision.

Not to belabor the point, but this isn't about ordering chicken or fish. It's about *who* you end up with. The decision, you see, becomes quite murky when two incredible options present themselves.

In the buffet of life, your entire future depends on tiny little decisions here and there. Do you resist the temptation at the dessert table and stick with your current bounty? Or will you always wonder how life *could have been* if you had only just tasted of it?

This is about potentially looking back, itchy with regret, only to find the path behind you has tarnished like an old septic tank. A relationship you neglected. A kiss you never shared. A smile you forgot to return.

Your previous options are now old and stale, while a whisper from the past mocks your choice like a malignant little friend. *Why didn't you zig instead of zag? Just imagine what could have been.*

When you get to this branching of your life's path, it's not enough to merely choose one direction. No, you must annihilate the rejected road. Lay waste to your other option, because to dance between the two will slowly unravel you.

And it will start with your fickle heart.

Chapter Two

Decisions

I never have been good at making decisions, but between Silas and Salinger, it has to be Silas. I need to put some distance between Salinger and I. You see, I don't trust myself. If I continue to entertain the notion that Salinger is an option for me, I will doom my relationship with Silas.

The unraveling of my life will be my own fault. And the truly sad part is, I've seen this coming down the pipes with laser precision and crystal clarity.

Denial. It tastes like treason in my mouth, but the reality is, I have divided my emotions between two men and hoped to retain some semblance of control over the matter. I have allowed myself to wonder *what if?* And I have hung on to the possibilities like a drowning man clinging to a sword. I have no business falling for two men no matter how great they both are. I need to detach my feelings toward Salinger and fix my relationship with Silas.

It's always been, Silas.

Chapter Three

Trouble

"Do you need some water?" Adelaide asks, as she pensively makes her way toward me. She has a crazed look in her eyes, while ironically her hands are motioning for *me* to stay calm. She can sense the devastation in the air. It resonates in my office—thick, like Silas' disgust and my own reckless folly.

I laugh stiffly at her approach, it's like she needs to disarm a bomb that's strapped to my chest. Her tall, lanky frame is stubborn in its advance, but I can see her outstretched fingers trembling. Her hair is pulled into a sleek bun that gives the illusion, or not, of her forehead and temples being pulled tightly back, which only adds to her look of alarm.

"Adelaide, relax. That was my boyfriend." As shocking to me as it is to her, my voice quavers and hardly makes it past my teeth.

"Oh...ok, well then....perhaps some coffee then?" She lowers her hands and begins to back out of my office. She's pensive, like she wants to believe me but Silas' wrath is still too oppressive, it has not yet dissipated.

"Nothing for me, thank you. This is all just a big misunderstanding. I'll get it figured out. Nothing to worry about. Everything will be just fine."

I realize I'm rambling, mostly to myself and then drop succinctly into my chair. Alone in the metaphorical rubble of my office, the air I suck into my lungs feels stale.

Adelaide resumes her post at the reception desk, but the wild look on her face has not yet diminished. She uses what must be sweaty palms to smooth her already slicked back hair, then busies herself tidying up her desk.

I grab my desk phone and punch in Salinger's extension.

"Yes?" his answer is preoccupied, and I know he's busy with the same end of month deadlines I have looming over me. I'm certain I only have about forty percent of his attention, but what I have to say requires all of it.

"Get in here." I slam the phone down before he can make one of his usual witty remarks. Then I begin seething.

***

Salinger takes his sweet time getting to my office. By the time he struts in, the vehemence I feel has soaked the walls.

"What the fuck?" he asks, seeing I am in no mood to play. He crosses his arms and widens his eyes at me as if annoyed I'm disrupting his productivity. When he cocks his head sharply, prodding me to answer, I snap.

"What is the matter with you?" He further narrows his eyes in confusion.

"What are you talking about, Jessie? I don't have time for this," he motions with his hand, indicating he doesn't have time for me and all my crazy.

"How could you do this to me?" my voice is softer now. "I mean, don't you care about me at all?"

"JB, land the plane. I have no idea what you're getting at."

"This." I hold out the rumpled stack of photos. He walks forward and then takes them from my hand. I watch his face as he looks through the pictures one by one. His expression doesn't change beyond his initial, interested eyebrow lift.

After far too long, I say, "Well?"

"Well what?" he asks, innocently looking up from the pictures.

"Well, did you get your money's worth?" I spit out. He's stunned by the abhorrence in my voice.

"What? You think *I* did this?" his question dangles in clumsy silence.

"Who else Salinger? Who else would do this?" My ribs are tightening and squeezing the breath from my chest.

"Who else? How about Silas, for one? He clearly doesn't trust you," then, with self-satisfaction, "Looks like Mr. Perfect has a chink in his armor."

"He didn't do it. He actually does trust me… Well, he did, anyway."

"Clearly not! Oh, look, one for our Christmas card," he smiles and holds up the 8 x 10 of me grabbing his package. I remember it vividly. The photo was taken out of context, but still looks severely damaging for my relationship.

"Salinger, it wasn't him."

"Well, it wasn't me either," he steps forward and drops the stack on my desk, "I'm serious Jessie, I had nothing to do with those."

"Who then? And why?" I start to shake, but it's from the inside, so Salinger doesn't notice. I can feel my relationship unraveling. It feels like in a cartoon, when a thread gets pulled and the person slowly starts to turn, and then ends up spinning around and around as the sweater disappears. I'm dizzy and suffocating, and the feeling won't stop.

"Easy, JB or you're going to hyperventilate. Do you need some water?"

"Why does everyone keep offering me water?" I ask, my breaths quick and shallow. "Is water supposed to save me from this personal hell?"

"Not exactly, but you are clearly on fire," he clears his throat, "Do you want me to talk to Silas? I will if you think that would help."

I scoff at the thought, "Only if you want a broken jaw. Tell me Salinger, would you like to eat your meals through a straw?"

"Don't be so dramatic. There is nothing in those photos that can't be explained. Well...maybe not the one with your hand on my dick." He assumes the posture of someone deep in thought as he slowly rubs his chin.

"Nope. Nothing to be done for that one."

"Salinger! This isn't funny."

"Honestly Jessie, aren't you more concerned that there is someone out there that has taken such an interest in you? Someone who is obviously following you and taking *pictures* of you?" he over-enunciates the last part like I'm a moron and completely missing the big picture.

"This is psychological warfare, Salinger. I'm not in any real danger. I don't think."

"Ok then, if it's psychological warfare, it's someone who wants Silas and hates you, or vice versa. It's obviously an attempt to cause friction in your relationship."

"I bet it's that bitch, Parker! She hates us both."

"Maybe. What about his ex-girlfriends? And what about Ruby's mother? Could she be stirring the pot?"

"There has been no sign of Ruby's mother for years, and what, *now* she decides she wants Silas and Ruby back? No. It can't be her."

"Ok, then. What if it is Parker?"

"I don't know. I need Devin for that," I crumple my brows while deep in thought, then ask, "How long does one really need to traipse the European countryside anyway?" I really do need to consult Devin, he thrives on this shit.

"Devin's trip must be very inconvenient for you."

"I know, Right?"

Salinger had delivered his last statement with a healthy dose of sarcasm. Unfortunately, it didn't dawn on me until after he had already left my office.

Chapter Four

What now

I skipped my class at the gym after work because I felt too emotionally drained to summon the necessary energy. Now home, I'm antsy with what can only be described as some sort of high-frequency current. It feels like an impending seizure or a gallon of caffeine. I can't sit still, I'm anxious, I'm talking to myself, and my whole body feels like it's purring.

I need to talk to Silas. I need to talk to Devin. And, I should probably eat the Chinese takeout that is sitting on the kitchen counter. It smells a little like burnt hair though, so I mentally cross that obligation off my list.

In an effort to quiet my buzzing thoughts and bodily agitation, I do a set of burpees. Then I slide the two-ton coffee table, one of Devin's designs, across the floor. I shove it right up against the TV console and then congratulate myself for not throwing out my back.

Now that I have more room, I do another set of burpees. Then another. And again.

***

Pretty soon, it makes sense to roll up the huge area rug that, according to Devin, defines the space of the living room. Only this time, I drag it into his bedroom and drop the thing at the base of his bed.

Next, are the wrought iron stools that generally sit at the kitchen island. Those heavy bastards now barricade Devin's closet, along with a few laundry baskets full of various designer knick-knack items. You know, candles, photo frames, artsy centerpieces, wall sconces, decorative pillows, and two unusually large vases full of fake limes.

By the time I finish with my silent tirade, Devin's bedroom is piled high with his belongings, and all the furniture that is too big for his room has been stacked into one, very packed corner of our condo.

While standing here in bare feet and the same skirt and top I wore to work, I realize just how crazy I look. I can see my reflection in the windows, now that I have taken down Devin's majestic, floor to ceiling curtains, and the horror is plain to see.

My hair has come loose from the clip, my eye makeup is smudged— giving my eyes a vacant and disturbingly hollow look, and my pencil skirt has ripped halfway up the side. I look feral like I've been raised by a pack of wild dogs. It is this very image of myself, that causes me to crumble to the floor, sobbing.

I don't know how to explain the photos to Silas, and if I'm totally honest with myself, I know he won't listen anyway. The pictures are irrevocably damaging, yet at the time my actions didn't feel deceptive or treacherous. Too playful *for sure*, but I hadn't kissed or slept with Salinger.

I'm ashamed to admit that I don't know what I would have done if Salinger *had* kissed me, or what would have followed if that particular door had been kicked open. I *do* know I was caught up in the moment, and at that moment, I hadn't been thinking about Silas.

Does that make me a bad person? Or am I just a girl with too many options after a lifetime of sub-par choices?

Besides the physical closeness in the photos, any emotional affair I might be having with Salinger is what it is, regardless of whether I'm at work or a bar. The fact is, I'm attracted to Salinger. His presence in my life has become *very* important to me, and I don't want to lose him in any capacity.

It might be shitty, but I like having him as an option. As much as I hate to admit it, he has been bubbling to the surface as a blue ribbon choice for quite a while now.

However, I *choose* to be with Silas. I see my future with Silas. I *want* a future with Silas. That is, if I haven't driven him away with my insistence on dancing with the devil.

***

Once I'm done crying and my eyes are good and puffy, I sit up and adjust my hair back into semi containment. I plod into the kitchen for some tissues and a reprieve from my own wretched thoughts.

I grab the remote and turn on Pandora. Hopefully, some music will drown out the sound of Silas wanting nothing to do with me anymore. Our relationship had been so promising, our future dazzling.

After a few ghastly bites of takeout straight from the Styrofoam, I drop the container heavily into the sink and abandon it for the tranquil consolation of my bedroom.

Once I finally decide to change out of my work clothes, I realize being idle is the antithesis of what I need, which is to keep busy. So, I get to work cleaning the condo, or as I like to think of it… operation distract my shitty mind from all of its shitty thoughts.

***

It's after midnight by the time I have mopped and polished the hardwood floors, wiped down all the baseboards, scrubbed the windows to an invisible shine and cleaned the kitchen and bathrooms to a meticulous degree.

The resulting brilliance would pass even the most stringent inspection by an OCD sufferer. The sparkling cleanliness of the condo creates a resounding echo. It sounds empty, and it pairs nicely with my hollow soul.

After a slight hesitation, I decide it's still a socially acceptable hour to head down to the parking garage and root the Spackle out of our storage unit. I need to fill the nail holes that pepper the walls so I can re-paint.

***

While I am rinsing the butter knife I had to use for Spackle, instead of the elusive trowel, I hear my laptop clatter with an incoming call. It's 1:45 in the morning, which can only mean one thing, Devin.

I sprint through the shiny emptiness toward my room, where I dive onto my bed and fling open my computer with still-wet hands.

"Hi," I pant.

"Hi yourself. Jessie, what the hell? Have you been rolled down a mountain of shit?" Devin asks with his trademark snark, before taking a sip from his dainty mug of coffee, or tea…or cynicism.

"What's with the red alert e-mail? All kidding aside, are you alright?" Devin asks.

"Hi, Love," Corey says, as his face crowds the screen. "You Ok?"

"What's going on? Surely it must be more than you have forgotten how to shower or brush your hair." Again, Devin. Again, cutting the pleasantries to skip right to the chase.

"This happened." I hold up the photo of Salinger licking my neck. Both guys lean in simultaneously to get a closer look. Corey gasps.

"And this happened." I show them our long embrace.

Silence.

"Aaaaaand, this happened." The damn crotch-grab. The coup de grace.

"Sweetheart! We have only been gone a few days. You have already fallen into Salinger's arms? What about Silas?" Corey seems stunned by my moral ineptitude. Devin just smirks.

"Someone sent these to Silas. They were taken when I was out with the girls."

"That doesn't look like *the girls,* Jessie," Devin says, with condescension dripping from his smiling mouth. I can't tell if he is teasing me or if he is excited to hear about Salinger in bed.

Corey just looks horrified. I can tell thoughts of Silas and Ruby are running through his head, and he is too sincere to keep the disappointment off his face.

"I called him for a ride home. *After* I called you guys *and* Silas. Anyway, it's not what it looks like. All my friends were right there next to us."

"While he kissed your neck and you rubbed him off?" Devin questions, in a drawn out voice.

"No, Devin! It was a joke, someone spilled their margarita on me, and my damn friends goaded Salinger into licking it off. The crotch grab was because I thought he was wearing a cock cage...*for his woman.*"

15

More silence.

"We hugged, and he drove me home. No kissing, no fucking…no cheating."

"Let me get this straight," Devin takes a big deep breath, and I wait for his genuine sentiment, his helpful words of advice.

"Salinger wears a cock cage?"

I drop my head in defeat.

"Honey, I think the bigger issue is that Silas is having you followed. I mean, thatright?" Corey has a look of pity on his face, and I don't like it directed at me.

"That's what I thought at first too, but it wasn't. I think it might have been Parker."

"Why would it be Parker? Because of the champagne stunt? I doubt it." Corey dismisses the idea immediately, and I realize they don't know about how she orchestrated my rape.

"Well, I kind of got her fired. She was part owner, and Silas ended up buying her out. Long story," I can only admit to a fraction of what has gone on between Parker and I, because to give any more credibility to the situation would invite too many questions.

With the exception of this, I have never kept anything from Corey and Devin, and I swear they can read the omission on my face.

"I don't know Jessie, it sounds more like someone is trying to discredit you. The truth will become clear soon enough. Why don't you just wait and see who makes a play for Silas?" Then Corey scrunches his forehead and adds, "Where do you guys stand right now?"

"He is piss—"

"Um, Hello!" Devin bullies his way in. "Do you even care that we spent the day in the presence of the Pietà? I mean, *excuse* me, Miss. Self-

16

Absorbed, but can you stop your egocentric ramblings for a moment? You should at least pretend to appreciate that Michelangelo was the greatest, most prolific artist of the 16th century."

"I'm sorry guys. You're right. The Pietà? Wow." I'm trying really hard to sound interested, but I can't force enough authenticity to read believable. My heartbreak is too poignant.

"For shit sake, Jessie! The man pioneered the Mannerist style of architecture! Does his greatness do nothing to penetrate your dark soul?"

"Devin, stop." Corey moves him boldly from view. "Jessie, it's the middle of the night for you. Have you even been to bed?" Corey's warmth cuts through my shaky facade, and I break.

The crying is instant, the shaking too. I have been somewhat able to repress my feelings, until now. All I want to do is climb up on Corey's lap and sob like a child.

"Sshhhhhhh, it's going to be ok," he promises without conviction.

Chapter Five

Changes

My alarm wakes me with a jolt and I sit up, dismayed by the blaring. The fervor in which I fling forward knocks my laptop to the ground, where it slams shut as it makes contact with the floorboards.

I've only had a few hours of sleep, as evidenced by the bags under my eyes and what feels like finely ground sand beneath the lids.

Without leaving my bed, I text Salinger that I'm working from home today, and to call me if he needs anything. He doesn't respond, but I imagine him snorting with derision before deciding not to bother texting back.

After hoisting my laptop back to my bed and a quiet but earnest prayer for it not to be broken, I open it up, and it flickers to life.

The truly beautiful thing about our condo is the open floor plan. The fact that I don't even need to get out of bed to go measure the space before ordering a new couch is fantastic. Plus, if the measuring tape were to elude me like the trowel did, I would just be wasting my life looking for it.

***

After I've pondered and agonized over every conceivable detail regarding a new couch purchase, I nearly reconsider. The options are endless—size, type, color, style, fabric? or leather? The process is head spinning, primarily because in the grand scheme of things, couches mean very little to someone such as myself. The vague seatability factors are erroneous and inconsequential to me, so I pay them little attention.

In the end, I decide on a taupe sectional made from some sort of velvety, micro-suede. It looks big and comfortable, both necessary for my lonely existence. After clicking *add to cart*, a window pops up, asking if I would like to add decorative pillows to my purchase. Without much thought, I add seven crispy white, creased, and puckered pillows to the cart.

Before my feet even hit the floor for the day, I have spent just over twelve grand of my savings. Oddly, my finger had not even hesitated before clicking *submit order*. Am I financially punishing myself or is it high time I finally purchase some furniture? Probably both, I'm not even sure it matters.

I'm now the proud owner of a farmhouse dining room table and chairs, a large sectional sofa with seven deco pillows, a reclaimed railroad-cart coffee table, a massive white shag area rug, a much too expensive sideboard for below the mounted T.V, a sofa table with matching end tables, sleek new bar stools for the kitchen island, and two gorgeous mercury-glass lamps. On the reasonable side of my prodigious spending spree is the fact that once you spend that much money, the shipping is free.

I feel bratty and entitled to this mega purchase. I've never lived on my own, though I am unquestionably well into adulthood. Beyond my bedroom set and car, I have never really purchased grown-up stuff. Even with the car purchase, my brother Johnathan did the negotiating, while I heeded his advice to keep my lips buttoned up and the heavy sighs to a minimum.

Adding to my lack of adulting, Devin and Corey do most of the grocery shopping and a lion's share of the cooking. Laundry I'll do though. Well, mostly. Unless I leave a load in the dryer (almost always) and Devin folds it neatly and delivers it expeditiously to my room.

So, now I'm wondering, how does someone so successful in business, who has fast-tracked up the career ladder and smashed through the glass ceiling, fail this miserably at adulthood? Is it possible I have been so preoccupied being a consummate professional that I have neglected to mature in real life?

Do grown ass women call in sick to work and stay in bed all day because their boyfriend broke up with them? Probably not, but I bet most women have other women at work to talk to about their breakups. Not me. I work in a very male-dominated field. Adelaide is too young, and the interns are too flighty. Me, I have Salinger, who is a large part of the problem in the first place, and probably prefers me single anyway. Plus his advice would be all jaded and angsty.

I suppose, as an adult with sort of the day off, I should go buy some groceries and paint…and alcohol. So I crawl out of bed, reluctant to face the day without Silas in it, and trudge to the shower.

Chapter Six

Renovate

Devin is going to shit himself when he gets home and realizes that I have paid two college guys to move all his furniture to a storage unit. The rest of his stuff is piled in his room, rendering the space useless to even sleep in.

We have not even done the required paperwork for me to buy the condo from him, and I certainly have not paid him yet, but maybe this will give him a little giddy-up regarding his house hunt. Besides, I am stretching my wings, finding myself, and all that other cliché bullshit people say in times like these. Well, you know what else people say in times like these? *Bottoms up.*

I crack my first beer before 10am and then chug it down. It would be helpful if I could actually swallow the lump of heartache in my throat. It feels like it's stretching my esophagus, like I consumed a golf ball or something. Sadly, I'll probably be hanging on to that little hitch-hiker for a few days or even weeks. I don't see the tide shifting in my favor anytime soon. I'm just hoping after Silas cools off, he will be ready to talk about it.

After opening all the windows and settling on a rather angry Pandora station, I turn to face the pile of drop cloths, rollers, and paint.

I decided on a color that's darker and richer than my sectional, but still taupe. I figure with the baseboards and ceiling already painted a crisp white and the area rug and newly purchased floor to ceiling, wispy white curtains, I will need some color.

The first coat goes on smoothly except for the spot where I touched the ceiling with the roller. Now that little smear of paint is practically lit up against the pristine white ceiling, while the vast white seems to glare at me, appalled that I should tarnish it so.

The cold beers go well with the job, as does the angry music. I had to choose something heavy in order to not be blindsided by a sappy love song. My emotions are only held in check by the fact that I am staying so busy. So busy in fact, the third coat of paint was utterly unnecessary, but I had deemed it useful for filling my time.

A loud knock startles me, so I spin around with the gasp caught in my mouth. I have the front door propped open for the sake of a cross breeze against the battle of the paint fumes. My neighbor Russ is standing in the open doorway with a goofy smile and an awkward half-wave coming from his wrist. I quickly lower the volume of the music, but the damage is already done.

"Russ, I'm so sorry! I thought everyone would be at work. I'll keep it down now that I know you are home."

"No worries, Jessie, I just came to see if you need a step ladder for the trim work," Russ smiles and steps in, looking around in shock.

"Did Devin already move out? We were going to have you guys over for dinner before he left." His sandy hair is clumped back into a loose ponytail that works as a disjointed duet with his delicately trimmed beard.

He and his girlfriend, Jean moved in the same time we did, and have been here the whole time. He is a website designer, and Jean sells advertising. They are sweet in a very soft spoken, gentle, never cuss kind of way. They say things like "Oh, my soul," and use words like,

"Persnickety." As a couple, I assume they always gently make love and never fuck or get a little dirty.

"He and Corey are in Europe. He hasn't moved out yet."

Russ looks around again with raised eyebrows. Apparently, he is skeptical of the vacant condo and Devin's status as an occupant.

"He will be just as shocked as you, believe me," I offer without really feeling the need to explain.

"Look at these floors! I never noticed the glossy finish before. They are stunning…they look wet."

"You know Devin. He has a very distinct opinion when it comes to interior design." I smile thinking back to the fact that the builder refused to finish the wood floors with a glossy polyurethane, so Devin sanded them down and refinished them himself before we moved in.

"Do you want a beer?" I ask, because there is not much else to say.

"Sadly, I'll have to pass on the beer. Jean is meeting me for lunch. Today is the five year anniversary of the day we met," he beams with pride.

"How cute," is what I say, but what I think is, *How lame of you. Why don't you just man up, skip the formal lunch, and make her toes curl while she screams your name?*

"Anyway, do you think you will need that step ladder?" he asks while rocking forward on his toes.

"Sure, thank you. I was wondering how I was going to accomplish the trim up there," I wipe my hands on old tattered jeans and then follow him next door.

***

We walk into Russ and Jean's condo. It's almost the same layout as ours, same enormous windows, same view of the neighboring buildings. The structural differences I notice right away are that they have a full-size washer and dryer laundry room where we added the half bath, and they have a huge pantry where we only have a small one next to our stackable washer and dryer.

The other big distinction between the two condos is the decorating. The difference is glaring, it's night and day. Or perhaps more like metropolitan chic vs. Susie homemaker.

Jean has decorated with quilts, baskets, lace doilies, and craft-show type dolls and figurines. Their living room contains a sensible couch and two armchairs, all in a matching floral print. There is a pallet of old wood on the floor looking weather-beaten and splintery.

If the janky structure next to the pile of wood is any indication, it appears as though Russ is in the process of building a bookshelf with it.

"That's a lot of wood, Russ," I chuckle after my statement because I can almost hear Devin say, *That's what she said.*

"Yeah, it's reclaimed barn wood from Jean's grandparents. They are finally ready to say goodbye to their ancient barn. Jean wanted me to build something from it, so we rented a trailer to haul some of the wood back here. There's only one problem."

"What's that?"

"I'm not a carpenter."

"Right."

"Now Jean just wants it out of here. She says she is tired of picking splinters out of her feet." I look from Russ back to the pallet stacked with planks of grumpy old wood, then back at Russ. Apparently, I'm looking for another time-consuming project.

"I'll take it," I announce.

He looks at me stunned, "I'll help you carry it."

***

Evening is coming on, and as I reflect on my day—Times I've checked in with Salinger…zero. Times I've checked work emails…zero. And times I have checked my office voice mail…also zero—I'm realizing that my job means very little to me right now.

My career goals have been accomplished with single-minded focus and the precision of someone who never questioned the importance of stability. However, that same stability now feels hollow, almost like it will never again be enough.

What I *am* thinking about, in an obsessive manner no less, is if Ruby needs help with her sight words, or what Silas is cooking for dinner. Or, and this is the biggest mind fuck, brain drain of them all—is Silas going to 1462 tonight?

Ever since Silas acquired full ownership of the club, he has been interviewing a constant supply of people to run the admissions and the new member orientations. I think he is having a hard time giving that much control to someone else. *He* wants to be the gatekeeper, *he* wants to decide who can participate. The problem is, admissions on its own is a full-time job.

Every Thursday through Sunday at five o'clock sharp, the membership office opens, and there is a constant flow of hopeful people and potential new members. The steady procession continues until midnight, at which time Mrs. Delacroix locks up and goes home to her perfectly quiet house in the suburbs.

I remember when I was one of the throngs of hopefuls. I had no idea what to expect, and sweet Mrs. Delacroix was my adviser and my introduction to Silas; aka Bishop, the warden of the gate. She stood sentry of what epitomized the old cliché *business in the front, party in the back.*

I've often wondered what Mrs. Delacroix's personal life is like. She is such an enigma. I don't even think Silas knows her first name. She's a walking paradox because she is such a proper, southern woman, that also happens to run interference at a kink club. Yet, upon returning home from working *at a BDSM club*, she looks as though she just led a fundraising event at her church, or been sipping tea at her country club.

Silas and I used to joke around that she probably keeps her slave husband at home in a cage, waiting for her to return. Although, I actually do think her husband is a very normal and well-adjusted person.

Just thinking about Silas conducting interviews and looking for a like-minded replacement, makes me feel even worse. He is relinquishing the position of club gatekeeper so he can have more time with *me*. Further, he is replacing his stand-in; that bitch Parker, because of her treatment of *me*.

The ache in my throat is so strong just thinking about him, I have half a mind to show up and interview for the job. At least I would get to see Silas. I would wilt under his cold, judgmental stare, and probably cry the whole time, but I would do it.

After entertaining the thought for an embarrassing amount of time, I decide I'm not ready to take our breakup to the club yet. So instead, I just stand here, in the paint fumes of my condo and stare at the pneumatic nail gun in my hand. I don't have the foggiest idea how to hook it up to Devin's air compressor, but the project I have in mind will take forever using a hammer.

I think about asking Russ, but then I have a vision of his pathetic attempt at a bookshelf and decide to forge my path alone.

***

I have managed to hang my new, airy chiffon curtains, thanks to the borrowed step ladder. They are currently billowing in with the gentle evening breeze. I like the sharp contrast of the stark white curtains and crown molding against the beige-y gray walls. The woman at the paint counter had said the color was the perfect gray-ige.

Eating has not crossed my mind all day. In fact, I've had the feeling of perpetual nausea since light first hit my pupils this morning, and it has not wavered for a millisecond.

My only saving grace has been these erratic projects I keep taking on. First the cleaning, then practically moving Devin out, then the paint overhaul, now this medley of wooden chaos. The pile of wood, I blame on Devin. If it were not for his creative genius and master craftsman influence, I would never have realized the value of a pile of old decrepit wood.

I take a last look at the pneumatic nail gun before I lay it on the floor, and then make my move toward the heap of wood planks. I start by laying the pieces out. Some are unusable, and some are diamonds in the rough, but the pile itself is the perfect representation of my state of mind. That is to say, haggard and only useful after weeding through the crap.

When I finish separating the wood, I have two groups. Straight, six-foot boards and a discard pile. The discard pile is where the splitting-open planks, join the giant nail-hole planks and the nasty ones with a weird, whitish mold on them.

The hammer, which is jammed through the belt loop of my cutoffs, goes particularly well with Devin's old Johnny Cash t-shirt. The ratty t-shirt hangs off one of my shoulders, and the hem is gathered into a hasty knot and tied at my hip.

I have paint on my knuckles and exhaustion in my eyes, yet I can't slow down, or I will fall apart. It's only been a day since Silas stormed out of my office, and I know I need to somehow explain myself. I need to address the photos, I just don't know how. I can't explain my attraction to Salinger and still convey my desire to be with Silas.

Part of the problem with me picking up the phone is that I know—with absolute certainty—that I was wrong. I can't make it go away. I can't simply apologize and bat my eyelashes at him.

Silas doesn't put up with anything less than total honesty. The expectation is not only for his sake but for Ruby's too. Even if he doesn't know the man in the photos is Salinger, odds are he will eventually find out. When he does, there will be no way for me to crawl out of the hole I have dug. The simple fact that this is the *second* indiscretion with Salinger makes the whole thing incendiary beyond repair.

My inability to explain myself so far is only because there is absolutely nothing I can say to him to defend my actions. Nothing that would help my cause anyway.

How do I apologize without sounding guilty of something? How can I insist Salinger was a complete gentleman without pulling the grenade pin? And furthermore, how can I maintain a friendship with Salinger and all the while keep the fuse lit?

My lack of response to Silas is because I'm afraid. I'm scared of saying too much, or of not saying enough, but most of all, I'm terrified of crossing a line that I can never step back from.

If I fully explain that I called Salinger for a ride and he dropped everything to come to my rescue, and provide all the deeply incriminating evidence about our scandalous evening, Silas will never trust me to be around Salinger again. The fact that Silas *already* suspects Salinger has feelings for me is damaging beyond measure.

Feeling nothing short of defeated, I find the section of wall where my newly purchased sideboard will reside, in seven to ten business days, and begin pounding a nail through the first plank.

I start just above the decorative baseboard. Once the first rugged slab is securely held in place, I pick up the next six-foot section and pound that one solidly in next to the first one, just above the white trim.

When I stand back to admire the first row, I realize I will need to cut the boards into different lengths, or there will be a crease up the middle of my accent wall. I need to stagger the sizes, and for that, I will need Devin's chop saw. Which means I need to find the keys to his shop.

As I wiggle into Devin's nearly impenetrable room, I ponder the stroke he would have if he knew what his bedroom looked like right now.

He appreciates structure and harmony in his space. Being able to manage his environment helps him balance the things he can't control, like his family, his difficult adolescent years or society's response to his lifestyle in general.

He is neat and likes order, but he can be lazy about his convictions too. So, he's not over the top about cleanliness, but he will only let things go so far before he snaps.

Often, if Corey is around, Devin will default to the little boy that just wants to be taken care of, and suddenly become helpless to pick up after himself. Corey, in his perfect human being way, will always nurture this side of Devin's feigned indifference. Although we all know Devin would take care of whatever cluttered item or dirty dish in a hot second should Corey falter.

I know Devin keeps his keys in the nightstand, but getting to them will take the athleticism of an Olympic gymnast, and more than a little balance.

Devin is a kinky guy. He has the stories to prove it, and a "toy box" looming somewhere in his room. I pause with uncertainty once the thought of discovering his stash of kinky sex toys and other various pervertables crosses my mind, but I push on nonetheless.

Easing the drawer of his nightstand open, I am rewarded not just with locating his keys, but by the lack of sexual instruments I was so nervous to discover.

The fact that his sex toys aren't in the nightstand does not in any way indicate his lack of ownership…it merely tells me, there are far more than could ever fit into a drawer.

His sexual playground is seasoned with prostate simulators, ball stretchers, anal toys, and urethral rods. I've heard graphic, sometimes unnerving, and guttural stories about each plaything; because Devin is vigorous in his sexcapades and exploitive with his tales.

Chapter Seven

Warehouse

I nearly tripped the alarm before hastily punching in the code, 7-7-3-4-* which luckily has not been changed in years. Devin chose the disarm code because it spells *hell* upside down. He finds it ironic, due to the heat of the gas forge and his metal working.

Devin's warehouse is 2,000 square feet of machinery, and it smells like billions of charged metal particles in the air, or, more aptly—like an amalgam of old blood and dirty pennies.

The front part of the space is very clean, tidy and Devin-esque. He has a comfortable set up with a sophisticated drafting table and adjustable, spinning metal stool. To one side is a seafoam green, vintage Amana refrigerator; complete with a boomerang-shaped handle.

Next to the fridge is an old school, stand up Ms. Pac-Man game—in all her fuchsia, blue, and canary yellow glory. The arcade game stands lookout, like a foundry mascot or a symbolic totem pole, just as proud as you please.

Devin's lack of showroom at the front of his shop was a deliberate stylistic choice. He prefers to exhibit his work at galas and exposés with all the regalia of royalty. These showcase exhibitions are annual soirées where he can flaunt his wares and secrete his ingenuity and brilliance.

Devin's success in the lighting design industry is evidenced by his endless waiting list of eager buyers. He has been forced to trim the demand for his work by requiring obscene design fees and staggering sales prices. However, his pricing is ironic because he would give the stuff away.

He has always had a unique eye for design that has morphed into something of an *I told you so* for all the naysayers of his past.

Really, he just loves to create, the financial gain is all but inconsequential to him. The money he has acquired serves him more as stone cold validation of his worth better than anything that can be purchased monetarily.

Finances are bittersweet for Devin. He is just not a guy who overly values money. He wants financial security sure, but he is not looking to impress anyone.

I suspect his upbringing has a great deal to do with his convictions. His family was wealthy, they were respected as upstanding citizens, and fundamental churchgoers. However, even though Devin had everything a kid from a materialistic family could possibly want, he had nothing of any real *value* to him.

He desperately wanted unconditional love and acceptance. He ached for even a modest understanding of his inner workings, or a smidgen of the most basic human desire—respect. Because none of these were afforded to him, his self-worth has been built on shaky ground.

No matter how much stabilization he backfills with, the foundation remains rotten, and can't be fixed monetarily. His success in life, when quantified by his obscene paychecks, still provides very little merit for him.

Unfortunately, he learned from a very early age, that money could not provide him with even a modicum of emotional security. That stability, deep seeded in most people, affords a person self-respect and emotional dignity, whereas Devin has had to mine his from barren quarries and impenetrable ground over decades of time.

As a result, Devin is a guy who donates a shocking percentage of his income to the Wounded Warrior program every year, but in keeping with the battle scars of his tutelage, he doesn't want a single accolade for it.

Anyway, getting back to his workspace, everything beyond the domestic scope at the front, is pure industry. Centered in the workshop is a hulking workbench that rests on locking casters. It's a proud island amongst all the equipment.

Lining the brick wall to my left, stands a drill press, metal lathe, jig, and power hammer. I actually know the names and functions of the equipment because of a very thorough introduction and tutorial from Devin.

Years ago, he wanted me familiar with his craft, so he helped me create my own lighting…um, sculpture. My masterpiece had turned into a blocky disaster, and it could have brought down the Titanic when all was said and done.

Devin hadn't felt the need to stifle my creative process with unnecessary burdens, such as any regulations regarding the weight of the thing against its basic connectivity. The whole process had been fun, but it mostly had just left me with a profound respect for metal workers and craftsman in general.

Devin kept the behemoth around for nearly a year, feeling a sort of allegiance to it and to me, but eventually, it ended up in the metal scrap yard to live out its days with the rest of life's discards.

Moving on, a row of metal cabinets are arranged against the wall to my right and neatly tagged with such labels as *bits, clamps, respirators and carbide inserts.* Next to the industrial cabinets are a row of various saws, standing staunch as the Queen's guard.

Devin's workbench is strewn with power drills and sanders, levels, and utility knives. Hanging from above is a bulky exhaust ventilation system. The gaping tubes span two feet in diameter and dangle from various points near the ceiling.

The back of the warehouse is where the forge typically emanates the otherworldly feeling of a post-apocalyptic sci-fi movie. The space is sectioned off by a rack of hammers, chisels, and tongs, with exploration beyond the massive cylindrical forge blocked by a huge cast iron anvil.

Next to the forge is a horse trough, full of dirty water and smelling of charged particles and brimstone. Devin refers to the trough as a *slack tub* and doesn't change the water nearly enough, judging by its rancid odor.

It looks to me like he has taken a propane torch and scorched the words '*Safety First*' into the brick above his protective equipment. I can't tell if he was being clever or defiant when he did it, but there is a certain irony in the act itself, don't you think?

As I wander around looking for his chop saw, it dawns on me how much I miss Devin and Corey. The ache in my heart has been steadily swelling just feeling Devin's presence in the shop, and I'm forced to acknowledge that I am no good as a lone wolf. Without Silas, Corey, and Devin, I am empty and desperately lonely.

There is an old saying that says, *you can't truly love another until you can love yourself,* but I have spent a couple of days solo now, and it's painfully clear that I'm not enough for me.

I can't be happy and satisfied without feeling the grip of neediness. I feel like I'm adrift in unnavigable seas, and the worst part is that I don't even want to try to maneuver through them alone.

I sink down to the grimy cement floor and allow myself to cry, with my face buried in Devin's stiff, battered, leather apron. It smells like gunmetal and the atmosphere of deep space; perfect for the black hole I'm trapped in.

***

The amount of energy I've utilized transferring the damn chop saw from Devin's shop to my condo, feels exponentially greater than what I would have used running an ultra marathon. Now I'm lying on the floor, panting and splayed out like a snow angel.

I start to giggle, though admittedly, it's quite a manic swing from my previous hour. I picture myself—winded in the elevator, bent over with both hands on my knees, trying to summon my last bit of strength just to muscle the cumbersome saw off the elevator.

I had managed to shove it across the floor of the elevator into the gap between the open doors while trying to catch my breath. Evidently, the doors had taken exception to being prevented from closing, so a shrill buzzer went off while the doors stubbornly and repeatedly attempted to close.

By that point, my back had refused to lift the little bastard again, so I just gave it another slow, yet mighty shove with my foot. This time it scooched far enough to actually catch the lip of the saw base in the elevator floor gap to the abyss.

Then, as if the squealing buzzer wasn't bad enough on its own, it had been joined by a clanging alarm; I guess, just in case you missed the death screech of the warning buzzer.

In a desperate attempt to quiet the noise, I had stepped out and tried to tug the saw from the elevator, while lifting just enough to free the metal lip. It must have looked like I was caught in a tug-of-war with someone inside the elevator. My face, beet red, my heels dug in…it was a sight, I'm sure.

Once my retrospective laughing fit subsides a little, I start to wonder what Silas is doing, and the giggles segway into whimpers. Soon enough, the tears come again. I roll to my side and sob, balled up like a wad of trash.

***

I'm cramming the pads of my thumb and pointer into my puffy eyes. As well as trying to breathe through the diaphragm spasms that are causing irregular and sharp inhales, in response to my crying jag. I need to call Silas, even if I can't exactly explain myself. I owe it to him, and I owe it to myself to try. I'm totally confident I will sound like a bumbling idiot, but it will certainly come from the heart.

I head to my room and shut the door, though I'm not sure why. I can feel the anxiety prickling at my skin while I pace the floor by the foot of my bed.

My lips are feeling blanched and numb, I'm sure it's symbolic of something wretched, but I grab my phone anyway.

Hi, it's Silas. Leave a message.

BEEP

"It's me. I just, I just… wanted to hear your voice and tell you, I love you. You should also know that, since our very first date, I have not kissed—much less fucked another man." Then in a much smaller voice, I add, "You are just going to have to trust me, Silas. Never mind what you think…you *know* me." There is a long pause before I finally hang up, then find myself frozen like a wax sculpture and looking at the phone as if waiting for a response.

Salinger feels like a loose end that I need to trim off. His very existence represents constant friction in my relationship; if I even still have a relationship. He will be an incessant question in my mind... *what if?*

Working with Salinger and being around him at all, is asking for trouble, but I can't *not* be around him. I won't close the door completely on Salinger, and this simple fact will probably be my downfall. I am a flawed individual, and worse yet, I'm not even willing to sever the gangrenous limb.

I wish I could look ahead, see where my path diverges and know what my future has in store for me. Option one, veer right and have this life with Silas...Option two, head left and have this life with Salinger. I feel like I'm being forced to choose a college major while still in second grade.

The truly gut-wrenching part of this whole thing is that having feelings for Salinger doesn't even lessen my love for Silas. You would think if I'm one hundred percent in love with Silas, there would be no room for other possibilities, but that's not how it works. Not for a selfish, emotional masochist like me.

I am simply going to have to tamp down any musings about Salinger and realize my traitorous, fickle heart will only destroy me if given the chance.

It's Silas. It has always been Silas.

I'm still staring at the phone, so I press my sister Alyssa's number. She has a no-nonsense wit that will cheer me up at the very least. Sometimes life is easier to maneuver once you see it through an objective set of eyes. Besides, she already knows most of the story, I just have to fill in the last shitty little bit.

I get her voicemail then hang up because the chance of her even listening to my message is slim. Even her recorded voice quips, *Are you sure you can't just text me?*

I crawl into bed and pull the covers over me. Next call, Mom. They should still be awake. On the fourth ring, my dad picks up.

"Jessie, my girl! What a nice surprise. Wait, are you in jail? Or do you need drug money?" He is teasing about my infrequent phone calls, but just hearing his voice causes my eyes to flood with tears.

"Hi, Dad," my voice cracks a touch, and I almost lose it.

"Is everything ok?" he asks, immediately tuned in to my quaking voice.

"Silas broke up with me." I have to hold my breath after speaking to keep the crying at bay.

"Why?" He genuinely sounds puzzled as to why anyone would even think about breaking up with me.

"He saw me out with another man," I say, leaving out most of the story because it sounds like napalm, even to me.

"Jessie, when are you going to realize you need to stop wondering if the grass is greener on the other side of the fence? That's just it, don't you understand? It is not…it's the same. There are weeds over there too. It might look really pretty and effortless, but that's an illusion."

"I know, Dad. I wasn't dating the other man, he's just a friend."

"Well, you just be careful of that little girl. You have a responsibility to her whether you know it or not."

"I'm trying to fix it, I just don't know how."

"Jessie, if you didn't do anything wrong, there would be nothing to fix. That tells me right there that you need to take accountability for your actions."

"Dad, it's not like it seems, I didn't even kiss the other man."

"Evidently you gave Silas *something* to gnaw on," he scoffs. "Plus, you're a beautiful woman, but that won't do you a darn bit of good if you're not an honest one. A beautiful woman who can't be trusted is a liability." He clears his throat, "Silas strikes me as a reasonable man, but even so, I'll bet he'd chew his own arm off if it meant protecting Ruby."

Chapter Eight

Night

I wake up in the middle of the night, shrieking like a howler monkey. The hoarseness in my voice tells me the screaming has gone on for a while. Even so, I don't immediately stop once I realize I'm awake. My body is shaking uncontrollably, and I'm drenched in sweat—my bed sodden with the mania of terror.

For me, the nightmares don't end with wakefulness. They hover around me like a bad omen, while the discontent settles in for hours. I lie back and remain stock-still in my bed, where the sheets have grown cold and inhospitable.

I'm always too petrified to move because I can *never* shake the feeling that someone or something sinister is in my presence, perched above my bed like an unseen gargoyle. My fear shivers are amplified by the cold, clammy embrace of the damp sheets, but I can't bring myself to get up and change the bedding or my clothes.

Usually, I can't remember the nightmares—or perhaps my conscious brain suppresses them, but I am *prodigiously* aware of being lit-up with terror. It's always the resounding fear that hangs on, not the nightmare itself. This time though, there is no dream amnesia, no repression of the details. This time I remember everything.

In the dream, I was standing next to a field of wheat. The stalks were almost five feet tall, with their wispy heads swaying in the breeze. The field went on forever, as did the infinite feeling of impending doom.

The atmosphere prickled, like an approaching electrical storm. Everything was quiet, yet the silence resonated as if I was underwater. I was trapped in this strange and otherworldly setting all alone.

The anxiety was closing in on me, heavy as wet burlap, while it swelled and receded like the breath of a dragon.

All of a sudden, I wasn't alone. An old woman had appeared at my side. She was silent, but she represented a malevolent force, like the crotchety old witch in those dark children's tales.

She turned her head in a slow, rickety way like her head had rusted to her neck and hadn't moved in decades. I could feel my heart beating— harder, faster, bigger, stronger; with the intensity building to a ridiculous crescendo.

When her eyes met mine, her face split into an inky black smile. It felt like she was draining the soul from my body with her ferocious sneer.

I could feel the acid and the vomit begin to pump into my throat. Then, quick as a whip, she reached into my body and yanked out my lungs, and flung them into the field.

I instantly could not breathe, and my eyes bulged with the strain. The instant my vibrant, pillowy lungs were swallowed by the wheat crop, the swaying field turned into a vast, surging ocean.

Without thinking, I lept into the churning water desperate to retrieve my lungs and restore my breath. As I was frantically searching the ever-changing, violent waves, I could hear the women's cackle; it was with me still as I woke screaming.

I try to comfort myself with a silent chant, *It was just a dream, It was just a dream, It was just a dream*, but it doesn't help, it never helps. I rationally try to remind myself that the nightmares are rooted in my anxiety. I reason, they are just my subconscious mind trying to purge the pent up, residual fear and uncertainty lingering from my "attack."

This is usually the point when Silas moves me to a dry area of the bed, covers my shivering frame with a new blanket, and snuggles me against him while he whispers his own chant into my ear, *Everything is going to be ok, you're safe now. Everything is going to be ok, you're safe now. Everything is going to be ok, you're safe now.*

In the first few weeks after my attack, he couldn't hold me like he does now. All he could do then was turn on the light and speak to me in a soothing tone until I fell back to sleep. Although usually, falling back to sleep took hours due to the massive surge of adrenaline, courtesy of my fight or flight response.

After a couple nights of this, and quickly running out of soothing endearments and self-loathing chastisements, Silas decided it would be more helpful to read to me.

At first, all he had on hand was a Dale Carnegie book about leadership. But he read it with such a soothing cadence, that he delivered me back to sleep under the prophetic words of the business pioneer. Since then, we have made our way through quite an array of fiction, and more recently, poetry.

I think the shift to poetry, accurately illustrates the winding down of my nightmares. Now, much less time is required to calm my nighttime sufferings. Sometimes I'm even able to drift off, safely in his arms, with nothing more than a few loving encouragements.

This is not the case tonight. No, tonight I remain in my sweat-soaked blankets. Cold, petrified, and missing Silas more than ever. It's going to be a long night. I gaze blindly at the ceiling while warm tears forge across my temples in constant supply. Otherwise, I'm too afraid to move or to even close my eyes.

KC Decker

Chapter Nine

Busy

In hindsight, the cleaning was premature. I glance around at the mist of sawdust coating every conceivable surface in the condo and wonder, *exactly when did I decide it was a good idea to build an accent wall out of old barn wood?*

In the light of the morning, through the wood-particle dust motes, I look at the planks laid out on the floor. They are positioned in a perfectly measured and cut rectangle, just how they will look once they're nailed to the wall. The care in which I took to make sure each plank was inconsistently staggered would make even Devin proud. Although, he wouldn't have tolerated my use of the saw without proper eye protection, not even for a second. His safety glasses were too big and kept sliding down my nose, so I decided they were more of a safety hazard and just left them hanging around my neck.

The next step in the Great Barnwood Extravaganza is getting the planks affixed to the wall. This will have to be done the old fashioned way—with a hammer because to me, the air compressor looks more like a nuke and I don't want to explode it while attempting to hook anything up.

It's a sunny nine thirty before I realize I need to call into work. I know Salinger will cover for me for a while, but I can't take that for granted. I try to blow the residual dust off the skim coat of my coffee, but when it does nothing more than ripple on the surface, I shrug and take a sip anyway.

I wonder when I stopped caring about seemingly insignificant things like sawdust in my coffee, talking to Devin before moving him out, or about going to work? Maybe those things really aren't insignificant, but I can't quite bring myself to care. It's like having PMS and *knowing* you're being a bitch, but not modifying your behavior in the slightest.

"JB, what the hell is going on? Do I need to send a search party out?" Salinger answers on the first ring, and his reprimand still manages to sound playful.

"No, of course not. I've just been working from home a little," I try to sound breezy, but it just comes out flat and indifferent sounding.

"Bullshit. You haven't even logged into your computer. Is this about the pictures?" Salinger gets right to the meat of it.

"No. I'm just feeling a little overworked, I needed a little time off, that's all."

"Uh, huh. Well, that's not really how it works, Princess. You see, we have quarterly reports due here soon, soooo department time isn't exactly an option right now."

"I know, I'll be back tomorrow. And I'll work late." The strength of my conviction sounds more like a soggy piece of bread than a real commitment.

"JB."

"What?"

"If I Facetime you right now, will I see you lying in bed, in a dark cave, with three-day-old makeup, and a tear streaked pillow?"

"No."

"Ok then, get your ass to work, we have deadlines."

"I mean, yes," I change course.

"That's what I was afraid of. Alright, I'll see you tomorrow." I can hear the resignation in his voice.

"Ok, see you tomorrow," I say after a pause.

"Jessie?"

"What?"

"Call me if you need anything."

***

After hanging up with Salinger, I address my next forced obligation—Devin and Corey. I take a few minutes to blow through their social media feeds and comment on their adventures like the good friend I am. I leave comments like, *Looks amazing!* and *Wow, that is so beautiful!* and then 'like' a bunch of their photos, and familiarize myself with their basic itinerary. I *am*, however, disappointed in the fact I have to muster the will to even do that much.

My apathy is getting the better of me, and I need to snap out of it. I'm losing sight of the people who love and care about me because I'm focusing too much on the man who currently does not.

I'm not at all present for the individuals whose affection doesn't swing quite so indiscriminately between sides of the pendulum, and that's not fair to them. I need to work on that, and soon, but first I'm going to call Silas again.

Hi, it's Silas. Leave a message.

BEEP

"Hi, I was just hoping you would stop brooding long enough to actually talk to me," then I pause as if he is going to reply. Realizing he is not, I charge forward, "So you just go right on ahead with your despondent little freeze-out because the silent treatment suits me just fine. In fact, you can keep marinating in your trumped up version of what *never* happened, because I only wanted to talk to Ruby anyway... We were right in the middle of a book, and I know she wants to know how it ends. Oh, and don't even *think* of stepping in and reading her the last few chapters... because *The Magic Tree House* bedtime routine is **mine**. I'm serious Silas, don't do it, you would mess up all the voices and wreak the whole thing. So, just, don't." Then there is another awkward pause, followed by some sort of verbal punctuation, "Bye."

"Ugh," I voice out loud, as I try to shake off the fact that I just left that rambling, angry, and all-over-the-place message, by flinging my arms around like I'm swatting at flies in the air. When my little outburst does nothing to erase the last five minutes, I stalk off in search of the hammer.

***

I'm still wearing what has fast become a uniform over the last few days, Devin's beat up Johnny Cash t-shirt and equally ragged cutoff jeans. I did have the sense to remove my itchy, lace bra before going to bed, but this morning I haven't even bothered putting it back on.

My dirty hair screams of complete and total abandonment. It hangs in wavy clumps, so I look like I belong in a late nineties grunge band. Completing the perfect image of failure to launch, is the fact that I haven't brushed my teeth in days. The disintegration of my basic daily hygiene is further evidence that I have plummeted into Fuck-it-ville.

I'm legitimately worried that if left to my own devices, I would just carry on like this forever. The simple fact is that I need people in my life like Devin, he would at least sprinkle me with lye and then hose me off.

Anyway, with nothing to keep me company except my own stink, I get to work hammering the planks of barn wood to the wall. I start off with visions of a maximum of five hits per nail, with four to six nails per plank depending on their length. Easy, quick and done.

Well, turns out reality is a bit different from the fantasy because I immediately wreak the first two planks when the nail creates a huge fissure that splits each board wide open. The process is further handicapped by the fact that I can't hit the nail straight to save my life, so right out of the gate, I have a bunch of bent nails and what has essentially become tinder. I figure the nails I'm using are probably too big, but even that is not enough to stop me as I surge ahead, already tired of this project.

***

After about two hours longer than I had planned on the entire job taking me, the bottom four rows are up. They look great, but I'm not even halfway finished, and I thoroughly hate this project. I should have gone to work, this is beyond ridiculous.

"You need a brad nailer," comes a voice from the doorway that both startles and delights me. I slowly turn around to face him.

"Silas," is all I can say and it comes out like a whisper. He is standing in the open doorway, completely composed and perfect. He's wearing work clothes though he has loosened his tie, causing it to hang a little crooked. He's not smiling, but he doesn't look angry either.

I'm not sure what to do or say. Literally, all I can think about is how I must look like a bargain counter, crack whore. I want to run over and throw my arms around him, but I'm not sure if he is here to reconcile or to bring some of my stuff back. Consequently, I just stand here gawking at him.

He holds his ground too, not saying anything, and giving nothing away as to his intent. Finally, I break, as tears fill my eyes and I quickly blink them away.

"I'm sorry. I was wrong. It was all playful, amongst friends, and completely taken out of context, but this time you have every right to be mad at me. I was wrong, and I'm sorry." In my hand, the hammer begins to slip, calling my attention to how sweaty my palms are.

"This time?" he asks.

"Yes, this time, because last time you were this mad at me, I was totally innocent. Remember when Salinger barged into my hotel room?" He snorts, but takes a step inside and closes the door behind him.

"Even though I was surrounded by my girlfriends, and idiot drunk, I let that go way too far."

"Did you fuck him?"

"Silas! No. Of course not. Do you think so little of me?"

"I'm not really sure what to think of you when I see your hand all over another man's cock."

"I can explain," I say weakly, as my mind races through how I can possibly express that I thought Salinger was wearing a cock cage, without sounding flippant.

"Is this where you explain to me that my dick isn't enough for you?" I'm stunned by his question, so I just stand here with a grimace on my face while a slow exhale tumbles out of me.

"Because the club is bursting with guys that would fuck you from the word go. I'm serious Jessie, if all you are looking for is to get railed and not have to answer to anyone, then just say it." His response is so callous, it's like there has never been emotion behind sex and all anyone even cares about is the carnality of the act.

"I said I didn't fuck him! Do you honestly think all I care about is getting *railed?* Don't you know how much I fucking love you? I mean…look at me, I'm a mess. I haven't even gone to work, much less eaten or showered!"

"You are a mess."

"And look at you. You aren't even fazed. Maybe *I'm* the one who isn't enough for you." Then a thought crosses my mind, and I can feel the color run from my face.

"Have you been fucking other women at the club?"

He stands there with a stupid, shit-eating grin on his face, but he doesn't reply. My stomach rolls.

"Oh my God."

Still no response.

I turn on my heel and walk to my bedroom, hardly able to keep the dismay from rioting in the form of vomit. I lock myself in the bathroom and aggressively crank on the shower. There is nothing that will be able to wash this feeling off of me, but I refuse to stand in the same room with Silas and the smug look on his face.

He has been with someone else.

The thought rips through my heart, as I yank off my clothes and step into the scalding water. He has now used sex as a weapon against me, and I can't defend myself against that kind of warfare. The emotional carnage feels like an Agent Orange leaden rice patty field. With time crops may grow, but will the ground ever reap a healthy harvest? Can I ever forgive him for sinking so low just to spite me? Or even worse, just to hurt me?

I'm not sure which comes first, the tears or the dry heaving, but I'm kneeling on the shower floor with my hands planted for stability, and both actions are violently and selfishly claiming my body. I remain on the shower floor until the water turns cold and merciless.

Under the chilly spray of the shower, I quickly wash my body, then aggressively scrub the greasy clumps from my hair. When I step out, I feel like half of the person who entered the shower. I feel empty and disgusted; burned by his needless revenge.

While forcefully brushing my teeth, I realize I have done this to myself. I should have followed Silas out of my office and pleaded with him to listen to the truth. All this time spent in pitiful isolation as my life unravels, and he has been busy burying his cock in any number of willing vessels.

Some coffee-laced stomach acid rolls onto my tongue. I spit it out with a mouthful of foamy toothpaste, then squeeze my eyes together trying to erase the image in my mind.

Chapter Ten

Still

I put on another one of Devin's hand me down t-shirts. Although rather than actually paying tribute to Bob Dylan, it's more so I can absorb comfort from Devin in the form of his castoff shirts. It's his comfort assist from across the ocean I suppose, through t-shirt osmosis. I've cut the neck hem out of this one too, so it hangs sloppily off my shoulder just like the Johnny Cash one that's still crumpled on my bathroom floor.

I'm not sure how I'm going to deal with knowing Silas has fucked around. I get that he owns a sex club and has unrestrained access to women, but I really thought we had something special.

It sounds so naive of me—and to even voice it, shows just how stupid and gullible I really am. Of course someone like Silas is going to partake in the gluttonous offerings at the club. In fact, the moment he felt himself single, all he had to do was *oblige* one of the countless women haughtily waving her sexuality in his face. Those women are everywhere, they sprout like fungus, and they care nothing for those whose heart they are helping to break.

I'm angry now, as I forcefully step into the first pair of clean underwear I lay hands on. They are boy shorts, and probably symbolic of no longer needing sexy panties.

When I glance toward the twisted sheets on my bed, I'm reminded of last night's nightmare, and my anger intensifies. Silas is the reason I even have those wretched nightmares, and now...now he is having sex with someone else! Well, screw him! Screw her! Fuck my nightmares! Fuck my job! And fuck my life!

Normally when I get this agitated, the first thing I want to do is go to the gym to burn off the crackling fury. Preventing me from doing so, is the fact I've hardly ingested anything except coffee and beer for the last few days. Consequently, I already see stars if I stand up too fast.

I could never get through a workout while feeling this depleted, so I settle for ripping the sheets off the bed with vicious abandon. They smell like a high school locker room and are still damp in sections from the profusion of sweat.

Still furious, I storm out of my room with the balled up sheets tucked under one arm. I stop short when I see Silas standing by the accent wall.

It's been well over an hour since I left the room to shower and cry. I was positive there was absolutely zero chance he would still be here. But here he is. Just standing there with his sleeves rolled up, nailing a piece of barn wood to the wall with Devin's pneumatic nailer.

I pause for a bit, struck dumb by his presence. Then, with fierce determination, I storm right past him to deposit my sheets in the washing machine. Adding the detergent pod and fiddling with the temperature buttons buys me a scrap of time to compose myself.

"What are you still doing here? Haven't you done enough damage for one day?" I spit out.

"Jessie."

"No, I get it. You thought I cheated on you, so you fell on the first little club whore who crossed your path."

"Jessie."

"Stop! I can't stomach any more. I bet you still smell like her dirty panties!"

He has the nerve to chuckle, "Jessie."

"Silas NO! If you have so little respect for me, for the fact that I love you, and your, your, daughter—that you couldn't even return my call before stuffing your face between another woman's legs, then FUCK OFF!"

"Fuck off?"

"Yes, Fuck off! You know, actual grown-ups talk about things that are bothering them before they just...just, lay waste to the whole sloppy thing."

"Is that right?"

"Yes, you Fucker! They actually have conversations and they *com-m-un-i-cate* with each other! That way, when one of them has **jumped to conclusions**, the other one can straighten him out before he goes off and pumps his seed into some little skank just to hurt the other one!" I'm panting, this rage is taking more energy than I've summoned in days.

"Yes Silas, communication really does save relationships. And not because people are never wrong, but because it stops them from doing stupid shit that completely annihilates the relationship!" I'm all in now, waving my arms and being more expressive than I've ever been in my life and I'm annunciating each word like he is dimwitted. I'm riled up, almost ready to throat punch the self-righteousness right through him.

"Are you done?"

"Am I done? That's a stupid question! I've only just started. I haven't even touched on how badly this will crush Ruby. Have you even thought about how you are going to explain this to her? And while we're on the topic of Ruby, how exactly are you going to teach her not to put up with any shit from men, when you are so busy dishing it out? Huh?" To my horror, and also completely dissolving my ferocious veneer, my voice cracks on the mention of Ruby.

"Your accusations are a bit laced with hypocrisy. Don't you think?"

"Hypocrisy? Do you even hear yourself? I put my hand on a dude's *jean covered* package, because he told me he was wearing a cock cage, and I was drunk and had no impulse control. YOU FUCKED ANOTHER WOMAN!"

"Done yet?" he asks, then tilts his head almost patronizingly to wait for my incoming tirade to pass.

"Yes, Silas, I'm done. I'm done with you always assuming the worst of me and then shutting me out while you pout like a child. I'm done because I will never be able to be intimate with you again without thinking about her wrapped around you. I'm just...done, with you." I'm broken now, not sure how much longer I can hold it together. Fighting with him had been cathartic, but now I have nothing left but disappointment and unabiding sadness.

I start to walk back to my room while still in one piece. I'm fractured, but not yet in tiny shards on the floor. I can hardly keep the heartbreak off my face as I brush past him.

I'm not even angry anymore, but I am totally devastated by the finality of it. When I said I would never be able to be with him without thinking about her, it wasn't all bluster. I know myself, and the knowledge of such a thing would hover over me forever. What's worse is that I would never be able to trust him again, I'd always wonder, and that's no way to forge a future together.

In the space of a heartbeat, he is pulling me into him. Suddenly I'm cradled against his chest with one set of his fingers entwined in my damp hair and his other hand at the small of my back, preventing my escape.

I struggle to get away before the tears come, but the attempt is futile because they are already here. I can smell his skin, his scent is so familiar and dizzying to me that it's almost cruel to infuse me with it. He always smells like faint, day-old cologne; warm and sporty and animalistic.

I'm comforted by his scent when he holds me in the night. I get wafts of him on my clothes while I'm at work. I can smell him when he becomes a part of me, his body slick with sweat and his intoxicating scent. I'm basking in it now, though it has the same pull as heroin for an addict. To know it's wrong, but to need it so intensely that nothing else matters.

It's ironic that he would try to comfort me because he is the one responsible for my pain. He has put the nail in the coffin, but he holds me tightly even so.

I have never wanted something so much, while at the same time wishing I could vanish into thin air. Being held by Silas was always a given. Never did I ever question if one day he would stop holding me. Soon his scent will no longer linger on my clothes, it will no longer permeate my skin, or swirl through the receptors in my brain.

How could I have let this happen?

I lose it, and the tears become sobs. I'm crying for my loss of the future we will never have together. I'm crying because I will miss the hell out of Ruby and because Silas will never hold me like this again. I don't want his pity, but I can't bring myself to break away from him.

He is so tender, yet unyielding in his embrace that it almost makes me change my mind. I can eventually accept him cheating on me with another woman. I could probably even learn to trust him again. I just don't want to lose him. Some of him is better than none.

He raises my chin to look into my face and evaluate my anguish, then his lips are on mine.

It feels for a moment like everything will be fine, like everything is back to normal. I kiss him back, and it's a fevered, hungry kiss. A desperate kiss.

***

He is holding my face in one hand and crushing me against him with the other. I'm melting, my resolve is slipping away. I could easily have him again, right here in my empty condo. I'm ripping at his shirt, yanking it open, wanting nothing but to feel his skin against mine.

He slides his palm up the back of Devin's over-sized shirt and feeling nothing but panties beneath, he grabs my ass and hoists me up. I wrap my legs around his waist and gasp when he buries his face in my neck. I can feel his frenzied breath against my ear, and it leaves a trail of traitorous goosebumps down my arms.

We are behaving like wild animals, it's like each of us is trying to get inside the other; not necessarily sexually, more like each of us is trying to possess the other…claim them. Own them. His mouth is on mine again, one arm holding me up, the other hand clawing at my back.

I tighten my legs around his body as if he's not close enough yet. I'm grasping his face between my hands and kissing him so fervently, it's as if I'm trying to pull him back from the other woman and reclaim him as my own.

He is yanking my hair and forcefully craning my neck back while he fumbles with his zipper. In a crazed manner, he slams us against the wall, all but knocking the breath from my body. He adjusts his clutch on me just enough to undo his pants, then lets them drop to the floor. Then he reaches around behind me and fumbles the wide crotch of my panties to the side.

When he plows into me, my body welcomes him like he belongs there, and my whimper is swallowed by his kiss. He is lifting and pinning me against the wall while he slams into me. His intensity is feral and seems almost primitive.

Before long, the passion with which we started starts to feel demanding and aggressive. This time it's different from the way he lovingly dominates me. Now it's like he wants to leave me marked and claimed before discarding me. So he can rest easy, knowing he was the last to be inside me.

The feel of his cock sliding in and out of my body reminds me that I am just a vessel to him. Someone he is finished with, but who still stupidly welcomes him into my warmth.

My thoughts start to spiral out of control. This very same penis, the one that feels just as much mine as it is his, has been pumping in and out of another woman. Who is she? Is she beautiful? Does he have feelings for her? Was the sex better than with me?

Then I'm consumed by the nagging question, how can I accept this treatment from him and still retain my self-respect?

"Silas stop."

"I can't, Baby, you feel too good," he grinds out, into my mouth.

"I can't do this." I unhook my legs from around his body and push against him with both hands on his chest. He adjusts his hold, so he's clutching my ass and pinning me harder against the wall, his cock still buried deep inside me. Now all I can think about, is him doing this to someone else. I start crying again.

"Just stop."

He doesn't even slow his stroke.

"Red." I'm crying full on now, so the word comes out weak and tortured; just like my lungs, brutally torn out and cast into the surging ocean.

He stops, but looks at me as if trying to gauge my seriousness, with his eyes pinched into a squint. Then he slowly pulls out, lowers me down, and steadies me until I find my feet.

He wipes my tears with both thumbs, but more follow, so he pulls me against him again. He rests his cheek against my head and cradles my body. The erection between us is no longer insistent, just evident and as familiar to me as the nose on my face.

"I'll never be able to forget about it, Silas. You need to go."

"Now you are going to kick me out? Before I've even gotten a word in."

"It's not your words that will haunt me, it's your actions. So, yes. Go." I try to pull back, but he doesn't release me. Pulling away from him is painful and I feel like a part of me will be left behind, but I have to do it.

"I haven't been with anyone else, Jessie," he speaks into my hair, and his words freeze time. I stop wiggling to free myself but remain quiet. I'm not even sure I heard him right.

"Did you hear me? I have not been with anyone else since I first laid eyes on you."

"If that's true, why did you tell me that?" I'm cautiously optimistic, but still unsure if I can believe him—now or ever again.

"I never told you that. You just went all crazy and assumed I did. I'm not sure how to even address the fact that you thought I *would*."

"You said you fucked someone from the club, Silas. Nothing was lost in translation, I heard you loud and clear." Now I'm getting mad again, does he take me for an idiot? Now the truth is no longer convenient, so he tries to alter the facts.

"No Pipes, you asked me if I had been fucking women at the club, and then didn't even give me a chance to answer. Though I shouldn't even have to dignify that shit with a response."

"You didn't deny it, and you looked guilty as fuck. You can't change your answer now because it suits you better." He exhales with exasperation.

"Actually Jess-ie, you could have slapped me in the face, and I would not have been more stunned. Or maybe flabbergasted is a better word, because I could never have guessed you would hit me with that. I have *never* given you even a sliver of a reason to doubt my integrity. Not *once* have you ever had to question my devotion to you. You want to have Devin's baby?.... Sure! You want Parker gone?.... Poof! You want to work side by side with a man who's in love with you?.... Great! But, you step out on me to cozy up to some slick dick, motherfucker you met at the bar?...Now you've gone too far."

"Silas, what happened with that slick dick, motherfucker *did* go too far, and I'm sorry. But you should know that those photos completely misrepresent what really happened."

"How's that?" he sounds skeptical at best.

"Well, first of all, they look like we were alone. The truth is that all my girlfriends were right there. Also, we were on a crowded sidewalk, not a private hotel room. And the crotch grab... I honestly was under the impression he was wearing a cock cage, and in my drunkenness, I was only trying to point it out to my friends— I know, beyond inappropriate, I know."

"Even if I buy all that, how do you explain the fact that he was kissing your neck... and you were practically creaming in your panties?" I flinch at his crude delivery, then answer the best I can.

"Someone spilled their margarita on me at the bar, my friends thought they were being cute, and they told him to lick it off. Again, we were ripped, it's not an excuse, but maybe an explanation for our lack of boundaries. As far as *creaming in my panties*, I believe I was laughing because I was surprised he actually did it." Silas ponders this information, deciding whether or not to press the issue.

"We never kissed, we never fucked, and he never touched me intimately, nothing. But I *am* sorry," I look up into his face with true contrition. "I will never put myself in a situation like that ever again, and you will never have to question *my* integrity ever again." I stretch up on my tiptoes and plant an apologetic kiss on his mouth.

"You really didn't get with someone at the club?" I ask, looking for clear assurance.

"No, of course not! I was at home licking my wounds. Plus, I'm pretty sure you have ruined me for other women." I breathe deeply for the first time in days and feel my shoulders relax by inches.

"How have I ruined you?"

"For one, you have my heart," his hands slide up under my oversized t-shirt, and he brushes his thumbs across my bare nipples. "And for another, you have my balls," his mouth closes in on mine while he continues to skim my breasts with his commanding touch.

He pulls the shirt over my head, causing the warm cotton to separate our mouths for the briefest of moments before we snap back together like two opposing magnets.

He steps out of his pants while I peel the ripped-open shirt down his body. The sense of relief I feel is indescribable. It's as if the sun had burned out, all the crops had died, and the animals had begun to starve—and then the sun decided to blaze again.

I think once you picture your future with a certain person in it, and proceed forward, factoring them into everything—house, kids, extended family, career, travel...life; it's debilitating to change course. All the neurons in your brain have formed certain pathways, chapters have been written, bonds created—the idea of something new is unfathomable. *This* is the state of insurrection where I'd mired. All the wheels were off the track, the proverbial bell that couldn't be un-rung had tolled, ashes were forged, the dye cast. And then, suddenly everything was back to normal. My misery thwarted. Harmony, finally, in place of discord.

Silas shoves down his boxer briefs and then slips the boyshort panties over the swell of my ass. He slides them gently down my thighs, guiding them with his hands ever so slowly, until they reach my ankles. Now I'm naked and he is on his knees.

He lays his cheek against my torso and wraps his arms around my body, holding me against him. The gesture is childlike until he lowers his mouth and drags his tongue through my slit.

My grip tightens in his hair. His touch is salacious, though his access is limited while he hugs my legs together. His breath against my electric flesh is dizzying, and his tongue brazen as he works at the button pressed between my legs.

His technique is something new for me. He places his lips near the top of my crease, then he kind of sucks, and kind of quivers his lips around the area of my clit. It's almost like how a bunny twitches its nose, yet there is enough suction to thoroughly engage my clitoris and send my pulse soaring.

I'm aware of evening creeping in, and of the darkness falling outside my well-lit condo. The sheer, billowing curtains do little to shroud my activities, as I stand naked in front of the same windows that look upon dozens of other windows.

At this point in my orgasmic climb, my head is lolling back, and my breasts are practically waving to the near-certain onlookers.

When I'm close, Silas eases his mouth away, takes hold of my wrists then sits down while guiding me onto his lap. Our position is sensual, and one of adoration rather than the standing wall fuck from earlier tonight. I cross my ankles behind him, as he eases himself into my acutely responsive body. The fullness of his erection stretches against my channel in increments as he pulls me into him, simultaneously boring deeper and deeper.

I wrap my arms around his shoulders and neck, while my breasts and abdomen are pressed into him. There is not even a sliver of space between us as I begin to rock against him, aided by the tightening of his hold at the small of my back.

Our kissing is passionate and all-consuming, like our lives depend on this very connection. I feel us becoming stronger as a couple with each passing minute, as he pours his energy into me and I do the same for him.

Despite the last few days, I have never felt so close to another human being. Not just physically close, but mentally—almost spiritually, like our souls are connected as well.

My body is hazy, flooded with sexual endorphins. My eyes feel shrouded and gauzy with the ethereal glow of our intense connection. Our bodies are completely united, to the point where I can't tell where mine ends and his begins. We have melded together and become one. To break this bond seems impossible, even reckless perhaps. We belong with each other, our bodies work so perfectly together, our minds so in tune with the other.

I don't know if it's our position and close proximity, our mental connection and emotional high, or our sense of relief to still be together as a couple, but I can feel the power of the esoteric. Now I fully understand why tantric sex is such a sacred practice; I feel spiritually connected, even elevated by it.

Our movements are slow and grinding, not at all fevered or hurried. I feel powerful, slightly above him and in control of our tempo but this is not about power. This is real emotion. This is raw eroticism stripped to its most basic and pure form.

He breaks our kiss to mumble, "I love you, Jessie. I need you with me, always." He is kissing me again, so my response is swallowed by his affection.

"Silas, I—" before I can say another word, his statement crystallizes. I'm overcome with emotion, so a fresh round of warm tears fills my eyes. I crane my head back while Silas buries his kissing mouth in my neck. The warm cascade runs into my ears and brings a shiver up my spine that I can feel throb in my nipples.

As if he too can feel the quickening, he begins to flick one with his tongue then tug it with pursed lips. My body is ringing with his erotic attention. My nipples feel like live wires, and the sensation is shooting straight to my clitoris. Our bodies have become slick with sweat and desire, as I begin to grind harder against his shaft.

"Silas, I can't do this without you. Any of it, my nightmares, Devin and Corey's baby, my job. Nothing matters without you."

He breathes against my skin, "You'll never be without me again."

"I love you," I whisper, as I raise his face to mine for a tender kiss. The sweetness of the kiss evolves into something more when I suck his bottom lip into my mouth then gently bite down while changing my methodical rocking into tight, circular motions.

He has one forearm around my waist and the flat of his other palm against my shoulder blades. He is pressing himself against my rhythmic movements, and I know he is getting close.

"Slow your hips, Baby," he pants, as he slides his hand from my shoulder blades up into my hair. The little tug against those sensitive strands of hair also manages to elicit a deep clitoral response as I feel myself vasodilate.

"I love the feel of you inside me," I groan, as I squeeze his cock and grind my clit into his pelvis. I'm getting close myself.

His breaths speed up, "I love being inside you." After a short pause, he adds, "Do you want me to come inside you?" His voice is rumbly, and the rasp of it makes even the innocent question sound dirty and sexy.

"Yeah, Baby, I want all of you," I whisper, and my voice sounds husky too.

He whispers into my ear, his stubble grazing against my flesh, "Yes Pipes, and **I** want all of you."

The scrape of his whiskers against my ear is the last bit of sensation my body can handle. I clasp tightly against him to ride out my orgasm while whimpering in ecstasy against the side of his face.

The spasms and clenching of my vagina is the last bit of sensation *he* can take. He cradles my cheeks between his palms but stops short of kissing me while he succumbs to his own release—his face twisting with the sheer intensity of it.

***

We remain fused together, slick and thoroughly satiated while our breathing and heartbeats find their normal rhythm. I'm at home in his arms, and I don't want to move except I'm as hot as a nuclear fusion reactor. I'm feeling light-headed from the exertion and my mouth is so dry, even the saliva gets caught in my throat.

Silas is perfectly content to remain just how we are and does little more than straighten out his legs.

"That was fucking sexxxy. I have never made love to someone like that. Never," Silas muses.

"Like what? The Lotus position?" I ask as I lie back between his legs, in search of cooler temperatures. My own legs are still wrapped around him, and as I lie back, I release his penis from its captive state within my body.

"Let's just say intimacy has never been a big part of my sexual past," he says. Then his grin broadens, and he leans forward, sliding his hands up my body until he cups my breasts. Squeezing both nipples between his extended fingers, he asks, "You know what I want to do right now?"

"Get me a drink of water?" I inquire.

He laughs, then drags his palms back down my body, across my hips and over the inside of my thighs, caressing them in a way that reminds me my legs are still wide open to him. He finds my vagina and playfully swirls his fingers through his own cum, dragging it through my lips and gliding it brazenly around my dilated clitoris.

I suck in my breath at the extreme sensitivity of my clit. Realizing even the slightest touch is too much, he brings his wet fingers up to circle the tips of my breasts in turn. Then he blows a cool breath of air across them, where they applaud his efforts by standing up straighter.

"Actually, I want to finish this fire hazard of a project you've started. But first, I want you to put that cock-tease underwear back on, and nothing else."

"You want me to just strut around, almost naked?"

"Yeah, I do."

"For the world to see?" I gesture to the oversized windows and beyond them, to all the potential voyeurs. He smiles, then eases out from under my thighs. He stands up to stretch, totally unconcerned with his own naked display and swaying penis.

"Let's knock out this tinder wall, and I'll tell you about the event at 1462 next month." I step back into the boy short underwear Silas finds so sexy, then walk over to the wispy floor to ceiling curtains.

Right before I pull them together, I pause for a bit. My heart rate picks up at the thought of being seen like this. Here in the city, it is not uncommon for tenants to own telescopes. I've even seen them myself and laughed at the audacity of the *stargazing* owners. As I stand here, looking out into the darkness at all the other windows, I feel my nakedness acutely. I can just about feel the eyes on me, and it flicks at my pulse in a way I wouldn't have expected. At the club, sure, but in my own home, with real neighbors?

I picture them in the dark, binoculars raised or gawking into the eyepiece of their telescopes, watching me, seeing my bare flesh and rock hard nipples. I can't move away from their view, the rush is too exhilarating. Silas steps up behind me and places a freezing glass of ice water against my chest, right between my breasts.

"Oh my God, thank you! I need this so bad," I say, then guzzle it down. I'm so dehydrated, I can feel it permeate my whole being, recharging the wilted feeling of every one of my body's systems.

When I'm finished, he takes the glass from me and presses it against my nipple, as ice cubes shift into their new assignments. He nibbles on my ear and gently exhales into it. The thrill of my erotic display now multiplies by a thousand. I can feel the secondary effect from the icy glass pinned against my breast, as it throbs between my legs.

Silas pours an ice cube into his hand, then puts the glass down on the windowsill. Then he holds the cube behind my ear and slowly drags it down the side of my neck. As the ice melts against my flushed skin, tiny trickles of water streak down my back and run across my chest, cascading down my cleavage. The ticklish dribbles raise goosebumps on my skin where the brutish feel of the ice, did not. When he bumps the cube over each nipple, I gasp and rest my head back against him.

He asks into my ear, "Do you like when strangers can see you like this?" I answer in the form of a moan, as he reminds me we are most likely being watched.

At any point in the last hour and a half, if anyone even glanced our way, they had witnessed quite a show. Fully illuminated, carnal fucking up against a wall, toe-curling oral sex, and sweet passionate lovemaking. So it stands to reason, people might still be tuned in to the show, and still very much gawking with undivided focus.

We've checked a lot of boxes for the voyeurs already, so why am I feeling such a charge displaying myself to total strangers like this? My heart is pounding in my chest. My panties dampen, and it's more than Silas' warm, residual cum, it's my own excitement.

He drops the ice cube back into the glass, then begins kissing my neck and fondling my breasts. His kisses are so gentle they make me squirm, but the commanding way he tweaks my nipples floods me with animalistic desire. The fact we have an *audience* makes the whole deed, naughty and raunchy and very forbidden.

I can see our reflection in the window, Silas is nuzzling my neck, but his eyes are on the hidden spectators. We look hot, and seeing myself like this… seeing what *they* see is shockingly indecent.

I can feel their eyes crawling over me, their attention focused on my tits as Silas drags his thumbs roughly across the tips. He is definitely putting on a show, and my pretentious nipples are prominently center stage.

He wraps his left arm across the front of my body and takes hold of my right nipple, boldly rolling and tugging it between finger and thumb.

He then slides his right hand heavily down my abdomen, allowing his fingers to creep under the elastic of my boy shorts.

When he drags his middle finger wetly through his cum and steadily up my crease, I moan with desire.

"Spread your legs," he says, as he makes eye contact with me in our reflection.

I do as he says, and he eases his finger inside me. He rubs my g-spot with each advance and withdrawal of his finger, and it's enough to make me writhe against his palm. Then he inserts another finger.

I grind against his erection with my ass as I press my g-spot into his fingers. He can feel me getting close to the edge, so he withdraws his fingers, first dragging the wetness between my lips a few times, then finding my clit.

He must still be cognizant of how sensitive it is because he hardly touches the electrified bundle as he begins to rub small circles. The light pressure of his magical fingers slowly increases, causing me to push harder against his shaft while quiet whimpers escape from my lips.

He is cupping my breast now, while gently strumming his thumb across the tip. My body is turned on from every conceivable erogenous zone, and my mind is so turned on by the exhibitionism, that I find myself moaning with near delirium.

He drops his hand from my breast then eases my underwear down, just enough to free his orbiting fingers from the confines of the elastic, but also exposing more of me to our viewers. After he does this, it's only seconds before my orgasm sweeps me under and holds me down.

***

After I come for anyone who happens to be watching, Silas adjusts my underwear back into place and turns me around to face him. He kisses me sweetly while instinctively supporting me against my freshly acquired rubber legs.

"That was hot, Silas," I say before I begin kissing his neck. My arms are wrapped tightly around his body, and I know he can feel my nipples against his chest.

"It was very hot, My Little Exhibitionist, I watched the whole thing in our reflection."

I kiss my way down his body, stopping at his nipple and flicking it with my tongue a few times before sucking it into my mouth. I pinch the other with my finger and thumb while he groans, and I can feel his hardness twitch against my body.

I drag my chest down his bare torso and then settle on my knees in front of his swaying cock. I tease the head with my tongue while I scrape my fingernails down both sides of his ribcage. His ribs are very sensitive for him, and I want to make sure all the sensation is not focused on his dick, not yet.

Luckily for Silas, my best friend is a gay man. Devin is many things but subtle, he is not, so I have learned an impressive amount from him about giving head. Devin is uniquely qualified as a giver *and* receiver, and he's never been shy expressing what feels good for a man. Silas has been the beneficiary of this knowledge on many occasions. However, I still have some tricks up my sleeve.

He slides his fingers partway through my hair and gently holds my head while his eyes drift to the ceiling.

I hold his erection a bit to the side and circle the base of his scrotum with one hand while I give a gentle tug, just to hold the sack around his testicles taut. Then I employ one of Devin's go-to moves. I start at the bottom of Silas' sack and lick up the middle, between his testicles and all the way to the tip of his cock. After repeating this a few times, Silas tightens his grip on my hair and groans with pleasure.

I know a huge part of what guys find sexy during a blowjob is watching it happen, so next, I dutifully look up into his eyes while I repeatedly and incessantly tap his sensitive frenulum with the fluttering tip of my tongue.

"Ohhhhh. Fuuuck. That's so good."

The hardwood floor is already hurting my knees and giving me the sharp sensation of having gravel behind my kneecaps, so I need to get him off quick. I close my mouth around his tip, wrap one hand around his shaft, then rotate my lips around the sensitive ridge at the base of his head.

I know with certainty this is the most receptive and electric spot on a man's penis, so I focus my attention here. I alternate slobbery pressure as my lips circle back and forth, halfway around, then back, against his coronal ridge.

The intensity of my focus causes Silas' grip on my hair to tighten. I can feel a few extra-tight strands of hair pluck from my scalp, and the sharpness of the sensation gives me the shivers. Silas, on the other hand, is nearly howling with pleasure.

When he comes, what he lacks in quantity he makes up for in intensity, as he shoots hot semen past my teeth to the back of my throat. As he rides the waves of his orgasm, I sink my mouth down his erection, both milking it and coating it with his seed.

Once I sit back on my heels and look up into his delirious face, I only have a small amount of cum to swallow, while the rest cools against his exhausted penis.

"You have an amazing cock, Silas. Look how it glistens for your spectators. I can almost hear the applause," I say, while seductively wiping my mouth and maintaining eye contact.

"Jessie, any applause you hear, is for your gifted mouth. Now come up here and give me a kiss, our attentive fans need to see how much I adore you."

***

We made quick work of my accent wall. Actually, Silas made quick work of the accent wall, while I cleaned all the sawdust and debris from the floor. Then we ate cold chicken legs from the fridge while sitting on the kitchen counter drinking the last of my depression beers. After our uninspired dinner, Silas showered while I put fresh sheets on my mattress.

Now, at last, we fall into bed exhausted. Silas pulls me against him and says, "I love you, Jessie. Thank you for not exploding my heart to go fuck another man," he laughs, but I know he is serious.

"I love you too, and you're welcome. Wait, weren't you going to tell me about an event at the club?"

"That's right, I was. Don't let my pathetic man-feelings get in the way of you hearing about it though," he laughs again, then pulls me in tighter.

"Silas, I love your man-feelings, and I don't find them at all pathetic, but I am about to fall asleep with my eyes open."

"Ok then, it's kind of like a talent show, and petting zoo all rolled into one fabulous party. Goodnight."

"Hold it." I'm not tired anymore. But I'm also not very inclined to go. "Petting zoo? What?"

"Well, talent show is really more accurate, but it's also interactive, thus the petting zoo term. It's hands down the most popular party of the year."

"Interactive talent show, huh?"

"Yeah, Babe, you'll get to see demonstrations of both Kinbaku and Shibari rope bondage, different types of suspension techniques, electricity and fire demonstrations from the best practitioners around the world. It's incredible."

"I'm still hung up on the interactive part."

"Ok then, if you are not interested in sampling from the exhibits, there are plenty of voyeuristic options too. There is the body-paint fashion show, a Burlesque show, oil wrestling, toy demonstrations, dungeon furniture exhibits..." He is ticking these examples off one by one, and I can tell he is excited.

"Are you telling me you wouldn't care if I got *interactive* at a sex toy exhibit?" I ask, calling Silas out about the ridiculousness of his suggestion, and peering up into his handsome face.

"Pipes, I'm going to be there with you. Plus, if I'm honest, I wouldn't hate seeing you wrestling another woman in the pit," he smiles, then goes on, "I love showing you off at the club, but if this fine ass is up on any of the dungeon furniture," he says while squeezing my naked butt, "You can bet, it will have been me that put you there."

Chapter Eleven

Work

Now that I'm back at work, I'm so far behind I can hardly come up for air. Salinger has done what he could to keep me slightly caught up, but I'm sure it has come at a price for him, like keeping him working late into the night. I saw him briefly as he buzzed past my office earlier. I'd say he was relieved to see me back, but the truth is, I'm not even sure he noticed me.

Quarterly reports are a massive time suck, and I will surely be here long after the office janitors have gone home. I turn to my set of double monitors and begin the slow grind that is my descent into numbers hell.

***

I've already worked through my lunch when thoughts of the club come trickling into my consciousness. The thoughts are distracting enough that in order to quiet the constant nagging, I need to entertain the musings.

Specifically, I'm thinking about the body paint fashion show. Silas said interactive, and it would be kind of fun to surprise him with a little body paint. The fact I can't stop pondering every nuance of it is what forces a quick internet search.

After wasting nearly an hour searching body paint, I'm certain of two things. One, Silas is going to love my version of *interactive talent show*, and two, now I'm really behind with my work.

I have hardly turned back to my spreadsheet when my cell vibrates with an incoming text.

Devin: *Might have to cut the trip short, Corey's mom has taken a turn for the worse.*

Oh crap, Corey's mom is a saint. She is an amazing woman, and she's the reason Corey is the man he is today. Before her stroke and her subsequent move into an assisted living home, she used to cook a huge southern meal and have everyone over a few times a year.

Now, hearing she isn't doing well, I feel guilty for not reaching out to her sooner. It's as if her dinners were the only reason we cared for her but in truth, we all love Corey's mom. Her animated stories about Corey should be transcribed and annexed for posterity so they can be kept for future generations. Then a thought hits me. *Future generations.* Corey's potential child may never get to know her.

I text back: *I'll go see her after work tomorrow. Can't today, I have to work late.*

His reply is nothing more than: *Give it to us straight, don't sugarcoat anything.*

Crap, so much work to finish and so many distractions. How am I supposed to get anythi—

"JB. Holy shit. Is this an illusion? Are you really here, addressing your responsibilities like a grown ass woman?" Salinger charges in, causing yet another distraction.

"Salinger, I only took a few days off. You needn't alert the press," I smile.

"Well, welcome back. I've been busy as fuck trying to keep both our heads above water. Are you feeling better? Has Silas gotten over himself?" His barrage of statements and hastily delivered questions make me think he's had a ton of coffee, and not much human contact lately.

"Thank you for your help and for keeping me on track. Yes, I'm feeling better."

"Thank Christ for that. Nash starts to chew on the furniture when I don't come home inside of a twelve-hour span." He turns to leave my office with nothing more than a twinkly-toothed smile.

"I'm going to order dinner in a bit, what can I get for you?" I ask his departing back.

He calls over his shoulder, "Let's do BBQ, it's going be a long night."

***

After two days and countless hours of redundant work and virtually no sleep, I crawl out from the rubble of my office like a Pompeii survivor. I've managed to have my quarterly reports timestamped and submitted with hardly a moment to spare. Salinger had abandoned ship hours ago, having completed his reports in a timely manner.

With my eyes clouded by the hazy film of exhaustion, I stumble toward the employee lounge to replace my coffee IV before heading out to visit, Maribel, Corey's mother.

Her stroke was over a year ago, but I have kept distant tabs on her through Corey. I know she has trouble with the left side of her body, but with continued physical therapy, she is expected to mostly recover.

Thankfully, her mind is still sharp thanks to quick-acting paramedics and the fact she was having tea with a friend when the stroke occurred.

The high probability of her being alone and powerless for a possible recurrence is what prompted Corey to find her a permanent residence in an assisted living community. Devin and Corey had agonized over the decision and spent months touring and interviewing possible caregivers and facilities.

Corey's bond with Maribel is something to behold. Ever since Corey's father passed away five or six years ago during his deployment, it has just been the two of them, and their closeness is really touching.

The way Corey's parents nurtured and accepted him for who he is, is diametrically opposite of Devin's upbringing. The difference could not be any more obvious than their personalities. Simply, Corey was raised with grace, and Devin, with grit.

***

As I make my way through the parking garage to my car, I begin to feel the weight of Devin's text. *Give it to us straight, don't sugarcoat anything.* What if she has taken a massive downturn and I have to deliver the news that brings Devin and Corey running home after a short European jaunt instead of a several month excursion?

And while I'm selfishly making this about myself and whatever news I will have to impart, I realize, I should have visited Maribel a long time ago. She is more like family to me than Devin's inept parents, whom I grew up with right alongside Devin. Poor, sweet Maribel. Hopefully, she is just fine with many years ahead of her.

All of a sudden, out of a sleep-deprived haze, I'm picturing her bouncing her laughing grandchild on her knee, and gleefully asking, "Who's Grandma's Big Girl?"

***

I'm in that weird state of limbo where it feels like everything is moving extraordinarily slow. Each slow-blink creates an audible *swish* inside my foggy brain. My tiredness is without bounds, limitless—yet I'm feeling squirrelly and amped up from the endless flow of caffeine.

The nurse looks at me sideways when I tell her I'm here to visit my mother. For some reason, I worry visitation might be restricted to immediate family, and I don't want to have to fight my foggy way in if they confirm as much. Her hesitation and suspicious look bring me right to the edge of my comfort zone.

"I was adopted," I blurt out.

Same disappointed look. She knows I'm lying.

"Late in life," I stubbornly continue even though it sounds ridiculous, even to me.

"Jessie, we've been expecting you. Corey added you himself. He even called this morning to make sure there wouldn't be any difficulties." She delivers this information sweetly, not with the patronizing tone I would have used.

"Oh. I'm sorry. Lack of sleep tends to dull my judgment. I was afraid—"

"You don't need to apologize for anything. Please come into my office so we can have a little privacy."

***

The plaque on the desk identifies her as Jolene Eisenbalm; Director, but when she closes the door and extends her hand, she introduces herself simply as Jo.

"So, just to give you some background, Mrs. Phelps has suffered some complications related to her stroke, and they have been exacerbated by her lack of mobility. Last week she was being treated for a particularly nasty bout of Nosocomial Pneumonia," she clears her throat while my blank look and dull mind try to catch up.

"As a facility, we're often hindered by the antibiotic resistance of certain bacteria, as well as, our community setting."

I nod, "Okkkay." So far nothing sounds too bad.

"On several occasions, it became necessary to utilize what we refer to as a fever blanket, in order to bring down her dangerously high fever."

"Fever blanket?" I ask.

"Yes, it's a blanket that circulates chilled water. It's one of many tools at our disposal that helps prevent organ deterioration and reduces brain trauma."

"Oh, my goodness!" Now we are talking brain trauma and organ deterioration, this meeting just took a drastic nosedive.

"Mrs. Phelps, is no longer in danger from her high fever, in that way she has stabilized." Jo's eyes are kind, but they mask potentially grave information, and I have the distinct impression that I'm being fed the facts, one baby spoonful at a time.

"Is she going to be ok?" I ask with hope in my voice.

"We can't be certain how much trauma her brain has suffered, but we are monitoring her for the possibility of DVT as well as limb contra—"

"What is that?" I interrupt, not even caring about my rudeness, while she tosses out medical terminology like I was her colleague.

"My apologies. Deep Vein Thrombosis is when blood clots form in the veins of the legs due to immobility. Another side effect of immobility are bed sores, of which Mrs. Phelps has several. Unfortunately, she also has some limb contracture difficulties."

"Can I see her?" I blurt out. It seems simpler than the anatomy/physiology lesson I'm currently receiving. Besides, with my brain cells already swirling around and bumping into each other, I'm not absorbing the information anyway.

"Yes, of course," she stands and directs me to the door.

Chapter Twelve

Visit

Any dullness I feel is obliterated when I see Maribel. She is huddled into a ball on her hospital bed. She looks as though she has aged twenty years in the blink of an eye. I have never seen her without her full regalia of makeup and perfectly put together outfit, consisting of a cinched waist and country club sanctioned A-line dress.

Her room smells like a pit of despair; damp and closed up, dark and lifeless. I get the eerie feeling that I'm sharing the floor space with the Angel of Death and my thoughts start to swim. How am I going to tell Corey?

"Maribel? Are you awake?" I whisper as I take a cautious step toward the side of her bed. The rolling cart that serves as a dinner tray when slid over her bed has been cast aside. On the cart is a mug of foul-smelling beef broth and cold, forgotten toast.

There is a stirring under the covers but no reply, while she rotates and unfolds her body. After some weary false starts, she fixes her gaze on me.

"That you, Jessie Hayes?" her body looks feeble, but her voice comes out fairly strong.

My voice cracks, "Yes, it's me."

"Girl, get over here an' give me some sugar!" Now she's sounding more like herself, though it betrays her sickly appearance.

I step forward and then sit on the edge of her partially-inclined hospital bed. When I lean in to hug her wilted frame, I falter with discomfort. It's really difficult to see her this way. She is a proud woman, who is never—and I mean never without her lipstick. She is clean; in a sponge-bath kind of way, but this version of Maribel is unfamiliar and unsettling to me.

She alternately kisses my cheeks, then squeezes me against her. She smells sharply of capsaicin patches dusted with the manufactured scent of baby powder, instead of her usual dignity and refinement. Her hair, however, has retained the ghost of its past with the essence of vanilla beans.

The whole image of her is so distressingly different than what I'm used to, I still can't reign in my emotions. I'm alarmed by her appearance, but thankful her mind is still sharp.

"Now, now, why you so sad, Jessie? Did Chevrolet stop makin' trucks?" she asks while holding my cheeks between the soft plains of her hands.

I chuckle while blinking away a tear. Her southern colloquialisms and sense of humor have always been part of her charm.

"Maribel, I don't like to see you like this. What can I get you?" I ask.

"I know, Honey, I feel like I been 'et by a wolf and shit over a cliff." She smiles, and although her left side droops a bit, I can recognize Corey's broad cheekbones and bright eyes in her face.

I laugh at her description. "You need sunshine and some fresh air. Would you mind if I opened the curtains and the window?" I ask. It's too late for sunshine, but the stagnant air needs to disperse.

"Go on right ahead and do anything you think needs doing."

"Are they feeding you ok?" I ask over my shoulder as I wrestle with the window locks and crank.

"Lawd no. Not one of em know how to cook a decent meal. All I been thinkin' about is sweet tea and buttery grits." As she sits up, I can tell she is struggling a bit. Whether it's lack of strength that troubles her, or a slowdown caused by pain, I can't be sure.

"You need more than tea and grits, Maribel, you need some chicken and waffles. I'll talk to Jo, because whatever that is," I nod to the nasty broth on the rolling side table, "Isn't going to cut it."

"Aren't you precious! But before you go doin all that, you get over here and tell me all about that hunky man you seein'. Corey and Devin never give me enough details."

I smile as I switch on the bedside lamp, and then reach for my work bag to retrieve my laptop.

"First, I want to show you Corey and Devin's emblazoned trail through Europe... What's the WiFi password in this joint?"

***

After a while, I can tell Maribel is growing tired. The lasting effects of her stroke are seen all over the left side of her face, which is more noticeable at this hour than it was before. My own exhaustion is creeping back in after a mighty second-wind, as well.

A man dressed in scrubs and an employee badge hanging from his pocket scuttles into the room. He sees the two of us, reclining in the raised hospital bed, crocheted afghan draped over us, and the glow from my laptop illuminating our faces.

We both look up at him guiltily, as if caught passing a joint instead of merely looking at pictures.

He shakes his head slowly. "Maribel, the AC is on, and here you are with your window wide open."

I'm the first to take offense to his reprimand of a grown woman, and say, "We just needed some fresh air, Nurse Ratched." Next to me, I hear Maribel snort on her stifled laugh as she recognizes the reference. The CNA stalks across the room and vigorously winds the window closed, evidently not a fan of Kesey's writing.

"Perfect, and if you could fluff our pillows next, that would be amazing." I'm not sure what has gotten into me, but I know what Corey pays for his mother's care, and shitty broth and toast with a side of passive aggressive caretaker is unacceptable to me. Also, probably because I haven't slept in so long, I'm not even pretending to filter my thoughts.

He tugs the curtains shut, and then stands at the end of the bed with his arms crossed mightily across his chest. I can't see his feet, but I'm somehow sure one is tapping impatiently.

"It's getting toward bedtime, Mrs. Phelps, and we still need to get in your respiratory therapy." His words are kind toward her, but when he shifts his gaze to me, his tone changes, "Visiting hours are over, Miss."

"So they are," I smile through teeth that are practically oozing venom and wait for him to leave, which he eventually does.

"That boy thinks the sun comes up just to hear him crow," Maribel says. I'm feeling extra punchy now, so her comment makes me laugh a little longer than it should.

"You need to jerk a knot in his tail, Maribel." I use one of her own sayings, as I clumsily roll off her bed.

"Sweetheart, you sound more and more like Devin every time I see you."

"I feel more and more like Devin lately. I think my mind is compensating for his absence." After I say this, I realize how much sense it makes. Devin and his snarky comments may not be here, but I'm so used to them, I can almost insert his presence into the room.

With that thought, I wonder if I'm starting to lose it, am I taking on his personality because I miss him so much? It's like I need his side of my personality to be whole. I shake my head to clear the wandering thoughts.

"I'm going to bring you some real food tomorrow, so hang in there, Mama M."

"Good, cause I'm so hungry, I could eat the north end of a south-bound goat."

Chapter Thirteen

Catch Up

With the manic pace of the last few days at work, it is with blessed relief that I find myself with nothing pressing to do. The office is a virtual ghost town, being both a Friday and on the tail end of the quarterly reports. I would have taken the day off too, except Silas has meetings all day for the new club. So, I might as well put my time in.

After leaving Maribel last night, I had texted Devin and Corey that things were mostly fine, but to call me this morning for the run-down. So far, no call.

My mind starts to wander to thoughts of the party at 1462. Silas said he wouldn't *hate* seeing me wrestle another woman, but that's not going to happen. I have no intention of rolling around in oil and then spending the rest of the evening looking like a greasy, hot mess. I would, however, like to participate *somehow*.

I still feel very underestimated at the club. It's probably my own insecurities about Silas' boundless sexual exploits, but sometimes I feel like I have to prove myself to the other women. I know some of them adhere pretty strongly to the notion that I'm too inexperienced to be with Silas.

In reality, it's not that I'm *inexperienced*, it's just that I'm not the overt, showy type that saturates the club. I've seen everything and more at 1462, but the aspects that interest me sexually are few and far between. I'm not into most of the underlying themes; punishment, pain, submission, or even multiple partners. *However,* there is an element that I'm finding myself more and more drawn to, something that makes my heart beat faster just thinking about it.

Exhibitionism.

Silas, in his infinite wisdom, has recognized my interest in this kink and begun to draw it out in various ways. First, was sex in the interrogation room. Which was just a big room with a table and two chairs, with a couple different handcuff options. It doesn't sound too exciting or exhibitionistic until you factor in the gigantic two-way mirror and the crowd of hidden onlookers.

Then there was the flashlight party, where except for flashlights, the club was pitch dark. Silas had me inclined backward on a liberator ramp naked, with my feet on the floor and legs spread open. My ass had rested at the peak of the ramp, and the blood had pooled in my head at the bottom of the sloping cushion.

In quite a bold display, he first went down on me, and then fucked me while thirty flashlights shone on my crotch and jouncing tits.

Somehow the whole thing had still felt a bit anonymous because, with the exception of a few light beam bobbles, no one ever illuminated my face. The anonymity was a complete illusion, however, because everyone knew they were watching Silas; and as an extension of him, me.

Then, of course, there was the sex in front of my window at home. This one had felt the most salacious, probably because I was in my own space and in front of my neighbors instead of a bunch of kinksters. In fact, ever since it happened, I have a hard time looking people in the eye within a few blocks of my condo. I'm always wondering if they *know* who I am.

I ponder if they have seen my o-face, or know I have a mole under my right breast and a vein in my forehead that's only visible while my head is rocked back during an intense orgasm.

I think sex at the club, private, or not so much, feels less raunchy because everyone there is sexually adventurous in one way or another, even if they are simply observing.

It might surprise you to know that a healthy percentage of club goers are non-participant, observers. Sometimes, this is the natural progression and the voyeurs are simply getting their feet wet. Sometimes there is never the intention of participating, only a desire to surround themselves with some uninhibited revelry. However, there is always an unspoken acceptance of whatever kind of sexual debauchery abounds. There is an expectation of nudity and all varieties of sex, so it becomes less taboo somehow.

Now, if you asked me if I would have flashlight sex in a different environment, with a different crowd, the answer would be a resounding, *No.*

At the club, I don't know if subconsciously I'm still trying to prove myself. Or, if I'm staking claim on Silas—who is a bit too adored by some the women for my liking. Or, if the pure exhilaration of showing off in such an explicit way is what I seek, but I definitely like the aspect of exhibition at the club.

Having said that, I'm still not the girl who is going to jump up and demonstrate a fucking machine at the club party. Nor am I going to dabble with the fire and electricity exhibits, or volunteer for the toy demonstrations.

Which leads me to question the suitability of the body-paint fashion show Silas spoke of. Now an idea is blooming in my chest and making me blush.

***

The internet, in its boundless wisdom, provides me with some very adventurous options for full body paint. Every conceivable variation of bikini, corset, team jersey, or occupational uniform is covered, as well as superheroes and jungle cats of all kinds.

I'm looking closely at a full-body painted cowgirl, when Salinger's entrance, preceded only by the briefest of knocks, fills the room with the awkward fact that naked, painted women are plastered all over my computer screen.

"Uh, working hard, JB?" Salinger asks, with a whisp of a smile wafting across his face.

"Yes, I am. Did you know it can take 6-12 hours for an airbrush body paint session?"

Salinger's grin broadens to epic proportions. "Why are you interested in body paint exactly?"

"What do you mean?" I ask. I'm stalling because his tone is a little too *knowing* if you know what I mean, and I'm not fast enough on my feet to come up with something clever to say.

"Are you modeling for the show?" he asks, and it's a direct hit, he knows about the club event.

I gulp down my smile, "I'm just curious."

"Uh, huh."

"So, uh…anyway, are you going to go to the party?" I'm trying to sound unaffected, but I'm also aware of my cheeks heating up, and I doubt Salinger misses my discomfort.

"I've got my bulk mail, mass marketing rollout, *personal* invitation, stuck to the fridge right now," he says, through a mouth that's trying not to smile. "Party of the century, I hear," he shifts his weight and holds my gaze with laughing eyes.

"So I've been told," I say flatly. Of course he knows about the party. This definitely changes things in regard to my painted almost-nakedness on stage. Salinger never attends club functions, I've all but stopped worrying about it, and now… now, the party announcement is hanging on his refrigerator. I bet it's under the magnet of his smiling, ballerina niece too.

"Too bad I'll have to miss it," he says, throwing me a lifeline.

Hope blooms in my chest. "Why would you miss the party of the century?" I ask, my voice a bit too eager.

"Sadly, I'll be in Las Vegas. I have my fantasy football draft, and a championship title to defend," he shrugs, and true to form drops the subject like a hot potato. "Wanna go grab lunch?"

"Yes, give me a few minutes to get myself set up for Monday, and I'll come to your office." I'm instantly relieved to hear he will be gone for the body paint show, but that isn't my only concern right now. If I'm really going to surprise Silas, I'm going to have to figure out how to be away from him for 6-12 hours the day of the party.

***

Now that I'm on my way home from a zero productivity work day, my mind is juggling what lie to tell Silas. I have to be unavailable, or I'll never surprise him. Unfortunately, one thing I know for sure is that I am the worst liar to ever draw breath. Silas will be able to read the deceit on my face before I even start lying, so the pretense has to be believable. More than that, I have to somehow connect with the artists without Silas knowing.

I've seen the schedule of performances and the docket of expert presenters and Silas is right, they are coming from all over the place. The fire expert alone is from Sweeden, and one of the rope bondage demonstrators is flying in from Japan.

I close the door behind me and instantly feel like something is amiss in my condo. The air feels different.

"You really need a statement lighting piece in here."

I scream and back into the door as adrenaline dumps into my system and my bladder nearly lets go. Only then do I realize Devin is sitting on my new couch. He is leaning forward with his forearms resting on his knees, and his hands clasped together.

My relief is so sudden that my legs feel limp, like soggy cardboard and oddly tingly, almost unable to hold me up. I take a cautious step toward him, unsure if he is angry about what I've done to the condo, or more precisely, to his stuff.

He stands and opens his arms, but still looks like an executioner attempting to comfort his ward. I walk into his arms feeling heavy. Not heavy from the scare or from worrying about how he feels about the complete overhaul of his home, but from the resonating baggage I carry from the rape. I have gotten better about expecting horror around every corner, but the millisecond it took to bring all those feelings back to the surface, is pretty poignant. It overshadows how excited I am to see Devin.

"Don't you think?" he asks, as he envelopes me.

"What? Don't I think what?" His question is foreign to me, his words incongruous and distant sounding. I squeeze my hug around him anyway.

"That you need a statement lighting piece in here? I think it should be something rustic and earthy to tie in with the accent wall, but in complete opposition to the chic furnishings. I'm thinking industrial elegance. I have just the thing in the warehouse."

"Devin, why are you here?" I ask, tightly against his chest.

"Well, because…you see, I live here. At least I think I do," he says as he loosens his grip on me.

"I mean why are you back so early?"

"Maribel of course," he says, as he flops back onto the couch dragging me with him. He smells like recycled air, or a long, cramped trip, but he looks fresh as a daisy—as usual.

"She is fine, just a little thin and maybe…somewhat frail. I'm taking her some fat and carbs for dinner tonight."

Devin laughs, "I can hear her now, *Don't nobody know how to cook in here,*" Then he raises his voice an octave, "*Not a one of them could find their ass with both hands crammed in their back pockets,*" his chest rumbles beneath my cheek.

Not moving from my position on top of him, I say, "I want to hear all about your trip, Devin. Start at the beginning."

Chapter Fourteen

Reunion

Devin and I enter the Assisted Living Center like two railway bandits. We're loaded down with goods, and hazarding glances left and right to see if we've been detected with armfuls of contraband. We make it as far as the front lobby because access is secure and nobody gets in or out undetected.

The director, Jolene Eisenbalm, smiles when she sees Devin, and then hurriedly ends her phone conversation. She rises from the reception area and comes around to hug him, inquire about his trip, and exchange other tedious chit-chat. She acts as if Devin's day to day life was of paramount concern to the woman.

She steps back from Devin to welcome me, though with distinctly less fanfare. "You know you can't bring food in here, right?"

"What food? Jo, these are just some simple necessities for Maribel's comfort, that's all. You know, some furry slippers, her favorite quilt…"

"What's in the box?" she asks him playfully.

"Don't be silly, Jo, that's just an air purifier for the soothing tranquility of white noise. You know how white noise has a calming effect on the nervous system?" Devin never asks for permission, one hundred percent of the time he would rather ask for forgiveness later, should the need arise. Not that he is actually sorry, mind you, he's only sorry you don't happen to see things his way. Another personality quirk garnered from his youth.

Jo nods in agreement, evidently in full support of the calming effect of white noise.

"Anyway, Corey is still here I assume?" Devin starts walking toward the locked door though we haven't yet been granted access. Then he asks, "So, Jo…has that rapscallion of a husband finally finished tiling the bathroom yet?" His question is over the shoulder, not even sparing a thought for the locked door.

"Just barely, can you believe it took so long?" she answers with a smile, charmed out of her gatekeeping responsibilities.

"Honey, I'd have been done in a day, and had dinner waiting on the table when you got home." he winks and blows a kiss as she presses the button behind the desk, unlocking the door to the forbidden city.

Once the door clicks shut behind us, I ask, "Devin, what are you going to do when she notices there is no air purifier in Maribell's room?"

"What are you talking about? We have one. You said the room was stuffy, right?"

Chapter Fifteen

White Party

After leaving Maribel in the skilled hands of Devin and Corey, I'm off to Silas' to get ready for tonight's White Party at 1462. Silas hasn't told me much about it except that there will be a surprise that I will love.

I've pondered this surprise for a few days now, and I have decided, based on the over-the-top types of parties Silas hosts at the club, that the wild card of the night will be paint. Come dressed in white, as in, a blank canvas, and leave with various artist's renderings or splattered with paint.

The irony of having paint on my mind, is that tonight is also my chance to dig around and find out how to get in touch with one of the body paint artists.

I'll need to line the whole thing up for the Exposition Party behind Silas' back, so this should be interesting.

I have packed several options of white attire to bring to Silas' each with varying levels of attachment and disposability factors. If clothing is to be ruined with paint, I will absolutely not wear the white leather skirt or the matching bustier with white Gucci heels. The middle-of-the-road attachment outfit is a vinyl bandeau style top with white vinyl booty shorts and tall boots. And the completely disposable outfit is a cotton shirt that laces up the front while still remaining open over my braless cleavage, and a white pleather skirt. I'll ask Silas' opinion about which outfit to wear while impressing upon him just how much I don't want the leather one ruined.

***

Silas opens the door dressed in athletic shorts and a white tank top. My eyes are drawn to the bulging vein in his left bicep, and I giggle, realizing he had just been lifting weights in preparation for the evening.

"Hey, Sexy," he says with a sweaty grin.

"Hi," my eyes drift over his smooth, muscled shoulders and across his broad chest. In response to my ogling, he chuckles, then lightly takes hold of my chin and plants a brief kiss on my lips, careful not to get his sensuous perspiration on me.

I step in and nudge the door shut behind me. "Are you sure you want to go out?" I ask as I look around for signs of Ruby.

"They will be right back, just went for ice cream."

"Then maybe we should shower?" I wiggle my brows suggestively.

"Yes. Shower," he laughs at my lack of subtlety, and then adds, "She still wants to finish the book you know."

"Oh, I have every intention of finishing the book with her. Don't you worry about that."

***

In the shower, as Silas tips his head back to rinse out the shampoo, I get down on my knees. While still rinsing, he says, "Jessie," in a warning tone.

"What?" I ask innocently as I watch sudsy water cascade down his smooth body.

"We should save it for the cl—Oh fuuuck," his tune changes as I suck one of his balls into my mouth.

"Hmmm?" I ask, but it's really more of a hum, which makes him squirm even more.

I know exactly what he is feeling right now. His testicles are so fragile that he knows I could really hurt him, but he is loving the sensation while he fights the instinct to protect his most delicate parts. It's classic…pleasure with the threat of pain; I know it well by now.

"I want us to be. Pipes, we need—Christ, that feels so good—Jessie—" He is stammering, and reluctantly grasps the base of his sack and gently pulls himself away from my sucking mouth.

I stay on my knees but sit back on my ankles and spread my legs wider apart. The angle of the shower spray is now hitting me squarely in the chest and flowing down between my open legs.

"I want us bursting with anticipation when we get to the club. We can't do this now, it will lessen the experience tonight," he reasons, as he sits down on the built-in shower seat still guarding his rigid penis.

"That's fine. You can wait," I say, as I start to rub little circles around my clit, and his eyes shoot straight to my open legs.

"Don't do that," it's a command, but he can't look away.

"I just want you so bad, Silas. Over and over and over again," I say, using the same tempo as my circling fingers. I'm teasing him and it is so much fun seeing the indecision on his face.

"The longer you continue that, the longer I will make you wait tonight," he says in warning. I graze my other hand across my breast and begin to fondle my nipple, knowing I've almost got him.

"If I have to wait tonight, I better take care of myself right now. Don't you think?" I exhale a moan, and the echo of it in the shower beautifully punctuates my intent.

He crosses his arms across his chest and smiles a wicked little grin. "Ok, Pipes. Suit yourself." Then he turns the faucet all the way to cold.

It happens gradually, first warm, then cool, and then straight out of the Arctic cold. It is shockingly cold, splattering against my breasts and making my breath catch.

I stop rubbing my clit but bring both hands up to play with my nipples, which are hard as stone and could probably cut through the shower wall.

The sensations of the icy water, my exploitive fingers, and Silas' stare are now steadily throbbing deep in my vagina. I stubbornly lick my lips and strain my head against the frameless glass.

The chilly water trickling down through my silken flesh and dribbling against my exposed clit is almost enough to get me off right here, but the competing sensations begin to intrude and take over. The overriding sensations are the ones from my knees against the hard shower floor, the quaking of my folded legs; growing tight from the cold, and the near chattering of my teeth. They all bring about Silas' shower victory.

"Fine, you win," I say in sulky defeat.

"Shit, Jessie, I thought you were about to come." He turns the water back to warm and helps me to my feet, where I stand on legs teeming with pins and needles. "What the hell would I have done then?"

"No chance of that now," I say through almost chattering teeth, then add, "You should know though, my hot, silky vagina that you love so much, will probably feel like the Reaper's cold fist for the next few days. So, joke's on you."

"That's what you think," he says as he starts to massage one soapy hand between my legs and the other to the back of my neck to pull me into a kiss.

***

After about twenty minutes of innocent kissing and hardly anything else, the water starts to turn legitimately cold, so Silas turns off the shower.

I'm ringing the water out of my hair and Silas is squeegeeing the droplets from the glass when we hear Ruby scream. It's a blood-curdling scream that launches Silas from the shower like he was shot from a catapult. He snatches a towel from the rack like an Olympic baton handoff before running mostly naked to Ruby's aid.

I follow quickly behind him but do a better job of wrapping the towel around myself.

Analise, Silas and I, all arrive to Ruby's bedroom at roughly the same time, all of us expecting blood or protruding bones. Instead, what we find is an openmouthed little girl, staring in astonishment at the three of us from the middle of her frilly, purple room.

"What's the matter?" Silas asks, panting as he holds the towel against his penis but nothing else.

"Wellll," Ruby says shyly.

"Ruby! What are you screaming about?" Analise asks, in a much sharper tone.

"There was a spider," she says with a shrug, but she sounds apologetic at the same time.

"Are you kidding me?" Silas asks.

"Daddy, are you and Jessie naked?" Ruby inquires with wide eyes, almost like she is trying to shift the focus away from the spider.

"We just showered, Ruby. I thought someone was ripping your arm off!"

"Analise can see your naked bum, Dad," she says, as if she is embarrassed for him.

"Ruby. Elizabeth. Bishop!" Analise scolds. "Your father's naked bum is the least of my worries! Now, where is this most frightening spider?"

"It's there," she points, "Under my shoe."

Seeing that Ruby has summarily dealt with the offending spider, Analise huffs and then walks back to her apartment, leaving the connecting door ajar.

"Dad, when you shower together, don't you see each other's privates?" Ruby asks, still hung up on the pervasive nakedness in the room.

"Ruby, it's ok for grown-ups to see each other's privates if they are in love. But only if both of them want to."

"But why would you *want* to see someone's privates?" she asks, her face twisted in disgust.

"Well, Honey, it's hard to explain, but if you love someone...uh—" Watching Silas flounder is always entertaining, but it's time to put him out of his misery.

"Ruby, when you are all grown up, IF you want to see someone's privates, then it's ok. But if you *don't* want to, that's ok too. You can wait until you are older to decide for yourself. Now, how many chapters do we have left? I'm so excited to see what happens!"

"I know! Me too. I told Daddy we needed to wait for you to get back from your trip before we could finish it. Can we read tonight?"

I glance at Silas, who looks sheepish about being caught lying to his daughter, but I'm happy he didn't tell her we were fighting.

"Of course. I'm going to go get dressed while you brush your teeth and get your pajamas on. Let's all meet here in ten minutes."

"Dad?" she asks in a quiet voice.

"What, Baby Girl?"

"Can you get that giant, smashed spider out of here?"

"Sure, just let me grab a shovel real quick."

***

Now that Ruby is tucked in bed for the night, Analise is back on watch and Silas and I can get ready for the White Party at the club. I'm wearing one of his t-shirts while I dry my hair and he sits on the counter enraptured by my flat iron and the whole process of a woman getting ready for a night out.

"Tell me more about the party, so I can decide which outfit to wear," I say, while wondering if I'm right about the paint.

"The only thing I can say is that it can get a little slippery," he says, not quite an admission of paint splatter, but still convincing. Now I'm pretty sure that I am right about the paint.

"Which outfit should I wear then?" I nod to the three options hanging from the shower glass. "The leather one was expensive though…" Hopefully, that is enough of a hint.

"I wouldn't wear the leather one, you will get too hot. And definitely not those shoes. Seriously, it gets slippery."

"Ok then. Which one?"

He slides off the counter and approaches the outfits. "These are pretty fantastic." He holds up the white vinyl booty shorts, "And what is this? A belt or a top?" he asks while pointing to the vinyl bandeau top.

"It's a top."

"Damn. I'm going to need to see that one on," he says with a devilish grin. I've already started to run the flat iron through my hair, but I put it down so I can pull the t-shirt over my head, leaving me standing in white lace panties and nothing else. "Ok, hand it over."

He hands it to me and leans back into the vanity with his arms crossed. "I just can't seem to understand why grown-ups like to see each other's privates," he says as he ogles my bare chest, "But if those were mine, I would play with them all day long."

"What do you mean? I thought they *were* yours," I tease, and wave them in front of him.

"Fuck, Jessie, they are on my mind all day."

"Careful, you sound like you only want me for my body," I pout.

"I *need* your heart and mind, but I *crave* your body. I think I would shrivel up and *die* without all of you, though."

I walk forward into his arms and rest my head against his chest while he squeezes me tight. "I think I would shrivel up and die without you, too."

***

Now that my hair is pin straight and my makeup is done, Silas has chosen for me to wear the latex booty shorts, the bandeau top, and the knee-high boots with four-inch heels. The high heels trumped his concern for my safety, but only because they are a work boot style, with a thick, rubber tread on the bottom. He actually deemed me less likely to slip than even himself.

Silas is wearing white linen pants, with the drawstring tied so they hang low. I can see the hip shelves that drive me so crazy, and it makes me burn even hotter for him.

He pulls a light, v-neck t-shirt over his head and then says, "You know what would be hot?"

"What?" I smile.

"If you wore one of my tank tops." As the idea blossoms in his head, his smile gets wider and wider.

"Are you talking about your wife-beater, muscle shirt kind of tank tops?" I ask.

He slowly but enthusiastically nods his head.

"You don't like this?" I can't understand why he wouldn't want me to wear the tiny strip of fabric across my chest, it's far too sexy for anywhere but the club…or the bedroom.

"Actually, I love that, but there is something so hot about picturing your tits rubbing against the inside of one of my shirts."

I can't argue with that, it is sexy in a mark-my-territory kind of way. "Let's see how it looks first, before I commit, I have an image to uphold."

He pulls open a drawer, but doesn't take the one from the top, he digs a little, then comes up with an older, more worn out one. "This should work," he smiles and tosses it to me.

I take off the bandeau top and then shoot it at him like a rubber band. Then I slide his tank over my sleek, flat ironed mane of hair. As suspected, it fits a little big, the armholes are big enough to show my ribs, and the swoop of the neckline hangs awfully low.

"Is this too much side-boob?" I ask before realizing that no amount of side-boob would be too much for Silas. He slowly shakes his head while looking as though he's been caught in a UFO's tractor beam.

"Should I tie it at the side? Or just let it hang? Or maybe tuck it in?"

"That's so fucking sexy. I don't think it matters what you do with it."

"It's too long though," I say, then add, "Let's cut it."

"Whatever you need to happen so that you wear that shirt, I am going to make sure it happens."

***

The first thing I see when we enter the club is a huge machine hanging above the main room. It's spilling bubbles from an opening that's as wide and gaping as a hula-hoop, in a constant, steady flow. Two stories below the mouth of the machine is the dance floor, and the partygoers are chest deep in bubbles.

"It's a foam party!" Silas says as he sees the look of wonder on my face.

"It sure is!" I say, and I can feel how lit up my face is.

"Let's get a drink, then we can go dance in it," he says, as he takes my hand and leads me toward the bar.

Everywhere I look, people are soaked and laughing like little kids. This is definitely on the lighter side of 1462 parties, and the atmosphere is charged with a whimsical, excited energy. The exuberance is completely contagious, and I can't wipe the smile off my face. I have never seen anything like this, and certainly not on this scale.

"I believe shots are in order," Silas says to the bartender, who is unfamiliar to me but clearly knows Silas well.

"Absolutely," he says as he waves over another bartender, who happens to be Erik, one of the ones I do know.

"What will it be, Jessie?" the one I don't yet know asks. I stick out my hand to shake his, and he tells me his name is Kurt, though I'm surprised I could hear him over the crowd.

"Nice to meet you, Kurt. Why don't you surprise us."

Right away he lines up four shot glasses and then hardly pauses before pouring a row of tequila in all of them. He grabs a rocks glass filled with cut limes from behind the bar and slides it, along with a salt shaker over to us.

Both he and Erik lick the part of their hand that's made for licking salt, and sprinkle it on. Silas slides me in front him, and from behind, he licks the side of my neck and sprinkles me with salt.

Neither Silas nor I, miss the fact that he is not the only man to lick my neck in the presence of tequila recently.

Just acknowledging their different techniques, makes me think about how different they would be in bed. Shivers run down my spine, and they're not all from Silas' ticklish tongue.

I lick the back of my hand too just so we can all take the shots at the same time. Erik dusts the moistened spot with salt, then raises his shot glass.

"To foam!" he shouts, and we take our shots.

Without a word, Kurt replaces the shot glasses with four more and I, somewhat slowly, realize it's so I can return the favor.

I turn to face Silas. Then I hook a finger inside the drawstring of his pants and then tickle him with my fingernail, hip to sexy, smooth hip. Then

I bend and lick that beautiful ledge on the left side of his body and sprinkle it with salt.

The shots go much the same, with similar shouts, "To foam," but this time Silas' dick begins to harden, and in linen pants there is nowhere for it to go but up.

He makes some inconspicuous attempts to hold it down while the bartenders wish us a fun night then get back to work.

"Need a minute?" I tease, but then I decide to take the opportunity to break away for a bit of investigating. "I need to use the ladies room, are you going to be ok by yourself for a little while?"

He kisses me and says, "I'll see if I can manage," though I can't hear him at all now due to a song change, and evidently, a popular one.

From behind Silas, so he can't see me, I motion to Erik to meet me at the other end of the bar.

When he works his way down to me, he leans over the bar and shouts, "You are really good for him, Jessie. You know that right?"

"Thanks Erik, that's sweet. Why do you think that?" I shout back, over the rambunctious crowd.

"Some of us wondered if he was capable of falling in love. You know? He has always been so focused on the club, so single-minded and frivolous with his affections…That didn't come out right… what I meant is that he has never shown any real emotion with women. So we wondered if he would ever find someone special. Looks like, he has."

"He can be tough. And single-minded, that's for sure."

"What?" he holds a hand to his ear in hopes of hearing me better.

I change tact, he can't hear me, and I'm not here for a lengthy conversation anyway, "I want to surprise him. Can you help me?"

"Surprise Silas? That's going to be tough."

"Yes, but can you help me?"

"Absolutely."

***

When I make my way back to Silas, I'm not too shocked to find him animatedly telling a story to a handful of his friends. There is also a couple of eager female club members that I have never seen before, nodding and laughing a little too hard at whatever story he is telling. As I walk up to him, he slides an arm around my body, fitting me perfectly against his side as he continues his tale without even a pause.

"So, I don't even know what to say at that point. Here Jessie and I are, covered with glorified hand towels and dripping water on the floor, and my daughter wants to know why grown-ups like to see each other naked."

One of the laughing women places her hand on Silas' bicep and says, "You just need to tell her that big people do big people things when they are naked," she throws her head back laughing, and tightens her talons on his bicep, "And that big people love to be naked together because it feels sooo good."

"You can't say that to a six-year-old, her head would explode with questions," I say, and it comes out very patronizing.

"Oh, Honey, you can say all kinds of stuff to a six-year-old, because they can't understand a word of it."

"You don't know my daughter," Silas says, "She came into the world understanding more than some of us. Right, Sweetie?" then he adds, "Let's dance," then whisks me away from the stupidity.

***

Silas walks us into the foam, and it swallows us with warmth. It feels dry, yet damp at the same time, and slippery but not like soap. My first thought, after how warm the foam is, is that I shouldn't have bothered straightening my hair because there is no way it will stay flat in this environment.

The dance floor is crammed with people and there is not much space to dance, but the crowd moves with a pulse of its own. At times, the foam is above our heads, and at others, it's waist deep.

When the foam is low, I can see all the slippery nakedness mixed in with the fully clothed, and also, why Silas wanted me to wear this shirt. The dancers are wet from their exertion and the close proximity, but also, I think, from the foam. As the cotton dampens, it will cling to my breasts, and my areolas and hard nipples will shine through like two warning lights in a category five storm.

When the foam revelers transition from dancing to unified, arm raised jumping to the song, I can see more than a few sets of eyes on my jouncing wet t-shirt submissions. I capture Silas' undivided attention by accidentally-on-purpose sliding the armhole forward and exposing my breast for a few seconds.

He closes the tiny gap between us by turning me and backing me into him, dancing right up against my body. In short order, his hands find my now laughably concealed breasts, and he begins to pluck at my nipples through the thin cotton. I roll my ass up and down his bulging erection as he nibbles on my ear from behind.

Silas and I are having such a good time dancing together that I don't immediately register the man in front of me talking to me. He is wearing white jeans and a similar wet tank top. He is handsome, and he knows it. Perhaps too good looking because I like that he is watching my tits with such unabashed interest, and when my nipple nearly pokes out from the gaping armhole again, I find myself wishing it would.

Silas begins dragging his fingernails lightly over the cotton above my nipples, and I'm coming undone, right in front of the handsome stranger, who steps closer and repeats himself.

"I'd love to know how those tits feel pressed against my chest," he says loudly, but it's hardly audible through the kinetic energy of the club.

I feel, more than hear Silas' rumble of laughter near my ear.

"Sorry, you can look, but you can't touch," I yell back.

"So, let me look then," the stranger says, with a naughty grin.

As if a broadcast news bulletin about an ensuing tit-flash on Bourbon Street went out, all of a sudden there is quite a bit of interest in the very things beneath the almost transparent cotton. For some reason, even though they are nearly visible already, I'm a little shy about exposing them completely.

A gentle wave of encouragement flows through my immediate vicinity, but my eyes stay locked on the handsome guy in front of me. Feeling surprisingly nervous, I hook my thumbs in the oversized armholes, then slide the damp fabric to the center of my chest. I do it slowly, until the flimsy tank is gathered between both naked breasts. My heart is pounding like crazy, but I let the stranger have a good long look before sliding the shirt back into place.

I turn to face Silas, and his mouth is on mine in an instant. We dance together for a while before Silas says, "I would also like to see how your tits feel pressed against my chest." So I help him ease his own wet t-shirt over his head. He drops it to the floor, most likely never to be seen again, and pulls me against his firm body.

He slides his hand down my back, and when he can't breach the tightness of my vinyl booty shorts, he curls his fingers around the swell of my ass, and ventures between my legs.

He finds no solid access, as his fingers wrestle briefly with the vinyl at my crotch, then give up and find the back of my head instead. By this point, we have stopped dancing and are completely oblivious to the crowd around us.

The foam has relaxed a bit by the time we surface from our kiss, and it is clear the climate on the dance floor has shifted. The nudity has grown exponentially, and right next to us a woman is bent over, getting ambitiously fucked from behind while going down on a gorgeous black man.

I have never had the urge to smack someone's ass before, but the guy getting head has the most perfect butt I have ever seen. Not only would I smack it, I would bite it.

"It's hot, want to get some water?" Silas asks.

I nod, and he gestures for me to lead the way.

"Have you met Damon before?" Silas asks.

"Which one is Damon?"

"That tall, panty dropping guy you were so enchanted with. The one getting sucked off," he smiles.

"Oh my goodness! I just want to bite his ass and rub all up on him," I laugh as I peel the hair off my damp back.

"Yes, the ladies sure do love him. He is one of the suspension experts here at the club." Then he wiggles his eyebrows, "Maybe you can volunteer to be suspended at the Expo."

"Hell no. I'm not letting anyone suspend me, not even him."

Now that we are out of the thick of the dance floor and have some space, I notice Silas' linen pants are clinging to his package, and they are just as see-through as my shirt.

"Wow, Silas. That is an impressive cock you have there. On display. For everyone to see," I'm laughing, but for some reason, it seems really scandalous.

"You like that?"

"I'm pretty sure everyone likes it. Swinging all free. Every swell and ridge completely visible."

"I wouldn't say it's swinging free, linen is pretty clingy," he smiles. "Come on, I'm thirsty," he takes my hand, and we head off to the bar, clothes clinging to our bodies and all.

Before we even make it fifteen feet, we are accosted by another batch of Silas' friends and a few more stargazing women.

"How is the foam?" Silas' buddy, Scott, asks.

"It was a little overzealous at first, but I think things have settled down some. Where have you guys been?"

"You know these ladies, we had to hit the webcam room first."

Then the other guy chimes in, "Had to eat a little sushi first."

His date, or girlfriend swiftly punches him in the arm, "You have to stop saying that! It sounds better to just say *eating pussy*. Don't you guys think it's better to say eat pussy than eat sushi? There is nothing sexy about sushi...but pussy—" I swear she says the word pussy twenty times before she is finished, and the whole time she speaks, her eyes dart back and forth from Silas' showy dick to his bare chest.

"What's the webcam room like?" I ask.

Scotts' girlfriend, I think her name is Meg, answers, "It's so hot, Jessie. There is a computer screen projected on the wall, so it's interactive and real people can watch from anywhere in internet space. But the best part is, because you can see what they type, you can do what they request. It's so fun, you guys should try it."

"That doesn't sound safe. What if an internet creeper wants to track you down? They know right where to find you." I'm stunned someone would even try it, and you can read the shock all over my face.

"It's not like that," Silas says, "I paid a hacker a ton of money to ensure safety from discoverability. There are all kinds of firewalls, proxy settings, encryptions and VPN's. Not to mention 24-7 security software with specialized webcam activity monitoring, and automatic DMCA takedowns," Silas shrugs, and when he realizes everyone is looking at him wide-eyed, he says, "What? I take member security very seriously."

"Do people ever ask you to do really weird stuff?" I ask, but my question is directed at Meg.

"Always, but if you don't like a certain person or they creep you out, you can end the chat with the push of a button. You can even block their IP address, it's awesome."

Scott jumps in, "Meg loves blocking people, I think she has a God complex. She's always like, **I banish you**…and poof."

Then the other girl, while still eyeballing Silas' crotch and very prominent cock head through the clingy pants, adds, "You should try it," then drags her guy off to the foam.

Scott waits until they are out of earshot, then says, "Sorry about Jacy. She evidently has a thing for men in see-through pants."

"She couldn't take her eyes off his dick," Meg says, "It's hard not to stare, but still. Show some restraint, Jacy."

"I know, I had to create a line in my head so I wouldn't look lower than Jessie's collarbone for more than two seconds at a time," Scott says with a hearty laugh.

Meg laughs too, then starts to drag him away with a lighthearted roll of her eyes, "Let's go, Honey, the foam waits for no one."

***

At the bar, we get ice water from Kurt, and I am reminded again of the projecting state of my nipples because Kurt has no two-second rule. My shirt is clammy and adhered to my breasts like a second skin; a very transparent second skin. It's amazing how boobs can stop a man in his tracks, totally mesmerize him, and render him near useless.

While I stand here, representing myself as masturbatory material for countless distracted eyes, Silas is talking to a couple I've never met before. My own concentration on my show-off nipples is broken when I hear Silas say, "Jake and Rachael, this is my girlfriend, Jessie."

We all shake hands, but Rachel doesn't let go of my hand, so I'm oddly tethered to the woman while she speaks to Silas, "So tell me, why do people call you Bishop?"

"You might be the only person that calls me Bishop past the admissions room Rachael, but it's really more for keeping a low visibility and some semblance of privacy, that's all. It's nothing pretentious or self-serving." He doesn't mention that it's his last name, and not used narcissistically as though he feels himself priest-like.

"Well, *Bishop*, are you guys looking for any company this evening?" she asks with a tilt of her head.

"Not tonight Rach, thanks though," Silas has turned them down even before her meaning crystalizes for me.

Silas casually takes my hand from her, then whispers in my ear, "Want me to show you the webcam room? We can see if it's empty."

119

***

The room is a lot smaller than the other theme rooms in the club, and the furniture is sparse, though the added lighting options are not. There is a bed with a leather couch at the foot of it, and an open laptop on a small end table. Out of the view of the computer is a large armoire, where Silas retrieves clean sheets and tosses them to the bed.

"What if my boss sees this, Silas?" I ask while I peruse the different types of additional lighting.

"No one within a hundred square miles can even access the feed, there is a geoblock on it for precisely that reason," he says.

"That's smart. So, what do we do anyway? How does it work?"

"When you are ready, we just log in. We can read the comments on the computer screen or from where they get projected on the wall, but it's really up to us as far as what we do. We don't even have to acknowledge the viewers if we don't want to, we can write our own performance. And Meg is right, any nut-jobs get blocked."

"Do we respond back to them?" I ask, completely intrigued.

"We can, or we don't have to."

"How do we know they are there?"

He smiles, "You'll know."

I find that I am more nervous than I thought I would be, but I'm also excited by the idea. My heart is pounding in my chest, and it feels like it fills my whole rib cage.

"Ready, Hon?" Silas asks, as he turns on a bright overhead light.

We take a seat on the leather couch, and then Silas slides the end table in front of us. There is an engraved plaque with a username and password etched into it, which is screwed into the table top by the keyboard. He types them in and then sits back with his arm draped over my shoulders.

Instantly, I see screen names flicker to life in the viewer list, and then they flood the screen. There are more than I thought there would be, much more. It's scary and exhilarating at the same time.

I was nervous to flash that hot guy on the dance floor, and he was but one person. Now, who knows, but there are a ton of screen names, and we haven't yet done a thing.

Silas starts out, "Hi everyone, I'm Dan, and this is my beautiful date, Katie. She has finally agreed to go out with me, even though it took all semester and an inordinate amount of begging on my part."

The comments pour in, too fast and too many to read all of them. The one that catches my eye is from CumDaddy405, "I hope you took her to dinner first."

Silas continues, "I see that you are all concerned that I may not have gentlemanly intentions, but I assure you, I took her out for a very nice dinner and a walk in the park. The only reason we are here is because it started pouring rain AND because Katie here, asked me what I like to do for fun. So I thought I would show her. What do you guys think?"

Unceasing comments, SpankinIt4U, "Show us her tits." 420EZRiderDad, "Are u gonna fuck r not?" BBCock4you, "Spread ur legs 4 us darlin." SkoobyRinger1984, "Let's c u fill all her drippin holes." Each message is filthier than the next.

Silas again, "Now let's not get ahead of ourselves. You see, Katie and I have not yet shared our first kiss. Who thinks I should give her a kiss?"

I don't even want to read all the ridiculous comments because the screen names are bad enough.

I turn to Silas for a kiss, but he only gives me a dainty peck on the lips. I see now how he is going to play this.

"Now that that's out of the way, I was thinking we could get to know each other." Silas's arm is still over my shoulders, and ever so slightly, he grazes his fingertips across my breast, almost as if on accident. A coy smile creeps to my lips. This side of Silas will be new and fun.

As he innocently continues to graze my barely concealed nipple, I really start to embrace the role play. It is fun pretending to be on a first date while nervously getting acquainted with each other.

The first time Silas and I had gotten *acquainted* with each other, we were total strangers. I had performed like a trained whore, bending over in front of him while he stripped me of my lace panties. There was no erotic tension or sexy buildup then. So it's fun to pretend now, to kind of go back to the beginning.

"Should we find out if Katie has sensitive nipples?" he asks, as his fingers flutter again over the tip.

I straighten up my posture, whereby pressing my chest forward, and the lewd comments accelerate. These viewers are like feral kittens at a tuna can, it's almost comical.

"Katie, they want you to sit on my lap, so it's easier for me to fondle your breasts. Are you ok with that?" Silas asks.

I nod my head and slide closer to him. Aware that I've been completely mute thus far, and essentially look like a deer caught in the headlights. I like that Silas is running the show, however, I'm afraid of portraying the image of a lost little soul; having things done to her. That particular role is decidedly *not* sexy. In fact, it's way too disgusting and criminal to feed into, so I decide to behave less passively. I can't have these internet trolls thinking I'm anything less than willing.

Adjusting myself above Silas, I fold my legs back, so I'm in a kneeling position over his lap. Now I'm perched in a kind of reverse cowgirl position. I can raise or lower myself accordingly, which I do, in order to slowly grind hip-rolling circles against his shaft.

"Wow guys, it looks like Katie is feeling frisky tonight."

I lean forward with my hands on his knees and arch my back, presenting my ass to Silas. He grabs each cheeky section of white vinyl and gives a hearty squeeze while helping my crack to slide up and down his erection.

I can also see that by arching forward, my once cling-wrapped tank, has fallen away from my body and is dangerously close to exposing two naked breasts through the low neckline.

The comments are a constant, streaming, blur that I disregard entirely because Silas has released his cock from the damp linen and shifted the direction of it. Now instead of facing up my back, it's forward, between my legs.

I can vividly feel his coronal ridge, even through the vinyl, as it rubs against my vagina. I widen my knees even further, lowering myself to create more friction.

"That's enough for now, Katie. Shiny latex is no friend to a bare cock head."

I pout exaggeratedly for phony theatrics. I want him inside me exactly like this. The sex wouldn't be quite so exploitive because the position is hot, while still being censored from the viewers. It's perfect, because I'll never be on board with a close-up shot of Silas penetrating me, or even a spread legged, naked shot of myself; geoblock or not.

As guarded and perfect as the position is for sex, the logistics of standing, removing my shorts, and then getting situated again are just too awkward for caming.

Silas helps me unfold my legs and sit back on his lap so my legs dangle over his. Then he spreads my legs open as he widens his knees.

This position is raw and exhilarating, though my crotch is still shielded by the vinyl. I lean back against his chest with my legs open, and settle in for my webcam close up.

Both of Silas' hands slowly creep into the gaping armholes of my tank. It's an experimental, boundary testing, offensive strike by the shy, respectful Dan. It's his sly journey toward first copping a feel, and then timidly fiddling with my nipples. This shy persona is new for me too, as I absorb the novelty of his unsure demeanor.

Silas plays with my breasts while I pretend it's the first time he has ever touched them. His character, Dan is timid and unsure, finding encouragement from the lewd comments. It's exciting in an inexperienced lover kind of way. Plus, Silas is anything but timid in any other circumstance, so the roleplay is different and provocative.

"Look at all these filthy comments. Everyone wants you to show them your naked pussy, Katie. Can you believe their audacity? Even with all this urging, I'm inclined to keep it for myself," he hums, while taunting the faceless viewers.

"I like what your hands are doing, Dan. You should have told me you were this skilled when you first asked me out." I smile widely while talking, mostly because the whole thing is such a farce it's hard to keep a straight face.

"Maybe we should all have a look at these perfect tits instead? Would you like to show everyone what my hands have been doing underneath your shirt, Katie? Or should we make them wait?"

"I like feeling your hands on me Dan, let's show them how talented your fingers are."

Silas withdraws his hands from the armholes and starts to circle each nipple with his pointer fingers, over the nearly transparent fabric. His movements are slow and deliberate, causing the tips to strain against his attentiveness and the damp fabric to adhere more closely to my flesh.

Soon the circles become more insistent. Then he changes the angle of his fingers and begins to scratch his short fingernails right over the tops of my rigid nipples. He is indulging himself as well as the viewers with such focused attention on them. By the time he begins to pinch and gently twist, I'm already dappled with perspiration and ready to get on with things.

I can't clearly see the computer screen, but the comments projected on the wall are visible, and quite insistent. They all want nudity and sex, though the wording is much more crass. When I see a flash of one asking Dan to choke me, Silas leans forward and with a few keystrokes, MeleeInTheDark4 vanishes.

Silas teasingly eases the neckline of my shirt down. Only a little at first, but my breasts are being revealed bit by bit. The neck opening of the shirt isn't big enough to reveal bare nipples, so he finds the bottom hem, and coyly begins to raise it up.

"Katie, is it ok if I lift up your shirt? Everyone wants to see your pretty tits." I nod, and just like that, Silas begins to raise my shirt. The pace is slow, like a drawbridge rising crank by steady crank.

When only the bottoms of my breasts are visible and my shirt is balanced across two hard peaks, Silas stops raising it and begins caressing my abdomen instead.

I think he stops so I won't feel overly exploited, but by nature of this webcam, we are clearly passed the notion of overexposure. I'm fine with strangers jerking off while looking at my tits—especially under Silas' skilled hands, and *most especially* with the geoblock set at one hundred square miles.

I adjust my posture causing the hem of the shirt to lift and revealing my stony nipples, but only just.

"Katie, why don't you read some of our viewer comments out loud for me? Only read the ones you want me to indulge though, because I will happily oblige any viewer comments you repeat," he says this with a warning tone that isn't necessary, because eighty percent of what flashes across the screen won't even be considered, let alone dignified through actions.

"Ok," I smile. This could get interesting. I scan through some of the suggestions and find it hard to land on a mild one. Most of them want to see us fuck, but it's too early for that, I want to trail them along for a bit before deciding whether or not to even have sex on screen for them.

"Ok, how about you…" I have to lean into the computer screen to read the comment correctly, "Lap at my titty."

Silas smiles then sits forward, tilting his head around my side. It's an awkward angle, but he manages to flick his tongue against my partially covered nipple a few times before he slowly drags the flat of his tongue over it. When he repeats the lapping motion, my eyes roll back before refocusing on the typed demands.

"They want you to lift my shirt up all the way," I say directly. He does as he's told, causing me to feel prickly and excited as my naked breasts come completely into their leering view. I feel the flutter of my exposure all through my body as I scan for another viewer request.

"Now, push my nipple back and forth *roughly* with your tongue, then suck it… *hard.*" He does, maybe even sucking too hard because it elicits a sharp gasp from somewhere in my throat.

Silas has a glint in his eye and a wicked grin on his face while peering up from my breast. I think he's reminding me of his commitment to following directions.

Without taking his playful eyes off mine, he flickers his tongue against ripe flesh. Then, he swirls it around and around my nipple…slowly—and with devious intent, before sucking it harshly again.

I'm still, as endorphins flood my system, vying for my attention. Then I say, "Now, sharply flick both of them with your fingers." I lean back against his chest, granting him visual access from his vantage point over my shoulder.

When he does as he's told, a shot of pain radiates from each tip to my vagina. The strength behind his initial flicks makes me hesitate to read the next demand, unsure if I want him to do what I say.

"Flick them *hard,* Dan."

When he does, it's hard to distinguish if it feels really good or really bad. I decide not to read any more requests for pain. They all call for my discomfort in the form of slapping or stretching or rough biting. Not a single viewer wants gentle touches or sexy caresses.

"They want you to finger me," I say, altering the crude semantics laid out before me like a smut buffet. It's a healthy jump from where we are at the moment, but Silas moves to oblige.

He adjusts me on his lap, spreading my legs by widening his, and plucking at strained nipples with obedient fingers.

My head rocks back onto Silas' shoulder as he gently tugs. The way I'm draped across him allows him to fiddle with my breasts as if they were his own. The orientation of his coddling presents my body like a lustful offering or a tribute to the many voyeurs in attendance.

By now, my nipples are throbbing with galvanized hysteria, and my spread legs funnel the titillation directly to my core.

For the second time tonight Silas tries to slide his palm under the tightness of my shorts, this time down the front, but he is unsuccessful.

He tugs the button open and lowers the short zipper, which creates a marginal amount of space for his explorative fingers.

"*Spread your legs wider, Baby,*" he whispers against my ear. Then he pushes his hand down the front of the latex. There is hardly room for his hand, so all he is doing is pressing a finger against my bare, slit.

Adapting to the restriction like the pioneer he is, Silas begins alternating the pressure of two of his fingers, so my clit rocks back and forth between them.

I have clamped down on my bottom lip while my face succumbs to the erotic strain. When I shift my head to the side and gently moan, Silas addresses the viewers.

"I think she likes this everyone. She is so wet, my fingers are drenched just from touching her pussy. I can't wait to feel how tight she is around my finger."

KumKwatt42 types, "*U need 2 get those titties bouncing.*"

"They want to see your titties bouncing," he says to me, then asks the camera, "These titties?" then withdraws his hand from my shorts, palms both breasts and begins to lightly bounce them.

I groan from the loss of pressure against my clitoris, and Silas accurately reads the cue. He drops his hand and begins seeking another route to fame, this time from the side, through the leg hole.

The vinyl bottoms are so skimpy and short, that with my legs spread open like this, and only about an inch and a half of fabric to either side of the crotch seam, access is easily granted.

Silas is able to advance his fingers and dally with my intimate lips, before he spreads them, opening me further though the view is still shrouded by vinyl.

The sensation of being spread open for the viewers doesn't diminish due to the scanty coverage that obscures their view. It still feels raw and obscene. My naked and primed, lightly bouncing breasts only add to the feeling of indecency.

Silas moves his hands down so he can pull against my inner thighs, forcing them wider apart, and then tickling my core when he slips a thumb beneath the vinyl.

"Katie, do you like when I touch you and caress your smooth pussy?" Silas asks.

"Yes," I whisper, completely lost in the moment. The feeling of exhilaration is ridiculously amplified knowing people are watching. The thought of countless strangers ogling my body while jerking off is very erotic and only serves to heighten my arousal.

We hear some distant screaming coming from the club, and while I figure it's just normal BDSM club sounds, Silas senses something different. He slams the laptop shut and practically launches me off the couch he gets up so fast.

"Something is wrong," he says in a panic, as he quickly ties his drawstring while hurrying toward the door. I snatch my shirt from the couch and follow right behind him, attempting to restore my own clothing.

Once through the door, Silas flat out runs toward the commotion.

He's right, something is very wrong.

Chapter Sixteen

Crisis

Back in the main room of the club, there is a large crowd gathered. The foam has stopped pumping, and the house lights are on. Erik appears by Silas' side and says, "911 is on the way, and the moderators are working to disperse the crowd."

"What the fuck happened?" Silas asks, but we are already pushing through the crowd toward the figure on the ground.

"Oh my God!" I say as I drop to my knees next to the young woman on the floor. Her jaw is clenched tight, and she's grinding her teeth back and forth. I grab her head, worried she is having a seizure. Her skin is sweaty and burning hot, yet in stark contrast, she is shivering as though she were freezing cold.

"What did she take?" Silas shouts to the onlookers, then again, **"What did she take?"**

Someone calls out, "I think she's rolling."

"Who was she with? Where are they?" Silas yells, to no one in particular, as he drops to my side. He opens her eyelids. Her pupils are so dilated there is no discernable iris, and her eyes are wiggling around and rolling back into her head as if they were loose and disconnected.

"Someone find her friends! EMS will need to know what she took. Do it, NOW!" Silas is commanding, yet surprisingly calm.

Someone brings cool, wet rags, and I do my best to mop the sweat and heat from her skin. I can hear strong male voices demanding people get their stuff and leave if they have nothing to contribute. There is also quite a bit of rustling behind us, verifying the rather insistent removal of the reluctant.

Silas looks into my eyes, and in a calm voice, he says, "Keep holding her head to the side and make sure her airway stays clear. You need to make sure her tongue isn't obstructing her breathing and also watch for vomit that may be in her throat. You're doing great."

Then he takes her hand, turns her arm over, and finds her pulse with two steady fingers. He focuses his attention on his watch, then after a few moments, says, "Her blood pressure is really high." Then he looks around at the remaining bystanders, and asks, "Does anyone know what her name is?"

"Her name is Jessica Talbot, she was here with two friends, but they took off," someone says from behind me.

Then five paramedics swarm in. A cyclone of activity begins as Silas helps me to my feet and tucks me against his side.

"What do we have here?" one of the paramedics asks, as he shines a penlight into Jessica's eyes. "Fixed and dilated, nonreactive. Get me a set of vitals."

"No one seems to know what or how much," Silas answers.

"Patient is cyanotic, I want an OPA and start bagging her, 15 liters per minute," he calls out while aggressively rubbing her sternum. "Get her on the monitor."

"Patient is tachycardic, blood pressure is 185 over 110," a younger version of the one in charge says, "Presenting as diaphoretic and severely hyperthermic, placing ice packs now."

"Do we have an IV yet? Push 1 mg Narcan," barks the one in charge.

All at the same time, one EMT is cramming a tube down Jessica's throat, another begins squeezing a bag, assisting her breathing, an IV is started, and her thighs and armpits are packed with ice packs.

"One mg Narcan, going in now," says the one who started the IV, as she depresses the syringe.

"Get ready for a fight, and have suction ready in case she vomits," directs the one in charge.

The medics work together in perfect synergy, as if calls like this happen twice a shift. It's really amazing, yet I'm still terrified I'm watching this young woman die. In fact, I think the remainder of the onlookers feel the same, as we all watch them load her floppy, unresponsive body onto the pram and strap her down.

A few of us follow the medics out and then stand in stiff, muted, disbelief as she is loaded into the waiting ambulance. The last thing we hear from the EMT's is to, "Run emergent, lights and sirens," then the back doors are closed, and Jessica's lifeless body is whisked into the night under the blare of sirens and flashing lights.

When they are gone, I can still feel the flashing lights against my skin, and still see them flicker behind my eyelids. When I finally take a breath, it's only in preparation of holding it again. It is in this way that I'm able to restrain the tears and the violent shaking that waits just below the surface.

"You think probably Molly or Oxy?" Erik asks Silas.

"I was worried she was speedballing, but the Narcan would have worked. Same with Oxy."

"Did you see her pupils? She had to be rolling, she was faced out!" Erik says, seemingly familiar with the drug slang these days.

Silas pulls me against his chest and wraps both arms around me, snuggling me against him and shielding me from needing to say a single word. "She was definitely on some kind of stimulant—likely Molly, but who knows what that shit is cut with anymore, you know?"

"No doubt. I bet something crazy like Heroin or even Fentanyl," Erik says.

"Not this time. When they hit her with the Narcan, she would have sat bolt upright, fighting and screaming within about a minute, instantly not high anymore. That's how Narcan works. Drugs like Heroin or Oxy, or Fentanyl, bind to opioid receptors in the brain. The Narcan essentially strips those binds and blocks the receptors. I've seen a guy who I thought was dead, wake up screaming and swinging at the EMTs he was so angry they wrecked his high."

"That's insane," Erik shakes his head in bewilderment.

"Yep, it is. Let's go back inside, this is going to be a huge shit show to contend with," Silas says, with a resigned sigh.

"Do you even hear yourselves? She might die! What the hell is wrong with you two?" I finally find my voice, after what seems like decades of mute disorientation.

"Babe, I wish this wasn't so commonplace, but the fact is, it happens all the time," Silas says, trying to calm the beast.

"Literally *all* I can think about, is that girls' *mother* doesn't even know that her baby may have just died on the dirty floor of a sex club! She's probably at home blissfully sleeping, while her child just overdosed—abandoned by her friends to die alone on the sweaty, foamy, cum soaked floor!" I know my fear is displaying itself as anger, but I don't even try to quell the storm.

"Jessie," Silas tries.

"She hasn't even gotten the call yet! That her beautiful child; the one with such a bright future and so much promise—is at the hospital... or maybe even the morgue! And all you guys can talk about are callous platitudes and petty disturbances! You act like it's some huge inconvenience for you!" I'm furious, but the venom spilled, surprises even me.

I think my mind is having trouble processing the last thirty minutes, so my mouth offers release, kind of like the valve on a pressure cooker .

"Jessie— Calm down. We are fucking scared too. And there is *no* part of me that will ever forget what her eyes looked like when they rolled back into her dead skull, so don't—" Erik winds up, but Silas interrupts.

"Stop. It's a horrible thing. None of what you said is lost on either of us, Jessie."

"She looked so young, you guys," tears well up in my eyes. What I mean to say, is that she looked so affluent. Not at all the street rat you expect to have a drug overdose. She is probably a college student from a loving, supportive home, and just got burned experimenting with the latest club drug. I bet her Prada bag is still in coat check.

"I don't get it," Erik says, as the door closes behind us, "In here, there is every conceivable outlet to chase your high—why someone would need to alter or enhance that, is beyond me."

"That is exactly why her friends left," Silas says, with disappointment in his voice.

"Wait, what? What do you mean?" I ask, no longer as angry but suddenly very confused.

"Didn't want to lose their memberships," Erik states, as if it should be obvious.

"No way. They didn't want to get arrested," I offer, hoping I'm right because the alternative is just too depressing.

"When was the last time paramedics arrested someone?" Erik asks, with his brows raised.

"No," it comes out a shocked whisper.

"There is a lot more to this than sweet little, *stupid* Jessica Talbot. There will be an investigation, and possibly a lawsuit, Jessie," Erik explains. "We aren't being callused we are just trying to get ahead of this," he says, as he rakes his fingers through his hair and looks to the ceiling as if summoning angels for help.

"I'm already ahead of this. Unfortunately, as my lawyer says, this type of thing is not an *if,* it's a *when*. I have precautions in place if, God forbid, someone tries to hit me with social host, or dram shop liability, or even a negligence claim," Silas says, confident but weary.

"How could you possibly be ready for this, Silas?" Erik asks, clearly the pessimist.

"You know all the employee drug screenings we do? And the repetitive training about spotting on-premise drug use? What about all the zero tolerance verbiage in the employee work contracts… not to mention all the paperwork our members fill out? You know all those detailed incident reports and membership revocation write-ups?" Silas asks.

"Yeah," Erik concedes, but he is still skeptical.

"Those types of things help me demonstrate that I am neither negligent nor intend to cause someone harm. And I most certainly do not provide that shit to people."

"And 911 was called, and we rendered aid… how could someone think Silas or 1462 was somehow to blame?" I ask though I have zero knowledge regarding civil liability.

"I just hope she doesn't die," Erik says, then looks directly at me and adds, "Because that would be devastating for her family, as well as a *total shit show*, like Silas said."

Chapter Seventeen

Gift

We are all at Silas' for a sort of welcome home dinner for Devin and Corey, and while Ruby entertains the guests of honor out on the terrace, I slide between Silas and his dinner preparations. Looking up into his eyes, I say, "We can reschedule, I know you have a lot on your mind."

"Jessie, I told you, I'm fine." He sets down the knife he was using to trim the steaks and leans down to kiss me. "It will be good to just have a fun, non-taxing evening at home."

"Ok, but they brought gifts, so I can't promise the night will be non-taxing," I wink, and then shimmy out of my spot between him and the counter to go open more wine.

It's been eight days since Jessica's overdose at the club. She remains in the intensive care unit, in a coma; not dead, but obviously not doing great either.

Since all the chaos, Silas has been in constant contact with his lawyer, insurance agent, and law enforcement officials. He is preparing for any eventuality and is reaffirming his compliance with the law at every turn. He has scheduled, not only employee training but *member* training about drug use and how to spot it, as well as basic life support classes for anyone on the payroll. No one is exempt from the classes, club moderators, bartenders, bouncers, even those who have their hands in the accounting and marketing have been roped in.

Before we left the club the night of the overdose, Silas had formally terminated memberships for Jessica and her, what turned out to be, five friends. As well as had all the bartenders and himself drug tested, and the premises searched for any indication of drugs, or intent to distribute.

He tries to portray calmness and professionalism and doesn't want to *burden* me with the details, but I can tell it's heavy on his mind, at all times. Even through my attempts to distract or realign his focus with nudity, sexual advances, or outright pornographic overtures, he has remained distant and in his own form of coma.

I think Jessica's status, hanging between this world and the next, has more to do with his state of mind then the threat of vicarious liability, which, at this point I know all about.

I am worried about her outcome as well, but where I need constant distraction from the worry, Silas needs quiet contemplation. Our two coping strategies don't exactly complement each other, so the disconnect has been hard for me.

Devin's stance on the matter is that it's her own stupid fault and if she dies, it will be for making a stupid decision and then stupidly following through on that stupid decision, end of discussion.

Corey however, shares the bleeding heart Silas and I have. He is upset for her family and realizes that it could happen to anyone. He recognizes that she could have been a first time, peer-pressured user, and not automatically an addict going down in the flames of her own making. Corey's compassion radiates, making it almost enough to circumvent Devin's lack of basic regard or even simple humanity.

***

While the steaks and baked potatoes are on the grill, the five of us sit around the fire pit. Ruby is snuggled into Corey's lap, where she asks for the hundredth time, "When can I open my presents?"

I am on my second glass of wine, and finally relaxing around the warm glow. "Yeah guys, when can we open our presents?" I plead and then wink at Ruby.

Devin stands, hands his wine glass to me and says, "Alright, fine. I'll go get them."

Silas sips his wine then asks Corey, "How is your mom doing? Jessie says she is eating better."

"She is doing much better, thanks. It's me though, I'm having a really hard time with her being in that place. It's just that ever since her stroke, she really can't live on her own. Really, ever since my dad passed away she has been going downhill. Her stroke just happened to be the confirmation I needed."

"It's tough, but you don't want to have to worry about her falling and breaking a hip, then being alone for hours or days. It's a nice setup anyway, it's like she has her own apartment there, and she gets rides to her appointments."

"Yeah, it's just not the same. I'll have to get used to a new normal, I guess."

"She is a funny lady. I enjoyed meeting her. You should have heard her grilling Jessie," Silas adds with an amused smile, as he places his hand on my knee.

"She said *I* was cute enough to sop up with a biscuit!" Ruby interjects proudly.

Devin walks out with an appetizer platter of cheese and olives. "Ok, here are your presents. Jessie, Kalamata olives from Greece, and Ruby, you get some really stinky Camembert cheese from France," then he quickly asks, "Now, who has my Shiraz?" while Ruby giggles at the serious delivery of an obvious joke.

***

After dinner, Corey brings out the real gifts, and it's laughable because there are so many. Three are wrapped in frilly paper with an obnoxious cacophony of bows. The other two are unadorned yet tasteful gift baskets.

"Ruby, we are making you wait, because you were the least patient," Devin says with a stern look. Then he snorts on a laugh, "Just kidding, yours are the best, so we're saving them for last."

Then Devin clears his throat. "Silas, you took a minute to grow on me, but I'm glad you did. We brought you an assortment of European beers," he says with a broad, genuine smile.

"Drink them in good health," Corey adds. "There's German Pilsners, Italian Peroni, Mythos from Greece, Kronenbourg from France, Mahou from Spain…so many taste sensations. Devin and I drank enough Peroni to sink a ship, and the Mythos, ahhhh, it's fantastic."

"This is amazing you guys! Really, thank you!" Silas says as he examines each bottle with keen interest.

"And now, sweet Jessie," Devin says, "Even though you threw me out of my own condo, to live out my days on the street like a common sewer rat… I have loved you since I met you. And what speaks to that love better than Spanish olive oil and Italian balsamic vinegar?" Devin says in the voice of a game show host, making us all laugh.

I blow kisses, first to Corey, then Devin. "Thank you, you're too kind. Just so you know, I haven't thrown you out of your condo, I have simply redecorated."

Ruby squeals with delight, the anticipation just too damn much.

"Go ahead, Sweetie," Corey smiles at her, effectively giving her the green light to tear into all the frills.

While Ruby busies herself with the nearly impenetrable bows, Devin tosses a small box into my lap, "Don't think our love stops at olive oil, Sister." He relaxes back, next to Corey and takes a delicate sip of his wine.

I open the box and take out a little machine with, what…a mouth— kind of. The box identifies it as a *Womanizer*.

"Devin insisted," Corey says, shyly. "It's from Germany."

"What is it?" I ask, as I inspect the marble sized, circular mouth.

"I think it's a personal massager," Silas says with amusement.

"Yes. It provides your *little girl* with a gentle, suction-y massage. Hours of endless entertainment really," Devin says with a conspiratory smile, just as Ruby finally breaches the surface of her first box.

"Ahhhhh! It's a ruffly, red dress! I love it!" Ruby says, as she stands to hold it against herself.

"It's a Flamenco dress from Spain!" Corey exclaims, matching her excitement.

"Open. Open. Open," Devin encourages when she hesitates, debating opening the other gifts versus trying the red one on.

She lays the dress neatly across the back of the patio sectional, then drops to the ground and tears into the next one.

"So, Devin and I would like to talk to you guys about something," Corey says, causing warning bells to sound in my head.

"I better get more wine then," Silas says as he rises to his feet. "Anyone need anything?" He is perfectly relaxed, though he must know what's coming down the pipes.

Ruby pulls out another billowing dress, this one with a long apron. Then she nearly drops it to the ground when she realizes there are little wooden clogs in the box too.

"I can dress up like a little Dutch girl! I didn't know you went to Dutch!" she says, her face lit like a Christmas tree.

I laugh out loud at her comment. Somehow she knows about the traditional dress of little Dutch girls, but nothing of their country.

"Honey, Dutch people live in The Netherlands," Corey corrects her. Then he looks sideways at me for daring to laugh at her innocence, but he looks like he wants to laugh too.

With hardly a moment's pause, she descends on the last box, strips out the bothersome tissue paper, and withdraws a traditional German Dirndl. She holds it to her body and spins around, exclaiming, "I love it so much!" Then she pounces on Devin, dress and all. She squeezes him in a tight, prolonged hug, then gives Corey the same treatment.

"Maybe we can have a fashion show tomorrow. It's getting pretty late now though, Rubes," Silas calls from just inside the patio door. He is leaning with his shoulder against the doorjamb, in a relaxed stance.

I know we have talked about me getting pregnant for Corey and Devin, but his calmness in the eye of the storm is really a testament to his character.

***

Now that Ruby is tucked in bed, we all settle back in around the flickering crystals of the gas firepit. The ambiance is comfortable and easygoing as I lean against Silas' side. His arm is draped over my shoulders in a protective manner. I feel like the family unit is finally back together, strong, settled…and calm.

That is, until Devin drops the bomb we were both expecting and asks, "Can we talk about a baby?"

Corey jumps in, alarmed at Devin's directness, "There is no sort of obligation here, we just want to see where you guys stand. And, if either of you aren't comfortable…that's it, we pull the plug. There are other options we can explore."

"Have you looked into the other options? I'm not even sure what is available to you," Silas says, not at all dismissive but certainly curious.

"There is adoption—domestic or abroad, and surrogacy—biological or gestational," Corey answers.

"We are open to all of them, but there are positive and negative aspects pretty much across the board," Devin says.

My heart breaks for Devin. All he has ever wanted was a loving family. His own nuclear family was such a colossal disappointment that he has yearned for a do-over his whole life. And Corey, he represents all that is good in the world. He deserves absolutely anything his heart desires.

There has never been a question in my mind about their abilities as parents. Really—and I'm embarrassed to admit, the only question has been, how do I give up nine months of my life? I would grant them a child in a heartbeat if it didn't require such selflessness on my part.

I've thought it over and over ever since Devin brought it up months ago, and really the first three or four months, I wouldn't even be showing all that much. I'd maybe have some lite morning sickness in the beginning, but that can't be that bad. So really, all they are asking of me is a mere five months of an oversized body. In return for a lifetime of their well-deserved happiness.

When I rejoin the conversation, they are discussing the financial logistics and the lengthy time commitment required.

"Who would be the daddy?" I interrupt.

Three sets of eyes turn toward me.

"We both would," Devin says, sounding confused.

"No, I mean *the* daddy."

"Oh that," Corey clears his throat, "We have already decided that, in the instance of a surrogate, we would mix our, uh…contributions. We would leave it in the hands of someone more worthy than us," Corey explains, a little nervously.

"So what exactly is the process?" I'm curious about this step, especially because they will be mixing sperm.

"In the case of a gestational surrogate, the donor egg would be fertilized outside of the womb, and then implanted. For a biological surrogate, she would track her ovulation through her temperature and the viscosity of her secretions," Corey clears his throat again, "Then, when the time is right, she would insert a little cup into her vagina."

"It's a timeless tale, really. Two dudes come in a cup, and then forty weeks later, the fruit of their loins emerges as a crying, fist sucking, cherubic infant," Devin adds, just in case I wasn't following along.

Silas laughs, which reminds me of his overwhelming benevolence in the matter.

"And who will bring me pickle juice and ice cream in the middle of the night?" I ask playfully.

"I will of course," Silas says with confidence.

"Uh, yeah, he'll have to, you kicked me out on to the streets," Devin says sardonically.

"You mean redecorated? It's for the best anyway, I'll need a quiet, contemplative space if I'm to ovulate properly."

Devin and Corey look at each other with similar looks of cautious optimism.

"Jessie, you are talking like you are considering this, are you?" Corey asks, though I know he is shielding himself from my answer.

"Oh. You guys, yeah, … I'm going to do it."

***

It was pretty late by the time Corey and Devin left, but now, Silas and I are finally getting ready for bed. Silas has been remarkably supportive of my Baby-Mama prospects, so I plan to reward his kindness. Yet he is still leaden with anxiety about Jessica Talbot, and all but disinterested in sex. I plan to do my level best in the retribution/distraction department though, even if passion is the very last thing on his mind.

In the past week, I have worn sexy lingerie, talked dirty, sent lascivious texts and pictures, and performed a surprisingly impressive striptease. All to no avail, well, to *some* avail. As in, the efforts have gotten me laid, but each time the sex felt more like a perfunctory lay.

It turns out, I don't take well to indifferent, cursory sex; not with Silas, it's too out of his character. Thus far, I haven't been able to solicit his complete attention, but I intend to change that tonight.

Following an eventful evening of wine, laughs and dozens of stories about Devin and Corey's trip, I'm feeling confident in his relaxed state.

My overt actions have only had a limited payout, so now I'm going to try subtle, and hopefully put him back in the position of hungry predator.

After a comically long pee, brushing his teeth, and getting undressed, Silas gets into bed. It's even possible he intends to go right to sleep.

My approach is coy, though no less of an assault. First, I undress in the bathroom, partially hidden from his gaze. Next, I pull on one of his white t-shirts, making sure he knows I'm not wearing anything underneath. Then I fiddle with my hair, pulling it up into a ponytail while making sure the t-shirt lifts enough to uncover the base of my ass.

Suddenly, supremely interested in something that may, or may not be in my eye, I lean in toward the mirror, further displaying myself. My movements are highly calculated to look natural and unaware, even innocent.

When I spit toothpaste into the sink, my legs are slightly parted. I know he is watching closely, but his view of my naked crotch is carefully guarded by my demureness, and not visible outright. Same goes for when I wash my face, same bent over stance, still granting him innocent glimpses of glory.

After drying my face, while still out of his view, I pinch my nipples and tug them to strict attention before turning out the light and walking into the dim glow of the bedroom.

"I know you have been really stressed out lately, so I want to help you relax a little," I say, as I light a soothing, Sandalwood scented candle.

The comforter lays lightly across his lap, and it doesn't escape my notice that he's not hard. This also is out of character, especially after my bathroom tease, but I'm not giving up.

He watches me with a modicum of interest while I open the nightstand drawer and take out the massage oil that he bought months ago but remains unused. Then I crawl up the bed toward him, hoping he can see down the v-neck of my shirt.

He's leaning against a stack of pillows, and all I want to do is straddle him, and drag my nipples over his chest while kissing him into full arousal. However, that's not my strategy for the night, and I'll need to stay the course if I plan to succeed, and I *do* plan to succeed.

"A massage?" he asks, more surprised than I thought.

"Yeah, Baby. You are under so much pressure lately. Not to mention your unwavering support about me getting pregnant. You deserve this." *And so much more*, I think to myself. "Now, roll over on to your tummy," I say, as I begin tugging pillows out from under him.

He rolls over, and I cover him modestly with the sheet from his waist down. Normally, I would straddle his perfect, naked ass with my similarly naked self, but again, that's not the chosen method for this evening's madness.

I massage his back for a long time, kneading the knots from his muscles and caressing his worries away. Once his muscles are lose and free from tension, I use long strokes up the sides of his spine, pressing with my thumbs all the way to the base of his skull, then swipe my way down his back with a lighter, more ticklish touch, then repeat the sequence again and again.

Over and over, I press and stroke between each rib with my extended fingers, slowly making my way to his sides, then lightly up to his shoulders and down his arms. Then I move myself up his body, no longer sitting on the sheet, but skin to skin, where I settle my hands on his neck for some more focused kneading with my thumbs.

After his neck, I proceed up to his scalp where I rub and lightly scratch with my fingernails until I'm afraid he is going to fall asleep. Quickly moving on, I take less time with his arms and ignore his butt all together as I move on to his legs.

I move to his side and then adjust the sheet to enable my touch. This time, I do expose his nakedness as I shift the sheet aside. Baring one full leg, his ass, and his other thigh, I begin. I use long strokes up his whole leg, gradually taking more and more liberties around his inner thigh region. I start with small, plaintive brushes against his scrotum while caressing in, then down his thigh.

I can't tell if he's, hard because his penis is tucked under his body, but I imagine it would get uncomfortable at some point.

After an extensive full body massage, and no attempt on his part to roll over and pin me to the bed, I whisper into his ear, "Time to roll over, Baby."

He takes his time rolling over, and when he does my efforts are rewarded with a semi-erect penis. I dutifully ignore it while I begin massaging the fronts of his thighs.

Silas brings his forearm up and drapes it across his eyes, effectively cutting me off at the knees with respect to my kneeling position, and open thighs.

As his dick hardens further, I feel a sense of accomplishment at having gotten through to his body. However his mind, and consequently his sexual engagement, are still miles away.

I pour more scented massage oil into my hands and begin work on his stomach and chest. This time I work from his side because if I were to straddle him now, even just his oily thigh, I wouldn't be able to retain my purely nurturing guise.

I move my knees next to his shoulder so I can lean forward to press and knead down his torso, and also raise the bottom of my shirt with my efforts. I purposely don't touch his penis, but I elude to it in a thousand different ways.

"Why don't you take your shirt off?" he asks, from under his arm.

I stop massaging him and sit back on my heels. This is the first time he has shown the slightest interest in anything beyond his thorough rubdown. I hesitate because I don't want him to simply go through the motions, disengaged, and with his arm over his face.

Then I strip off the shirt, slowly, and while pressing my ass and tits out. When my hair drops free from the cotton fabric and falls down my back, he is solidly looking at me, no longer shielding his eyes.

"Now, why don't you come over here and sit on my face," he says with a quiet, yet commanding tone that kicks up my heart rate.

I place my palms flat on his chest, fingers pointing toward his hips, and massage down his body with a firm pressure again. The difference this time, is he helps me change position as I raise my leg over his face and bring my knee down on the other side of his head.

This time when my anointed hands make it to his erection, they don't hesitate. While trying to support myself with one hand, I use the other to guide his penis into my mouth, and then slide it down further to cradle his balls. While I suck his cock and gently massage his testicles, he is shifting beneath me, adjusting a pillow under his head.

Once he is satisfied with his position, he rubs the palm of his hand up and down my back, bringing it to rest on my hip. He takes a few swipes up my slit with his tongue, then grabs both ass cheeks, spreads me open, and pulls me down against his face.

It feels ridiculously good, not just because I'm craving him so badly, but because the change of angle puts his tongue's flection directly on my clit.

I stop sucking for a second, overcome with sensation, and then realize I'm no longer handling his balls all that gently. I quickly let go, afraid to hurt him.

He groans then murmurs into my glistening flesh, "Do that again, Baby."

I can hardly focus with his wet tongue against my eager body, but I do manage to fondle his ball sack again. I place my thumb and middle finger on the front and back seam of his sack and gently tug my fingers along that line, between his testicles. I'm careful not to squeeze them, but the gentle pressure against his balls as his sack tightens makes him groan, and slow his eager tongue.

It becomes impossible for me to suck his dick, cradle his balls, *and* hold myself up any longer, so I release his sack in order to grip the base of his cock.

One should never underestimate how difficult it is to give a proper blowjob while being serviced in a similar manner. I'm conflicted between wanting to pleasure him, and the primal urge to ignore everything except his fluttering tongue against my body.

Silas alternates pressing his tongue against my clit, with nudging it back and forth while it's strained against his tongue, utilizing the same amount of pressure for both.

When I begin to whimper and climb toward release, he switches to another method. His next technique on this occasion is roughly flicking my clitoris, and then very gently sucking it into his mouth so it's pinched in suction with its hood and my inner folds.

His mouth is magical, but there is something raw and supremely pornographic about my position that ratchets up the eroticism for me. I am literally wide open, with my vagina hovering just above his face and my spread ass cheeks clutched in his hands. Add to it the fact that I'm slowly bobbing up and down his shaft, and the scene is downright vulgar.

His reverent tongue coaxes me ever closer toward orgasm, and I moan around his rigid penis, which in turn, brings a moan from Silas. The change in vantage point for me, allows me to carefully drag the flatter, insides of my front teeth against the sensitive underside of his cock head, which is driving him wild.

As I get closer and closer, I have to release his slobbery dick and lay pressed against his body, because I no longer have the ability to hover.

He releases his grip on my ass cheeks to grab my hips and pull me closer, tighter against his mouth. I make a hollow attempt to finish him with a hand job, but once my climax hits, all I can do is ride the waves while he grinds his face against my ecstasy.

I come so hard, I'm distantly surprised I don't smother him in the process. Once the spasms begin, he abandons my clit, instead, savoring the inside of my vagina as it pulses against his tongue.

"Silas...fuuuck," is all I can say, and even I don't know what it means. I think it's a combination between, *Holy shit* and *Get inside me.* I slither forward, sliding my sweaty frame down his massage oiled body. I graze over his hardness until his buoyant shaft springs up between my open legs.

Silas sits up and moves his legs from beneath me, awkwardly lifting my dead weight and sitting back on his heels. Now I'm draped over his lap like a limp starfish, with my legs extended to his sides, my useless arms flung out, and my glossy vagina pressed against the base of his shaft.

"Jessie, I'm going to fuck you so hard." His demeanor has gone from slightly apathetic, to downright savage. He plunges into me, grinds his cock against the tightness, withdraws and repeats this unrelenting sequence, again and again. His grip on my hips is fierce, and he only releases it to smack my ass every few thrusts.

The tingling numbness in my rosy ass cheek distracts from the punishing depth of his cock, but still, the urgency is building deep in my belly again. I'm able to somewhat rise to my knees and forearms, but I am still completely presented to him.

His hands move to tightly grip my ass cheeks, and his thumb repeatedly drifts over the entrance of my previously discussed, soft limit.

"Damn, Jessie. I want your ass so bad right now." The vigor in which he is fucking me at the moment scares me to think of the prospect of his dick in my ass. However, his dirty talk and probing thumb send darts of adrenaline soaring through my veins.

"Can we push your soft limits?" he asks, his voice husky as his thumb continues to explore.

"Maybe a little, not your dick though," I answer, in clipped syllables against his pounding hips.

He spits on my crack and rubs his thumb around before beginning to delve inside.

Suddenly, all I can hear is a pounding in my ears, and a terrifying panic closes around me. My body goes completely numb, and I feel like I'm about to die.

"Stop," I whisper, and it comes from an automatic place, deep within my consciousness.

Silas doesn't hear me.

Now I start to tremble. At first, it's just a shallow tremor, but the panic works its way into a violent shaking.

"Please stop," again a whisper. I am no longer aware of his body slapping against mine, or his thumb pressing into me. I feel as if I've been buried in sand, and each time I try to open my mouth to speak, the sand rushes in; filling my mouth and lungs. I feel pinned down, I'm suffocating…It's like I'm slowly dying.

I crumble to the bed, and the jarring motion brings me to the surface, just for a moment.

"Red," I whisper, and then the tears come.

Silas stops moving, "Did you just say, red?"

I can't answer, I've been swallowed by something and it's already starting to digest me.

"Baby?" he asks again, but his voice sounds like it's from another planet, and I'm gradually dissolving in the belly of a beast.

He pulls out and then turns me limply over. "Pipes, are you ok?" He looks alarmed, but he's a million miles away.

Once my body is free of his, I start to crawl away from him, tugging myself along with anesthetized arms.

"Jessie, you're scaring me," he says.

"Don't touch me. Get away from me."

When he reaches out to me, I begin screaming.

Chapter Eighteen

Panic

I'm wearing one of Silas' gigantic sweatshirts while wrapped in a blanket on the couch. My trembling has slowed, and the sense of panic has mostly subsided. Ruby sits protectively next to me on the couch, rubbing my back and cooing sweet affirmations.

Silas is still pacing in front of us when Analise hands me a mug of hot tea. She sits down next to me, her and Ruby buffering me against the world.

"I use to have nightmares when I was your age too. Right after I lost Richard. They lasted for years." She strokes my arm in solidarity as she continues, "Night terrors, they called them back then.

I take a shaky sip of tea that burns the roof of my mouth, but I take another anyway. Maybe I want to punish my body for turning on me. Or is it my mind that smacks of betrayal? It seems the two, united in mutiny are conspiring to destroy me, one panic attack at a time.

"What was the nightmare about Jessie?" Ruby asks, "Maybe it will help to talk about it because when you're awake, you realize the monsters aren't real."

I smile at her. I wish it were that easy. "I don't remember, Sweetie."

"Well, monsters don't exist and you're safe now," she says as she pats my knee with reassurance.

I'm not safe, and I certainly don't feel safe. Apparently, *my* monsters have deemed it open season, and now persecute me while I'm not even sleeping. I was wide awake this time.

Ruby is naive. She is too young to realize that monsters *are* real, they do exist. They lie in wait and then pilfer from the unsuspecting. They steal your sense of safety, and they rip the security from your bod— Suddenly, a dark epiphany clarifies in my mind.

My rapist spit on me to lubricate himself.

Silas sees something on my face, and it causes him to snap to attention.

"Ok, everyone back to bed. Jessie is just fine, as you can see. Now, let's all get some sleep," he announces, as he hustles Ruby back to her room, and Analise back through her lock off, this time closing and locking it behind her.

***

Back in Silas' room, it's now me who is pacing back and forth.

"I'd say I'll never push your limits again, but that's not even what this is about, is it?"

"You spit on me."

"Did you take that as disrespectful? Jessie, I was in *reverence* of you. I probably should have used lube but at the time—"

"When you raped me. You spit on me."

His mouth drops open. He wants to discredit, or challenge my statement in some way, but he is struck dumb. His mind skitters and grasps for the truth in the memory, but he can't seem to remember.

"It had nothing to do with you playing with my ass, or pushing my limits, Silas. That *one tiny thing* brought me right back there. I was locked in that moment."

"Oh my God, Sweetheart, come here," he extends his arms to me, but his embrace has all the appeal of an unsprung bear trap to me.

"No."

"Jessie, I love you. Come here, I want to comfort you."

"I want to go home, Silas," I say, and my voice doesn't even sound like my own, the texture is somehow gone.

The look of anguish on his face is almost enough to change my mind, but to trade his suffering for mine would be to go all in and lose anyway.

He has been through so much lately. I don't want to add to his burden, but this…this *is* his burden, and we are both saddled with it now.

"Can…can I come with you?" he asks pensively.

I can't answer him, because what I know with absolute certainty, is that I can't be near him right now, as in proximity. I don't want him to touch me. I don't want to smell him. I don't want him breathing on me. If something so trivial can put me right back there. If something so minuscule has the power to trigger *that* feeling, then no.

During the panic attack, I had the genuine thought that I was dying. Actually, for better clarification, it's not even that I was *literally* dying, it's worse. It was that I *needed* to die, just to end the torment. Now, if that thought doesn't fuck with your rational mind, you are a stronger person than I am.

Regardless of all this making any rational sense, the idea that Silas has the innate ability to make me feel that way, is terrifying. And, I'll do anything not to feel like that again.

"Can we just talk tomorrow?" I ask, and then I watch his heart break. His eyes fill with tears, but he nods in understanding.

Now *my* heart breaks. He is the best thing that has ever happened to me, and now I'm pushing him away because I'm scared of his potential to trigger me? What the fuck is wrong with me? I already know what my life is like without him. I'm a God-damned basket case.

I resist the pervasive urge to flee, in the hopes I can make him understand.

"Silas, I'm afraid."

"I'm afraid too," he says, as he sits on the edge of the bed and puts his face in his hands.

"I'm afraid that I can go from totally present, having delicious sex with the man of my dreams…to wanting to die, in the space of a heartbeat."

Face still covered, he nods into his palms then sharply sucks in his breath, and I realize he is crying.

Still clothed in nothing but his sweatshirt, I step between his own fleece covered legs and cradle his head against my abdomen. I can't let this fear win. I can't let the monster devour me.

I realize I'm crying too. Then he wraps his arms around my hips. He doesn't say anything, but he doesn't have to, I know he too is tormented by monsters. The monsters of his actions, the ones he can't take back, the ones that still have the ability to crush us.

I loosen my hold on his head, and he allows me to slip through his arms while I sink to my knees. I lay my cheek against one of his thighs, and he folds himself over me. It's the soggy embrace of two tortured souls.

We remain like this for a long time before either of us speaks.

"Please don't shut me out, Jessie. I'll do whatever you need, just please stay," his voice is muffled as he speaks softly into my hair.

"I'll stay."

***

We get into bed, and Silas surprises me by evaporating any of my concerns about self-preservation.

"I received a custody petition from Amber's attorney. She wants custody of Ruby, says she was coerced into signing the documents, and that through fear and intimidation I have knowingly and purposely withheld her parenting rights from her." After he says this, he looks at me almost in challenge. It's like he is laying it all out there as if to say, *You think things are bad now? Well, buckle up, because I'm adding some fuel to the fire of PTSD, Jessica Talbot, and a looming lawsuit, so things are about to get worse.*

My mouth is open, but I'm not sure what to say first. I start with, "Can she even do that, after all this time? I mean, what are her chances of actually getting custody? Wait—does Ruby know? Silas, how long have you known about this? Hold it, is this why you have been so preoccupied and distant? It's not about Jessica Talbot at all, is it?"

"Wha—"

"You have known about this for a while haven't you?"

"Jessie, what do you want me to answer first? Yes, I've known about this for a while, and yes, she can petition the court for custody."

"Holy shit, when it rains, it pours."

"I know. I feel like one more, tiny thing is all it's going to take, before I'm front and center of my very own psychotic break," he says, as he leans back into the pillows, crossing his wrists behind his head. He looks drained, totally depleted of emotion.

"Why didn't you tell me?"

"At first, because I didn't think there was any merit behind her petition. Later, because I didn't want to worry you. And now, because I'm in the God damned eye of the hurricane, Jessie. Everything is falling to shit, and I don't fucking know what to do."

I raise my hand to run my fingers through his hair, then I change course, and coax him to lay his head in my lap. He lies there, arm slung over my bare thighs, while I toy with his tousled strands and ponder my next move.

I'm worried about myself and my fragile state of mind, but this is all so much bigger. Any looming panic attack is just one turbulent element in the pyroclastic surge threatening to erupt.

"Tell me everything. If we really are in this together, you need to be more forthcoming. Then we will tackle the chaos together; all of it." The request is directed at myself too. If we are to tackle the chaos together, I can't push him away or constantly fear him triggering a panic attack.

The thought alone speeds up my pulse, and I have to ignore the cold sweat dampening my brow. I assume no one has ever conquered their demons without a fight though, so that's what I'm going to have to do. Tamp down the fear, stay, and fight.

He takes a deep breath and begins, "Ok, from the top. I have been following Jessica's progress through a resident who is also a member of 1462. I know she woke from her coma, but she has some pretty significant brain damage. Now, she has been transferred to a different facility, and I can no longer keep tabs on her."

"Can't you just call the hospital and ask where she has been transferred?" I ask.

"No, HIPA laws prevent them from telling me anything. In fact, my insider could easily lose his job, if not his medical license if anyone found out what he was doing. I have tried calling a handful of possibilities though, and just asked to be transferred to her room, you know? To see if anyone would bite. So far, nothing."

"I'm glad she didn't die, Silas."

"Some things are worse than death."

"At least she still has the *potential* to get better. What about a lawsuit?"

"Nothing yet. My attorney feels pretty confident I'm covered in that aspect though."

"Maybe it's time to stop concerning yourself with Jessica Talbot, unless something surfaces regarding a lawsuit. I mean, there is really nothing you can do now."

"Should I reach out to her family?" he asks, and I can tell he has been mulling over the idea for a while. It's noble that he wants to, but it won't get him the answers he's looking for.

"No, in fact, I think you need to extricate yourself from the equation as much as possible. I don't want you on her family's mind at all, Silas. It's sweet of you to worry, but it's not getting you anywhere. There are other things that require your attention now. You have already done what you can for Jessica. Not to mention, you had *nothing* to do with her overdose. It's not on you. You need to shift gears now."

"You just took a thousand pound weight off my shoulders," he whispers. It's as if he needed permission to sever his self-imposed responsibility to Jessica Talbot's overdose.

"I think I need to find a therapist," I say, and it sounds random, but the thought is overdue. I personally need to figure out how to excise the tumor of my rape and the subsequent anxiety, because I'm chasing the wrong tail when I push Silas away. I realize that with complete clarity, and the resulting calm settles around me.

I can fix this. I can take a proactive approach, and instead of being a victim of my rape, I can be a survivor of it.

"I will go with you. I mean, I know you want to do some counseling on your own, but I think we should do some together too," he chuckles, "Did I just suggest couples counseling for us? Holy crap, my life really is off the rails isn't it?"

"I think you are right though. I need help. We need help."

"I will do whatever it takes, Jessie. I hope you know that."

I smile down at him, at all his worry, and I feel exactly the same. I will do whatever it takes to see him through his own storm.

"Hon, we need to talk about the Amber thing. Everything else can wait," I say as I twist a lock of his hair around my finger.

"I know, but the whole thing scares me so much. I can hardly breathe when I think about it."

"What does your lawyer say?"

"That court approval is always necessary when relinquishing your children. He says I should have filed a petition with the court years ago like he told me to."

"Wait, I thought Amber dropped Ruby off and then disappeared?"

"She did. My attorney told me back then that I needed to file a petition with the courts to terminate her parental rights, citing abandonment. Jessie, you have to remember, a child had just been dropped in my lap, a child that I didn't want," his voice cracks with the admission,

"I *wanted* Amber to change her mind and come back. Plus, I wasn't even sure she was for real, if she really was abandoning her. She needed to be gone a year, with little or no communication before it was considered true abandonment. Once the year was up, it wasn't really on my mind, nor did I ever think she would pop back up."

"Silas?"

"Fuck!" he exclaims, beyond disappointed in himself, and full of self-reproach.

"Silas, did you ever file the petition?"

He doesn't respond, doesn't even move.

"Silas?"

"No, and now I stand to lose my daughter," he takes a shaky breath, "I own a fucking BDSM club. I have a full-time fucking nanny raising her, and someone has just overdosed at my fucking sex club. What kind of a father do you think the court will see me as?"

For once I have nothing to say. No answers for him, and what's worse, is I know exactly what kind of father the court will see him as— sexually depraved and unfit.

"And, as if that's not bad enough, Amber is claiming I have kept her from seeing Ruby through intimidation, and that she fears for her own safety as well as Ruby's."

"What are we going to do?" I ask.

"I'll have to discredit Amber, prove there has been no intimidation, and present myself in a much better light. I've already hired a private investigator. He's working on her, and what she has been up to for the last five ye—"

"Silas! I can't get pregnant now! How will that look?"

"It will look like I'm a family man. They don't have to know the baby is not mine. You pregnant, shows stability for our family and for Ruby. That and the fat ring I'm going to put on your finger. So actually, you getting pregnant is going to help us keep my daughter."

"Did you just propose? Because that was the worst proposal in history."

Chapter Nineteen

Details

The objective of this week seems to be ironing out all the details, of which there are innumerable amounts of. Nevermind the endless flow of work details that are staring me in the face right now, I'm talking about all the personal ones. Silas calls this process, *getting our ducks in a row,* and they consist of various mundane tasks.

On his end, Silas, who is certain he is under investigation by Amber and her team of legal eagles, is working to change his partnership role in the new club from active to secret partner. He is also meeting with the investors of 1462 later this week to negotiate his role there too.

He explained to me last weekend, during our 'eye of the hurricane talk,' that he had controlling ownership of 1462 while Parker had been an active partner. Once he bought her out, he was only left with the investors. Apparently, the investors have no say in the business, they just collect their percentage of the profit. So, needless to say, Silas is pretty stuck with his ownership role in 1462, and any investigation into his assets or businesses filings will dig up as much.

The difference with the new club, is that now he is changing the business structure to bring in more partners, in addition to the investors. He decided rather suddenly that he no longer wanted to be the face of the upcoming club or any that follow, due to the personal ramifications; namely his parental suitability. By assuming the role of secret partner, he can keep a lower profile and hopefully be seen as a legitimate businessman rather than a sexual deviant.

Amber's team will no doubt attack his character and try to portray him as perverse and aberrant, but I think Silas' decision to downplay his role in BDSM is actually following a natural trajectory. The fear of losing his daughter because of his unconventional activities is driving the bus, but his desire to be on the cutting edge of the BDSM world is being overshadowed by simply wanting a secure financial future and a happy, dare I say, *normal* life. I think he is realizing what it is he wants out of life, and more and more, it's becoming less about the clubs.

Another of his ducks needing alignment, is his own investigation into Amber. His private investigator wants to meet with Silas in a week or so, to go over some of his findings. Silas wants me to be there for this meeting, but I'm not sure what good that will do. I'll just ask a bunch of questions, Silas already knows the answers to, and get fired up about whatever Amber has done with the last five, unencumbered years of her life.

Pretty much anything she has accomplished after ghosting Ruby is going to piss me off. Don't even get me started about the fact she has never so much as sent a birthday card, and now wants custody of Ruby—because I'm already about to start looking for Amber in dark alleys. Anything incendiary I hear will just make me want to drag her by the hair into a gladiator arena to take care of her myself.

Somehow, Silas isn't worried about the hot-headed level of emotions I'll bring to the table when we finally do sit down with the PI, but I am.

Moving on to my list of details that need to be ironed out, I have to meet with my lender about buying Devin's condo and get her any necessary paperwork. I need to get in touch with a therapist and make an appointment, that is if I ever get a minute to actually research one that specializes in my kind of crazy. I have to track down the airbrush artist who will do my body paint for the exhibition party at the club, which is less than two weeks away. I need to travel for work, or lie to Silas about traveling for work. And, last but not least, Corey, Devin and I are taking Maribel to dinner on Wednesday, where we will bestow the knowledge of her impending status as a grandma.

All of this, on top of a very busy work week. The overload of work is presently evidenced by the rapidly blinking phone on my desk; indicating a bunch of voicemails, and an ever-expanding inbox of unread emails.

One thing noticeably absent from my to-do list, however, is the trip to my doctor's office to receive my next birth control shot of Depo.

Chapter Twenty

Analise

Silas has given Analise the week off and bought her a plane ticket to visit her family. She had been overcome with gratitude for this, of course, but I can see the writing on the wall. I believe her future nanny status is in jeopardy, though I don't know how Silas could do it without her. He hasn't said as much, but he knows he is under surveillance and probably wants to demonstrate his devotion to Ruby as the ever-present, doting father. The dad who has no need for a live-in nanny.

After an abbreviated trip to the gym after work, I arrive at Silas' sweaty and still in workout clothes. Ruby opens the door with a mischievous grin on her sweet face, and it stops me in my tracks.

"What?" I ask suspiciously and then look around for an ambush.

"I have something to show you," she giggles, as she takes my hand and leads me to her bedroom.

Silas is sitting on her bed, looking relaxed in loose cargo shorts and a white cotton shirt. I'm not sure what I expect, but nothing seems amiss.

"Hey, Babe. Say hello to, Stewart."

"Huh?" I'm confused, because Stewart is my dad's name.

Ruby jumps up and down with excitement, "It's so awesome! Isn't it, Jessie?"

Just when I'm about to speak, I see it move on Silas' lap. It's a hedgehog, and damn if she didn't name him after my dad, just like she said she would.

"Uhh. Yep, he is awesome," I answer, as I look into his pointy white and brown face. He looks perfectly content, all balled up in Silas' lap.

"Actually, he is a *she*," Silas says, just to clear up any needless confusion. "Named, Stewart," he says while stifling a laugh.

"Want to hold her, Jessie?" Ruby asks, as she strides over to scoop Stewart up out of Silas' lap. "African Pygmy Hedgehogs need to be held often, so they don't become anxious or mean. Right, Daddy?"

"That's true, Rubes."

She gently brings the ball of hedgehog over to me, and deposits her succinctly into my palms, poised as if nervously waiting for communion.

I'm surprised by the feel of her, not too pokey or rough, just a warm little ball in my hands. I raise the new addition to my face and say, "It's nice to meet you, Stewart," and then I look at Ruby and say, "Tell me more about these little guys."

"Well, Stewart is four months old, she eats mealworms and crickets—"

"Freeze-dried ones," Silas interrupts, "And store bought hedgehog pellets," he chimes in, as if I will object to live crickets and mealworms inside, or because he did.

She continues as if no interruption had occurred, "They are nocturnal, and they are absolutely *not* rodents, they are insectivores," she gives Silas a pointed glance, to which he feigns utter shock and dismay at her accusation.

"Where will she sleep?" I ask, while laughing at his dramatic response.

"In her cage," Ruby points to a large aquarium. It's almost hidden from view, on the floor at the foot of her bed. It's full of various hedgehog items, like a tiny bed, a fleece hat, a curved PVC pipe to burrow through, and a wheel to run on.

"Ok, looks like she's all set then. I'm going to go wash the gym off, then should we go get some dinner?"

"Yes," Silas says, "I've been waiting all day to take my girls out."

***

After dinner at Ruby's favorite Mongolian grill, we walked a few blocks for ice cream, while Ruby chattered excitedly about school, her friends, and of course, hedgehogs.

The topic of Analise's future and of Amber's play for custody never arose, but they had bobbed beneath the surface of every conversation. Every twinkle in Ruby's eyes or giggle on her lips served as a reminder about co-parenting with Amber, or worse, loss of custody altogether.

The wildcard for me, regarding Amber's dubious plan, is that she's claiming Silas has kept her from seeing Ruby. Fear and intimidation are weighty words, and if she can spin them to convince a judge she's afraid of Silas, the judge may agree, especially after they factor in the seedy underworld of BDSM clubs, and drug overdoses.

I remember as a kid, my aunt and uncle used to take in foster kids, tons of them. I also remember how hard it was for them to see their foster kids returned to really terrible situations. Often, the courts sided with birth parents even if the situation at home was bleak, or as long as the parent(s) completed a mandated class or rehab program. The preference of the court

173

was to keep kids with a biological parent unless the situation was catastrophically bad. So, as a consequence, a lion's share of the kids were returned to really crappy environments.

I mention this, only because I know that Amber will have to be seen as a catastrophically bad parent to lose this case. Short of living in a meth house or a string of felony convictions, I can't think of how this will work out without Silas having to share custody. I don't happen to think he will lose custody altogether, for the above reasons, but I worry that Amber, as Ruby's birth mother, won't be bad *enough* to be denied joint custody.

Now that we are back at Silas', we are faced with the task of tucking Stewart into bed. Actually, tucking her into her fleece hat would be more accurate, as the three of us ring the perimeter of the cage, peering down into Stewart's brave new world.

Ruby had toted her new pet around with her like a mother marsupial, while she brushed her teeth and got ready for bed. Stewart, balled in the 'pouch' of the fleece hat, and Ruby clutching the hat to her body.

"Well, goodnight Stewart," Silas says, hoping to get the bedtime routine rolling toward completion.

"Yes, goodnight Stewart," I say, trying not to laugh.

"Goodnight, you little cutie," Ruby says, then blows a kiss into the cage before climbing up on her own bed. "Daddy, do you think Stewart needs a nightlight, so she is not scared on her first night?"

"No, she's nocturnal, doesn't she have x-ray vision or something?" he teases. Then he leans down to kiss her forehead, "Ruby Begonia, I love you so much. You are more important to me than oxygen, do you know that?"

She wraps her arms around his neck and holds him there, until he flips her covers back and climbs in bed with her, fully dressed. They hold that embrace for a long time, and I know how important it is to him, so I back out of the room and head to the kitchen for a glass of water. I need something to help me swallow this lump in my throat.

***

When Silas finally comes into the bedroom, he stands at the foot of the bed and stretches his arms up while yawning. When he reaches up, I can see his loosely hanging shorts and a glimpse of his bare abdomen. Even though I had only planned on talking tonight, a shy blush crawls up my cheeks anyway.

"I thought Ruby's middle name was Elizabeth?" I ask, trying to divert my thoughts.

"It is. A Ruby Begonia is a flower. I used to call her that when she was little. She always thought it sounded hilarious, that's why I still call her that sometimes now." He pulls his shirt over his head with one hand and then holds it loosely balled in his hands while assessing the look on my face.

"You got something on your mind, Pipes?" he asks playfully.

"Just those abs."

"Good because it just so happens that I do hundreds of crunches a week so you will notice them."

"I've noticed." I lean back suggestively and wait.

"Damn, Girl! You're insatiable," he smiles a wicked smile, "I can't lock the door though, Analise isn't here."

"Maybe you could just take me gently, under the covers… nice and slow."

"You got it, Babe. Just let me brush my teeth," he says, and then zips around the corner into the bathroom.

Even though I've already brushed my teeth and washed my face, I follow him into the bathroom and sit on the edge of the tub. His t-shirt hits my thighs in the mid to upper range, but I cross my legs demurely just the same.

"Are you thinking of getting rid of Analise?" I ask.

"No way, I need her too much," he spits into the sink, pauses, and then adds, "I am thinking of not having her live here anymore, though."

"I knew something was up."

"Now that I'm not doing the admissions, I'm not at 1462 every night." I nod, he's not wrong, but Analise is a huge convenience for us.

"I only go to the club at night with you, and we don't really go enough to require a live-in nanny, just a steady babysitter."

I like the idea of Analise not being here, but I'm hesitant to commit to it.

"Day to day business with the club and real estate can be done after I take Ruby to school. People do manage to parent a *single* child without a full-time nanny, you know," his statement, though a bit laced with sarcasm, is entirely true.

"Maybe have Analise do school pick up and evenings twice a week?" I offer.

"Yeah, that's what I was thinking. Plus, we don't need Analise underfoot, do we?" he saunters over to me and reaches out his hand.

"She has probably seen enough of your thrusting, naked ass anyway," I try to say with a straight face. I fall apart giggling when I picture Analise's face one of the times she walked in on us, mid-day fucking. You'd think she'd been sucking on a lemon. We *were* on the couch in the middle of the afternoon while Ruby was at school, but Analise really didn't have to bring Silas' mail over *right* then. Silas laughs too, as he pulls me into a standing position.

"Now, let's talk about *you* being here full time," he says as he lowers his lips to mine.

"I'm about to buy Devin's condo, all I have left to do is sign some paperwork from the Title company," I say, hardly parting from his minty mouth.

"You can own a condo… and live here," he says between kisses, reaching to cup my jaw with one hand.

"You mean, in Analise's lock off?" I tease, as he raises the bottom hem of my shirt, pulling the whole thing over my head. Now I'm naked except for some skimpy red panties.

"Analise's lock off will be my commercial real estate office, as I intended when I bought this place."

I'm not sure if I want to move in, and I don't know what to say, so instead, I slide my hand down the front of Silas' drooping cargo shorts.

I slowly coax his semi into a full-blown erection. When he decides that my hand is too restricted by his clothing, he lifts me to his hips and carries me into the bedroom, wrapped around him like a cheap suit.

After depositing me rather heavily onto the comforter, he drops his shorts and gets on the bed. He crawls forward, backing me down in the process. Then makes his way up my body.

"These are sexy," he says, as he snaps the hip string of my panties like a rubber band. "They are going to make it difficult for me to *take you gently, under the covers… nice and slow.*"

He grabs the remote for the lights and windows, and as the room is going dark, he begins kissing my neck and coating my body with goosebumps.

We clumsily get under the comforter, and he raises my arms above our heads, holding my wrists with one hand while he supports himself on his other elbow. He is kissing me slowly, tenderly, and the thought of him taking me gently makes my whole body radiate.

Silas is so good at fucking that it's easy to get caught up in it, but he is equally as good at passionately making love. So much so, that when he slows down like this, I can't imagine ever wanting it any other way.

He releases my wrists to caress down the side of my body with the backs of his fingernails. Our mouths are perfectly in sync, and we kiss like this for an eternity, like a new couple that's too nervous to explore each other's body.

I'm cradling his face with my hands, holding him against my mouth when he finally skims his thumb across my nipple. Just once, but the jolt it sends through me after all the chaste build up, is shocking to my virginal system. One bump across my nipple feels sinful and reckless.

"Si-las," I moan into his mouth.

"Open your legs for me," he whispers.

When I do, he slides his hand down my stomach and in between my legs. If the brief touch to my nipple made my heart race, then his wet, probing fingers are going to bring me out of my skin.

"Aahhhhh," I exhale, while my back involuntarily arches against his body.

"You are so warm and silky," he breathes, "Are you ready for me?" As if my wetness wasn't indication enough of my primed and ready state, he evidently wants to hear me say it.

"I'm ready Silas, make love to me," I say, and it's hardly audible.

He lowers his lips to my breast and grazes over the tip a few times. The sensation is intensely ticklish, and just before I start to squirm beneath him, he flicks it with his tongue a few times, alleviating my automatic response to the tickle.

My nails are absentmindedly dragging up and down his back. When he sucks my nipple into his mouth, my hand shoots to the side, gripping the sheet into a tight fist while my other fingers move to tangle in his hair.

The result of our extended foreplay is that every caress, every breath, every motion is amplified. When Silas' explorative fingers spread me apart, I grind my teeth with the need to feel him press into me. His finger dips in, making me groan, but it's not enough. I need to feel him *stretch* me open with his advance. Pushing in and dragging out, forcing me to expand around him and accept his girth.

The desire to be taut around his hardness and bursting full of him, makes me tremble with need. He lets up on my nipple and adjusts himself on top of me.

"Are you shaking?" he asks as he brings a hand to the side of my face, lightly stroking my cheekbone with his thumb.

"I just want you so bad, Silas," I say, in a clipped whisper that sounds like my jaw is chattering from the cold.

"I'm a little nervous," he admits, "Nervous to trigger a bad reaction." He sounds bashful and unsure of himself. I literally had not even thought about it, not for one second.

"It's ok, I'm good," I say.

He pauses, still a bit unsure, and then he guides himself in, just the tip at first. He watches my face, searching for any indication of anxiety or discomfort. Then he kisses me sweetly as he presses slowly in, all the way.

The feeling of our bodies uniting so passionately, so tenderly, is poetic in its simplicity. The natural way in which we kiss, while Silas rocks gently against me, the way he pulls back to look into my eyes and whisper, *I love you, Jessie*, is so intrinsic it feels almost spiritual.

When my trembles turn into moans of transcendence, Silas is looking into my eyes, and when my moans turn into explosive spasms deep in my vagina, he joins me in my release.

We are clamped together, face to face in allegiance to one another, and slicked with warm sweat. I feel so close to him, not just physically but emotionally. It's like something has been unlocked, another chamber in my heart or something; a compartment only a select few are ever permitted to access.

I hug him against me, feeling his penis soften from within, and never wanting to let him go. His weight against me is heavy but comfortable, and I close my eyes to rest.

Suddenly a thought occurs to me, and it strikes like lightning.

"Silas," I say sharply.

He lifts his head in alarm, "What's wrong?"

"We didn't use a condom, and I didn't go in for my shot yesterday."

He lays his head back down, "I don't think you can get pregnant after one day." He may be right, but we have to be more careful. If I'm going to carry a child for Devin and Corey, I certainly can't get pregnant with Silas' baby.

He kisses my throat and then moves down to nuzzle between my breasts with his raspy face. I squeal and kick off the comforter trying to free myself. He pins me there, and slowly drags his scruffy chin across my nipple.

I arch away from him, my body rioting against his stubble. When he starts to flicker his tongue against the chafed tip, I let go of him, dropping my arms to the sides and surrendering my breasts to his flirty campaign.

"Daddy?" Ruby loud whispers, while standing at the side of the bed.

Silas yanks the covers awkwardly over my salacious display, and tries to casually roll off me, "What's up, Sweet Girl?"

"What are you doing?"

"Just, uh… changing places with Jessie."

"But why were you licking her…there?" My hands are covering my face, and I can't for the life of me think of how to explain this with the least amount of childhood trauma.

"Ruby, do you need something?" Silas asks, also at a loss for something intelligent to say.

"Stewart is keeping me up."

"What, why?" he asks, scrambling for coherency. One second he is trying to explain his tongue on my naked privates, and the next, the nighttime wakefulness of the resident African pygmy hedgehog.

"She won't stop running on her wheel."

"What should we do? She's nocturnal, Ruby," he says, as if an explanation for Stewart's primal sleep patterns will be enough to coax Ruby back to bed.

"We'll have to move her cage in here," she says with authority.

"Do I look crazy to you?" Silas asks as he sits up, holding some covers over his naked midsection. "Why don't you go ask her if she minds getting her cardio in the living room," he suggests.

When Ruby scurries off, he stands and walks naked to the dresser to retrieve some pajama bottoms.

"Your naked body is going to get me in trouble forever, isn't it?" he asks, as he steps into the flannel PJs.

My blazing red face is still covered with my hands, so my voice comes out muffled, "I'll just preemptively book her a therapy appointment right after mine."

"You know it will come up again too. Darn inquisitive mind," he shakes his head.

"I know, just brace yourself for a very uncomfortable conversation with a school administrator," I laugh, but the thought makes my insides clench, *Mrs. Harper, did you know my Daddy likes to lick boobies while he is naked?*

"We need to get better at this, that's all there is to it," he says.

"I disagree... *Daddy*. You're already way too good at it," I tease, as I move the sheet to reveal the offending breasts, and pout my lips. Then I burst out laughing, as he smirks then rounds on his heal to go evict Stewart.

Chapter Twenty One

Intel

I'm running really late for the meeting with the private investigator. Silas had asked me to meet them at the restaurant at six. I'm nearly twenty minutes late by the time I charge through the doors of the bustling Italian bistro. Immediately, I'm baptized in the unapologetic aroma of garlic, it seems to dust the surface of everything like residual Mount St. Helens ash.

I see Silas right away and make my way over, ignoring the greeting and subsequent objections from the young hostess.

He stands and kisses my lips, then eases my chair out with a smile.

"I'm so sorry I'm late, my production meeting ran way over schedule," I sit, relieved the PI isn't here yet.

"It's ok, Nate won't be here for a few more minutes. I thought we could relax over a glass of wine first," he smiles and hands me a stemmed glass of fragrant Merlot.

"I need this so bad," I take a tentative sip, and then relax my shoulders for the first time today.

"I know work is really busy right now, thank you for being here for this."

"Whatever you need," I say, then wink at him before another decadent sip of wine.

"It will have to be a relatively quick dinner, I need to pick Ruby up before 8:00." He reaches for the basket of bread, "I need to be cognizant of teenage babysitter's bedtimes nowadays it seems."

"Where is she?"

"There's a sitter who lives in my building, advertises herself in the newsletter; CPR certified, tons of references. She is a sweet kid, I feel kind of bad though, within five minutes of meeting her, I left her with Ruby and took off."

"At least she's in your building. That's really convenient."

"Yeah, but her mom seems like a stickler for the curfew though, and 8:00 is pretty early." He takes a bite of bread, and then says, "Thank God Analise will be back for the Exposition party, that's going to be a late night."

"That reminds me," my heart starts pounding, "I will be traveling for work, but I'll be home in time to meet you at the club that night."

Silas stops chewing, "You're traveling for work on a Saturday?"

"It's complicated, but I promise I'll be back for the party."

He swallows heavily and looks like he wants to say more, but thankfully, Nate chooses this moment to descend on our table.

"Silas Bishop, in the flesh! It's great to see you again, Man," Nate says, in a deep baritone voice as he shakes Silas' hand.

"It's good to see you, Nate. This is my girlfriend, Jessie," Silas gestures to me, just before my hand gets swallowed by Nate's bear paw of an appendage.

"Awesome to meet you, Jessie. Shall we get started?" he asks, wasting zero time with me before turning to Silas.

Before I can even respond, Silas suggests we order first, and so begins my evening of being mostly invisible.

***

Nate jumps in with both feet, and not for the first time, he gives the impression of someone who rarely sits still. His energy fills the room, and his deep voice and hearty laugh garner a fair share of attention and furtive glances.

I would guess him to be in his forties, though the amount of sun baked into his skin over the years tells a different story. In fact, if you were to picture a bounty hunter that follows a tip to Aruba, lives in a van on the beach for a few years while surfing, cozying up to the locals, and drinking 150-proof rum drinks by the bonfire at night, then you've got the image just right. Except now, he is wearing khaki pants and a Tommy Bahama button down shirt, and his hair, though rangy, is combed back into a short ponytail.

Nate eats with the appetite of four grown men and hardly stops talking long enough to sop up his sauce with a hunk of bread, but once he is finished with dinner and pushes his plate to the side, he is all business.

"Alright, let's get to it then, shall we?" he asks, with bushy brows raised.

Silas glances at me, then back to Nate and nods. I can tell he is nervous to hear whatever Nate has uncovered, so I lay a hand on his thigh and give a reassuring squeeze.

He places his hand on top of mine, and says, "Alright, what have you got?"

"First, this chic is *hungry*. I can tell that right out of the gate."

185

"What do you mean, hungry?" I ask, assuming he's not speaking about Rigatoni, at least not anymore.

Distracted, or reminded that I'm sitting at the table with him, Nate glances at me for exactly one second, then redirects his attention back to Silas.

"She is pretty deep in financial trouble. A basic records search into her property holdings shows me her home is in pre-foreclosure. I also looked into her business filings, and her business tanked eight months ago. Up until recently, she has mostly been able to keep her head above water because of her divorce settlement. She got the house and three years of hefty alimony payments, but those payments have all but dried up. My guess is that she sunk them into her business and then lost her ass. Now, it's only a matter of time until she loses the house."

Nate waits a beat for Silas to respond. When Silas doesn't, he goes on, "I'm working on search warrants for her phone records and content, and for electronic data discovery and computer forensics. Shouldn't be too hard to prove she hasn't tried to contact you, and she doesn't seem to have a leg to stand on, with her threat and intimidation claim. I would say, you're in a good spot," he surmises, as he sits back to chew on the straw of his iced tea.

Silas still doesn't speak, it's like everything is taking extra long to sink in.

I attempt to save him from having to respond, "Well, that's a lot of great inform—"

"Any other avenues you think I should poke around in?" he asks Silas.

"I think all I need is her lawyer's contact information, and I've already got that," Silas says, still a bit underwhelmed.

"Great. We'll talk soon then," he stands and scratches his stomach, then remembers something with a flash of clarity, "What about

186

surveillance? You think you have what you need, or do you want images too?"

"I have what I need. Thanks, Nate," Silas answers in a deadpan voice, then stands to shake his hand.

When Nate is gone, I turn to Silas, excited, "Babe, I don't even think she wants custody! It sounds like she is fishing for—"

"Money," Silas says, confident in his appraisal.

"That's fantastic! We won't have to share custody at all, or worry about Ruby when she's with her. Honey, what's wrong?" I ask, totally perplexed as to why he isn't doing backflips.

"What's wrong? How about I'm not the fucking Bank of America? Everybody who looks at me sees deep pockets, and they want a piece of me, that's what's wrong. If I get a vicarious liability suit slapped against me, or God forbid, a wrongful death suit, it will be for money, lots of it. If I want to pay off Amber in return for signing over her parenting rights, it will cost me a ton of money. You know what else? I'm not even close to having Parker paid off yet. You know why? Because *that* cost me a ton of money. What the fuck? Am I a mother fucking gravy train? Everyone looks at me and sees a fucking payday!" he is angry, and people are staring at us.

"Ok, Sugar Daddy," I pat his hand, "That's enough, let's go home."

He stays frozen in his chair, slowly shaking his head as if he can't believe he didn't anticipate Amber's ulterior motive.

I wave down the waiter; which I have never done before due to the extreme rudeness it requires, but I need to pay and get Silas out of here.

Chapter Twenty Two

Proactive

I hated that I could tell the wounded soul that had waited in the waiting room prior to me had been a smoker. The rotten cigarette stench still hung in the air and made the waiting room feel small and claustrophobic. A weak attempt at clearing the negative energy had been made in the form of a white sage, aromatherapy oil diffuser. But the diffuser, while choking on its own vapor, had done little to distract me from the fact that I was about to lay myself open to the judgment of a stranger.

Once I'm finally settled in my new therapist's office, I immediately hone in on the tweed couches. They are gray but have a yellow thread running through the pattern, as if in defiance of the monochromatic demands of the fabric. The yellow flies in the face of reason, and is very distracting for me. I find myself wondering; if I find the frizzy end of it and tug the wretched thing out, would my therapist be relieved? Might she see me as a brave pioneer who simply can't tolerate the audacity of its bold placement? Could she even admit that everyone before me had wanted to do the same thing, but for some reason, they had shown more restraint?

The yellow is appalling, but the accent pillows are even more rebellious than the thread. Their wild pattern speaks of anarchy within the ranks. Really…how am I even supposed to feel comfortable here?

Shouldn't there be quiet chanting from Buddhist monks seeping in through unseen speakers, and a comfortable leather couch to lie on? And really, the lighting is much too fluorescent and blazingly bright for a safe place in which to unburden oneself.

In a nutshell, I feel about as much at ease as a witch living near Salem in 1692.

The therapist breaks my concentration with her repeated question, "Jessie, what would you like to talk about today?" Her eyes are brown and hard to read, or see beyond, they are not the blue ones I had envisioned. Her features are sharp too, hardly the comely face I want to confide in. Really, she is too young altogether to have much life experience under her belt, so I'm pretty skeptical about her ability to help me. How is this little whipper-snapper supposed to guide me through all my phrenic distress?

Her prying face loses its composure when she hears my response. It's the truest statement I can muster while distracted by the aggressive decorative accents.

"I'm a freaking mess. I tried to put myself back together, but now the tape has lost all its stick."

***

Optimism. Lately, the word itself has felt more like it stems from a strange dialect, or like it's fancy jargon with no solid concrete meaning. The thought of being optimistic has hovered around, but not quite landed—like it's more of an idea or theory, and not so much an actual *feeling*. But when I leave the therapist's office, I feel like spinning around until I get dizzy and fall down. I'm like a kid, light and free; buoyant almost, and finally optimistic.

I had made a month of twice-weekly appointments on my way out, and sincerely considered extending it several additional months. Suddenly, there was so much more I wanted to talk about. Not just my panic attacks, but *everything*. Therapy had felt like an extension of my own consciousness, almost like a fail-safe for my buried thoughts and resentments. It was an extra filter for external stimuli to go through before hitting the processing section of my brain.

It was freeing and enlightening, and I should have gone months ago. I *am* proud to have taken this step, though, however awkward I may have presented myself. To finally react in a proactive manner is the first step in changing my status from victim to survivor.

Oddly, the door I had entered into the waiting room of the dispersed smoker air, had been dark and unobtrusive. Yet the exit directly from the therapist's office, to avoid uncomfortable patient overlap, led into a well-lit, nicely appointed hallway. There was a floral scent to the air, and I would almost swear to God, there was birdsong in the distance.

***

After swinging by the title company on my way home, to deposit a few signatures on some paperwork, I find myself in possession of an actual property deed. Now, I'm a legitimate homeowner.

When I get home, all I want to do is flop down on the couch and do absolutely nothing. So, after plopping my folder of notarized documents onto my new coffee table, I do exactly that.

This morning I had felt like the world was closing in on me, with not just one appointment after a full day of work, but *two*. Both needed to happen, but in the oppressive manner of too much to do and too little time, I had been completely overwhelmed.

Now I can finally relax. Tonight, Silas is facilitating Analise's move into a cute one bedroom off 3rd, Corey and Devin are with their realtor looking for a house, and my ringer is still on silent.

I have my forearm slung over my face, and I can feel the tension of the day begin to drain away. I can't yet muster the required energy to reach for the remote, but I feel at peace with my stamina delay.

"I know, Right? It's the most amazing thing I have ever seen!" Devin calls out, as he virtually Irish step-dances into the room.

"Devin, why so loud?" I ask, keeping my arm over my face and realizing the two and a half seconds of peace I had enjoyed were now over.

"*I said…*It's the most amazing thing I have ever seen!" he repeats, not at all out house hunting with Corey.

"Fine, what are you talking abo—" I start to say while removing my arm shield from my face. Lying on the couch, and especially from this vantage point, I wonder how I could have missed it in the first place.

Hanging above my new living room setup is a one of a kind, Devin lighting design. It's the most garish thing he has ever made, and it's not even lit yet. I'm silenced by its unassuming grandeur.

"Am I right? I was working on it for the Pfizer's gallery, but in my heart, I knew you should have it. It's a statement piece, just like I said you needed," he lifts my knees, and then sits down, adjusting my legs across his lap.

"It *IS* the most amazing thing I have ever seen," I say, wide-eyed. It's on the small side for a Devin piece, and it appears delicate. It almost looks like a chrome leaf pile of fragile, gauzy, petals and vines. It reminds me of one of those magnetic desk sculptures for your office. The irresistible little toys with a platform base, and hundreds of little magnetic slivers that can be sculpted and reshaped while wasting countless productive hours at work.

With Devin's, the dainty filigree shapes come together in a swarm around the center of the oblong chandelier and peter out at the top, bottom, and edges, which only adds to its look of fragility.

"It's fucking amazing, Devin. I don't know how you manage to make metal appear light as air… or how it's even held together, but I love it." Then I knit my brows and ask, "Did you say it was originally for the Pfizer's gallery? Devin, how much were you going to sell this for?"

"I dunno… fifty-five or sixty, but I was going to do three of them for that price."

I gulp.

"I would rather you have it anyway," he says, as he slides off my shoe and starts to massage my foot. Then he says conversationally, "I think Corey and I finally found a place."

"Really? Where?" I ask.

"Not far, but…" he trails off.

"But what?" I start to get a little nervous, because he isn't looking at me, and he's really focusing on rubbing my foot. Devin is the kind of guy who says exactly what he is thinking—to hell with his filter, so it's his demeanor that worries me.

"It will be a partial gut job, well…maybe a total gut," he says as he finally looks at me.

"Oh, I thought you were going to say you want more for this place so you can afford it," I say relieved, because after dragging my feet for so long, I finally made it official, mere hours ago.

"OhMyGodNo! Jessie, you're going to have a baby for us, I would give you this place and the next one," he says, aghast.

"What is it then? You're usually so direct."

"It's just that…Corey and I…might need to live here a little while."

"Ok, what's the dif—"

"Like, eight to twelve months longer."

"Devin, I've lived with you my whole adult life, what's another year? Plus, I'm hardly ever here."

"It's just a lot of dick in a small place. Are you sure you're good with it? You're already doing so much for us."

"Devin, am I sure I'm good with it? Yes. It's you moving out in a year that I'm not so sure I'm ok with."

He smiles and tips his head back on the couch. "I know, right?"

***

When Corey walks in, Devin and I are still on the couch, sitting mostly in the dark and talking about living like sister wives on a compound with all of us, Silas and Ruby too.

Corey exaggeratedly taps the rocker switch that illuminates the entire room with Devin's lit, statement piece.

"Aahhhhh," I say, as I admire the chandelier. I thought it was amazing before, but now it's a thousand times grander. The forest of shadows cast across the ceiling even looks fluid, and artistic.

"That's right! I had to hold that thing while Devin wired it. It's a beast, don't let its prettiness fool you," Corey smiles and drops onto the other side of the sectional. "Sister wives, huh?" he asks, good-naturedly.

"Yeah, since Devin makes my annual salary in forty-five minutes, he should be the money maker, you for sure should cook, I'll spit out babies, and Ruby can be the baby's personal tutor and fashion assistant."

194

"What about Silas?" Corey asks.

"Oh, he will be too busy servicing Jessie and looking handsomely aloof—"

"He will be the face of the compound, the business manager," I add.

"As long as you are signing up to spit out babies, I want to make sure you and Silas are not having any second thoughts. Especially you," Corey says. He has been very guarded about the whole thing, like he is expecting it to fall apart.

"I'm fine, Corey, and so is Silas," I try to reassure him, a little surprised by my own confidence in the matter.

"Ok, but maybe we should hold off on telling anyone, just in case," Corey says, and I know he is specifically referring to his mom. We had talked about telling her this week, but even then he hadn't been sure if we should.

I tend to agree and have already decided not to tell my family until after I'm already pregnant. Not that they wouldn't eventually support the idea, I'm just not open to other opinions on the subject. I'm sure I will hear all sorts of input from my family, so it's better to quell the murmurings by presenting facts, and not eventualities.

"Fine with me," Devin announces, with no plans to include his family anyway. "Let's order food and watch a movie."

Chapter Twenty Three

Exposition

Now that the long-awaited day of the Exposition party is here, I feel like a horrible, deceitful, traitor as I sit in my car outside of the club. Silas had been understandably skeptical about the validity of my business trip, and his doubts only increased with my flightiness about the details of it. I had insisted I needed a chunk of the day to tie up loose ends and would fly home in plenty of time to make it to the party.

I obviously want to surprise Silas by participating in the body paint fashion show without his prior knowledge, but the road here has been so full of badly delivered lies and precious few details, that I worry about what he is thinking.

I happen to be a terrible, inconsistent liar, and because Silas can read me like a book, he definitely smells a rat. Most likely, a rat named Salinger, which makes the lie that much harder for him to swallow.

Silas has been a good sport about me working with Salinger, but I know deep down beneath his cocky, confident exterior, he has an insecurity when it comes to him. Especially when it comes to me traveling with Salinger, and *for sure* when the trip is outside of normal business hours, like 3:30 on a Saturday afternoon for example, like today.

I just hope once Silas realizes why I lied, and that I wasn't off gallivanting around the country with Salinger, he will be able to put down his suspicions and fully trust me again.

Aside from my outrageous lies, Silas has had a rough week with Ruby too. Whereas Analise practically clapped with glee at the idea of downsizing her role and moving into her own place, Ruby had been despondent. You would have thought Silas was suggesting she relinquish the flesh from her body, the way Ruby had cried and pleaded with him.

The Amber thing has left him with a chapped ass this week as well. He wants to present his offer and hopefully be done with the whole thing, but his attorney is in Alaska fishing and insists the lack of immediate response will only work in their favor.

Then, of course, is the cartridge of Sarin gas hovering above Silas' head regarding a potential lawsuit from Jessica Talbot's drug overdose. All in all, the poor guy hasn't been able to get out from under his considerable stressors this week, and here I am, feeding him lie after lie, and making him question where I stand. I can't wait to be done with the whole messy lie and enjoy the festivities tonight.

If all the box trucks coming and going from the club are any indication, this party will be on another level than other club parties. You would think the circus was coming to town with the amount of rigging, trusses and lighting consoles going in. Then there are the soundboards, risers, and video screens.

The pace is manic, and according to Silas, it's been going on since four o'clock this morning. As soon as the cleaning crew finished cleaning up after last night's *Blacklight and Graffiti* party, the production crews were able to get started, and from what I can see, they haven't let up since.

I'm getting frustrated just sitting in the car waiting for a text from Erik, but he needs to make sure the coast is clear, and that I can slip into the body paint room undetected by Silas. I didn't go through all this trouble to blow my cover now, how ever shaky it may be.

In fact, I should check in with Silas now, because once the artist starts with the airbrushing, I doubt I'll be able to. I text him because it's safer than calling. Plus, this way he won't be able to catch me off guard.

Hi, Sexy! Heading to the airport in a few hours. Can't wait for tonight, I'm dying to see you.

He responds right away, before I've even put the phone down.

Come in through the alley, and go straight past the catwalk to the back room. Do it in the next few minutes, or wait to hear from me again. It's not from Silas, the text is from Erik, and it's finally time to make my move. I grab my giant bag, full of clothes and makeup for after the show, sling it over my shoulder, and cross the street, toward the alley.

***

Once in the 'back room' that Erik directed me to, I realize it's just a big, open area with a loading dock and huge pull-down, garage style door.

The smell of paint is in the air, coating the insides of my nostrils, though the room is heavily ventilated and the commercial sized garage door is wide open. Inside the concrete room, sections of the walls and floor are covered with plastic, serial killer style.

There are a handful of naked women in various poses, each with varying levels of paint on them. There appears to be an airbrush artist for each model, complete with their own station of equipment, lights, and fans.

"Are you Jessie?" I hear, before seeing the man striding toward me from over by the loading dock. He is wearing low hung jeans with a dangling wallet chain, and a tight black tank top. He's good looking in a

199

bad-boy way, in that, he looks like he was just released from prison, but had a modeling contract waiting for him upon his release. He has neck tattoos that disappear under his tank, but none visible on his arms.

"Yeah, Hi," I say, reaching out my hand to him, "It's nice to finally meet you, Paco."

"You as well, Jessie," he says, shaking my hand without his cocky brown eyes ever leaving mine. "You're lucky you ended up with me. You ready to steal the show this evening?" He has an air of confidence about him that wasn't apparent from our string of texts.

In his messages, he had wanted to know what my ideas were and what type of aesthetic I was going for. Now, with a single handshake and penetrating gaze, it's clear that this is his exhibition, and I will be painted to his specifications.

I know he is famous for his work, Erik told me as much, but I'm not exactly starstruck, so I wouldn't mind his ego joining me back down here.

"I'm not really the show-stealing type, but you go big," I say with a nervous laugh that makes him look sideways at me.

"We better get started then, show starts at ten. Come on," he wastes no time, as he turns and strides away from me.

We walk to an area that's been set up right next to the loading dock. In fact, the location is highly visible to the outdoor, impromptu smoking section where workers are congregating while taking a break from club setup.

"You're not shy are you?" Paco asks, "I like to have as much ventilation as possible."

"Actually," I start, but can't think of a good reason that I would be fine strutting down a catwalk mostly naked and painted, but not ok with smoking Roadies stealing glances.

"It's ok Jessie, I'm pretty conservative with my model's modesty. Some of them, not so much," he gestures to the collective group next to us.

"Ok, great."

"Usually our models wear thongs and pasties, but not for club events like these. So I'm gonna get pretty intimate, but only in a purely professional way. If you ever feel uncomfortable, I want you to tell me," he insists.

"Ohh-kaaay," there is hesitation in my voice, and that's only a speckle of what's resonating from the rest of my body. He clearly said, no thong and no pasties.

"I do this all over the world, and it can become a bit mechanical for me to paint the intimate contours of a woman's body, but I never want a model to feel objectified in the process. No matter how disconnected sexually I am from my work, the fact that I am erotically close to you, can certainly push your comfort boundaries," he explains, sounding professional and not at all lecherous or exploitive.

"So, you said I will *not* be wearing a thong, and you will be painting… my intimate contours?" I ask as liquid embarrassment brings heat, not just to my face, but my entire head. I had researched the whole body painting thing, and seem to remember flesh colored panties and some very androgynous looking nipple covers.

"Contours and then some," he says, as he makes his way across the tarped floor of his workstation to turn on the air compressor. It whirls to life with a pressure building hum and seals my fate. This is about to happen.

I am really deep in this, I have lied to Silas for a week and a half, and I have volunteered as Paco's muse. If I turn tail and run, he won't have art to exhibit, and that is exactly why these artists have flown in from all over the place.

"Go ahead and get changed into a robe. You can lock up your stuff in the lockers by the dressing room. Just hang on to your key, or better yet, pin it to your robe," Paco says.

"Ok, where ar—"

"The dressing rooms are back the way you came, just hang a left by the door," he is busy fiddling with his airbrush, pressing and releasing the raised depressor on the top of the silver pen-like machine. "Oh, and make sure your hair is pulled back and completely off your body," he yells after me, with the afterthought.

***

As I make my way back to Paco, dressed only in a ridiculous gold, satin robe that hardly covers the swell of my ass, I pay more attention to what's going on in the space. Music is playing loudly, and it's the aggressive kind you would expect to hear in a warehouse full of highly artistic people; or perhaps a slaughterhouse, or b-rated horror movie. The music sounds a lot like the screaming of my inner monologue, but I proceed toward Paco anyway.

To my right, I see a table lined with water bottles and several different snack trays, for those who don't mind a light dusting of paint particles on their food. There are impressive trays of finger sandwiches sitting next to sloppy jars of mustard and mayonnaise. The fruit tray is nothing short of bountiful as it overflows with ripe juiciness. The cheese platter holds an assortment of gourmet and unidentifiable cheeses, crumbled or sliced, then laid out in a way that probably took someone twice as long as it should have.

Just beyond the snack table, a model sits on a stool, fighting with whoever is on the other end of her phone. She is hunched forward, with her untied robe slipping off one shoulder and displaying her partially painted collarbone and upper arm.

I smile as I walk past her, uncomfortable with how her eyes follow me while she spits venom through her phone.

From what I can tell, there are approximately ten women, and only a couple of men being painted. Some of them stand confidently, arms loosely to their sides and chests puffed out, just as proud as peacocks to be displaying their complete nudity. Others retain at least partial concealment from their robes or their breast cupping hands.

For now, I can't tell what the final looks will be, but one model has flames licking up her legs and is being asked to bend forward so the artist can access between her spread thighs.

Another model, one of the men, is looking up at the ceiling in what looks like utter mortification, as his boner is airbrushed by a male artist who could not care less about the state of his model's arousal.

It reminds me how Paco had said he is sexually disconnected from his work, and that it becomes mechanical for him. I'm happy to have that level of professionalism in the room, especially when I'm about to drop my own robe.

"Jessie," Paco shouts from across the space, "Quit lolly-gagging and get over here."

I quicken my pace, only now realizing how timidly I'm walking, as I take it all in.

"Sorry," I call out, while watching the executioner and his blade grow larger in my field of vision. Yep, this is about to get real.

Chapter Twenty Four

Model

"Alright, Mamacita, you ready?" Paco asks, as I stand stupidly in front of him, shifting my feet on the tarp beneath them.

I am very naked inside the robe, and supremely uncomfortable with the idea of taking it off and standing before him with not a stitch of clothing on.

"How about you just hold it open so I can get a few sketches down for placement?"

"Ok...sure. That's a good idea," I stammer, while trying to untie the knot in the satin sash. My hands are trembling, as I attempt to loosen the knotted mess. It feels like it has been tightened by two supernatural, opposing forces instead of by my own freakish need to conceal myself.

"Let me help, I don't have manicured nails," Paco offers.

I nod and drop my hands to my sides. I really didn't expect to be this nervous, it feels like it's the first time I have ever been naked in front of someone besides my own mirror.

Paco tries to distract me with erroneous questions, but they have minimal effect on my chattering nerves.

"Did you follow my directions? No heavy lotions, right?" he asks, but all I can do is stare at his prickly, shaved head while he takes a knee in front of me to loosen the tie.

After an awkward moment spent memorizing his hair pattern, the sash falls to my sides. The robe stays mostly shut because Paco leaves it that way when he stands back up. Apparently, he still has enough patience left to leave my unveiling up to me.

"And you exfoliated really well, right?" he is trying hard to distract me.

"Yes, I followed all of your directions," I say, still nervously gearing up to expose myself.

"Let's do this then."

I can feel the blush on my cheeks as I ease the robe open. It happens slowly like it's hung on rusty hinges, but my nudity gradually comes into Paco's view. First, just my bare sternum, belly, and thighs; clamped shut against my naked girl parts. Then, in tiny increments, my shy breasts present themselves while I hold my breath against the focused scrutiny. Now I understand the male model's look of mortification, as he gazed toward the ceiling.

"Now, that wasn't so bad was it?" Paco asks as he reaches for his airbrush, "Just another pair of tits, and a smooth undercarriage. I've seen hundreds, you know."

"I'll loosen up, it's just at fir— HHHSP!" I suck in a sharp breath, as a cold blast of compressed air and wet paint hits my body.

"It's all good, I know you'll loosen up," he says in a comforting tone, as he sprays a few more outlining strokes. "You naked is just as I expected... Hideous," he smiles but doesn't look up from his canvas. "Open the robe a little wider, please."

I open the sides of the robe more, standing like a flasher and hyper-aware of what the cold blasts of paint are doing to my nipples.

"Ok, you can close the robe. I'm going to get the layout on your legs next."

"So, what did you decide on for my body art?" I ask, much more comfortable now, with my robe loosely closed.

"You don't know?" he asks, surprised.

"Uhhh, no."

"The theme is Gods and Goddesses," he says while applying light spray strokes with complete confidence in their placement.

I try to picture a goddess theme with ethereal, flowing garments, but it doesn't feel authentic for a fetish exposition party.

"I originally wanted the Norse Goddess, Freya, but as soon as I found out you have long red hair, I went with the Celtic Goddess, Macha. Do you know the story of Macha?"

"No, I've never heard of her," I admit, "But I *have* heard of Freya. Isn't she the Viking Goddess of love?"

"Not just love, but war as well. She's known as an insatiable seeker of pleasure and thrills. Total party girl. She was accused by Loki of having slept with all the Gods," Paco laughs and slowly shakes his head, seemingly delighted with Freya's incorrigibility.

"Oh, that's right. Wasn't she also entitled to the souls of half of the bravest warriors killed in battle?"

"Yep, they got to spend their afterlife screwing her in the land of Folkvangr," he says longingly, with a dramatic smile on his face.

By now I'm used to the cold spray, and I don't startle every time he dusts me with it.

"Ok, turn around; I need to get your back sketched out."

"Are you disappointed you can't do Freya?" I ask while turning around.

"Not at all, I'll rock anything. Miles is doing Freya, he will murder it. He's so good," Paco says, pointing past me towards the artist named Miles.

His model is one of the ones who think their nakedness lights the sky. She is standing boldly, presenting her tits and spread open legs to the openness of the room, though Miles is presently painting her shin. His artistry does look fantastic. I can already see the look of leather-wrapped fur coming together as Freya's 'boots.'

"Alright, I'm gonna need you to lose the robe, but you can hold it to your front if you need to."

I slide the robe off, displaying my naked back and ass. As much as I want to cover up, I'm cognizant of the paint laid out in wispy lines. "Will I smear the paint?" I ask.

"No, but you will eventually have to ditch the robe, Jessie."

"Tell me about Macha," I say, tossing the robe to the side, and hoping he can distract me from the fact that my still unpainted tits are pointing toward a room full of people.

Even with the basic layout of airbrushed lines, he has somehow managed thus far, to have left my breasts and entire pelvic region completely free of paint.

"First, you have to unlock your knees. This is going to take a while, and I've had models hit the floor before," he says this, as he sprays an arc of paint down my right butt cheek, "Spread your legs more and bend forward, I gotta get your wedgie just right."

While I do as I'm told, I'm aware that I'm bending over for the smoking crew, if they happen to be looking. I close my eyes in embarrassment while Paco holds my cheeks apart with the finger and thumb of one hand, in order to continue his disappearing hemline, right inside the crack of my ass.

"The Goddess, Macha was a total bad-ass, warrior chic. She represented both sex and battle because she was beautiful and alluring yet fierce and warlike at the same time. She was seen as protection, success, victory, and *fire*," he says, enunciating the last word with a loud, drawn-out whisper.

As Paco continues distracting me with meaningless details about a Goddess I will never think of again, I'm starting to feel marginally less uncomfortable with my nakedness. However, my arm placement always feels awkward and unnatural. It doesn't feel right to just let them hang down, because Paco is moving around me, and I feel like I'm always having to move them out of his way. For now, they are crossed in front of me, kind of framing my boobs.

"Macha's powers protected the Celt's lands from invaders, which is why she is seen as a war Goddess and a guardian," Paco is rambling on about my Goddess, but I'm grateful because as long as he is talking about Macha, he is not picking apart my body in his head.

"Ok, hands on your hips, and stand up real tall."

I move my chin up and back, trying to keep my face out of the fine mist, but my stance feels really ridiculous. I must look like a misplaced superhero or something.

Paco keeps talking, "You know Bonfire Night in Scotland? It's a festival to invoke the blessings of Macha. The massive bonfire is thought to look like her streaming red hair, and the flames banish evil spirits. People dye their hair red for the festival, and dress in red, and…they eat red things." He stops suddenly, and looks around, "I really should have another fan, you are not drying fast enough. He places the airbrush on his work table, and then looks back at me, "Go ahead and take five. Get a snack and some water, I'll be right back."

Paco is crazy if he thinks I'm just going to *take five* and go mingle with the others. I'll just hold my superhero stance like an idiot.

So far the paint looks good, it's obvious I will be *wearing* tall boots and some very cheeky booty shorts. He also has some kind of shoulder armor going on, but the beginning stages are pretty basic, and there is still no chest coverage at all.

By the time I see Paco returning with a box fan, I'm starting to wish I had used the extra time to go get a drink, at least I could have washed the paint fumes down my throat.

"Girl, you haven't moved an inch," Paco says with a playful smile before he puts down the fan and then turns to walk toward the concession table.

He returns with a bottle of water and a skewer of pineapple chunks, speared through with tender basil leaves separating the fruit.

"Truly, this is going to take a while, you'll need to eat and drink here and there."

"Thanks, Paco," I say. I like that he looks me in the eyes when he talks to me, even when my nudity vies for his attention. His eyes don't even dart to my breasts for quick looks here and there. It puts me more at ease with him as my artist.

"Tell me your vision," I say, as I twist the top off the water bottle then take the proffered skewer from his outstretched hand. All he needs to do now is dangle some grapes above my head for me to nibble on, and I'll really feel like a Goddess. As a matter of fact, the paint flicked box fan would have to go too, he really should fan me with a giant leaf or palm frond.

"Yeah, ok… so, my initial vision was to incorporate Macha's alter ego of Mórrígan. You know, her aspect of death?" he says, excited to discuss his visionary arc.

"I wanted to do part of you as an old crone, and the other part, a vibrant, powerful war Goddesssssss," he says, with a flourish of his arm. Then he rifles through his workspace and finds his sketchbook.

"See, right here," he flips to the correct page and then taps it with an excited finger.

"Paco, did you draw this?"

He beams, and looks like a proud kid, his tough exterior all but melts away.

"It's incredible," I say as I take in all the detail. Both aspects of the Goddess are captured on a hugely endowed, anime-style drawing.

"Art is all I've ever been good at," he says, shyly. "We were dirt poor when I was growing up. I used to get in trouble at school, just to get sent to the principal's office. He would leave me in his office by myself and make me write some dumb-shit phrase over and over. I would steal every pen and piece of paper I could get my hands on," Paco's shoulders rumble with his stifled laughter.

"The funny thing is, I always left the pencil I was using right on the table, so he never suspected a thing. Sadly, it was the damned pencil I wanted in the first place, not the pens."

I keep hold of the book while he continues to move around me, spraying, and then backing up for perspective and a critical look.

I appreciate how he keeps talking, though I'm not sure anymore if it is for my benefit, or if he is just a talker. I'm starting to think his brain is focused on his craft, and his mouth is just there for company. He isn't even looking for responses from me anymore, just keeps right on talking and telling stories.

"These drawings are amazing Paco, you are very talented," I say while I flip through his sketchbook.

"Like I said, all I've ever been good at. Lift," he says, referring to my arms, as he makes his misty way up to my abdomen.

"And just so you don't think I'm a total pendejo, once I started making money, I made an anonymous donation to the school. I'm not gonna have that karma following me around."

I raise the sketchbook higher, out of his way. His face is only a couple feet from my bare vagina, and it's very distracting, so I fixate on his fully rendered drawings of Macha.

They are very sexy drawings; the kind of comic book art young boys masturbate to. Now I have a vivid idea of how I will be painted, and it's very skimpy.

Based on his drawings, the boots will hit just above my knees. They look bunched and gathered, and like they are held on with leather straps and ties.

The caramel colored skirt is pleated, and micro-mini short, as in, it stops at the edge of my vagina lips. The back of the skirt rides high on my ass cheeks and shows a red panty wedgie beneath, as well as a red garter belt and red fishnet, thigh-high stockings.

The drawing of the top looks like leather belted shoulder armor. It will encompass my upper chest, from my armpits all the way to my jaw. It has three, thick clasping buckles that run shoulder to shoulder across my collar bones and above my boobs.

There is also a worn looking belt that will buckle right below my breasts, with two perpendicular straps that connect with the collarbone belt. The vertical straps next to my boobs run up the sides, then over my shoulders, where they come together at the back of my neck.

My tits will essentially be framed and accentuated by buckling, leather straps. As for breast coverage, Paco has sketched a few different options.

One possibility is a skimpy red bikini top with almost no coverage, another is a torn white top that tucks beneath all the buckles, and the last option, if you can even call it that, is nothing at all…just balloon sized, Anime jugs with bright red, pointy nipples.

"Paco," I say, breaking his concentration.

"What do you need, Mama?" he asks, while he stands and twists to the sides, stretching out his back.

"Which top are you going to do?" I ask.

"I was waiting to see what your…until after I saw what I was working with."

I'm not sure what to say, so I don't say anything, but I hope he doesn't decide on the naked ones, I still have to walk across a stage tonight.

"I still haven't totally decided, maybe a combo," his answer is evasive, and he raises his brows sharply three times, adding to its cryptic delivery.

"I can't have naked breasts, Paco."

"Newsflash, Sister, not only will you have a naked rack, but your whole body will be just as naked," then he asks, "How did you come to the decision of doing this anyway?" his question is skeptical, like he wonders if I lost a bet or something.

"I want to surprise my boyfriend."

"Cause, most models strut their shit down the runway, naked titties jiggling the whole way. I'm just hoping you don't walk it with one arm across your chest and one hand covering your pussy," he laughs.

I hope he's teasing because he has already been hovering over, and scrutinizing my naked body for more than an hour, and if I were *that* shy, he couldn't exactly have done that.

"I'm counting on not feeling so naked once I'm all painted. That's what everyone says anyway."

"Naw, Girl. You won't feel naked. I'm just playin with ya. But I *do* hope you jiggle your titties a little, you are showcasing my work, and you can't be all prude about it."

"I'm not going to be *all prude about it*, my boyfriend runs this club, you think I would do this and then *not* work it?"

"I'm just sayin. You watch, Miles' model…Freya, will get to the end of the runway, drop it like it's hot, then spread her legs wide open, so everyone can see just how thoroughly she is painted." He cracks his knuckles then adds, "I'd bet my life on it."

"She must think her vagina is pretty or something," I scoff.

"Trust me, she will make the crowd howl."

***

After a few hours, my body paint is really coming together. Paco is putting some finishing touches on my garter belt. Where it meets the thigh-highs, it actually looks like it's clipped on. It even has a realistic looking bit of frayed red ribbon tied on the garter clips.

During our time together, Paco has educated me about the various Gods and Goddesses that are coming to fruition all around me. The model with flames going up her legs, is Pele, the Hawaiian Goddess of violence and destruction. She is looking just about finished, with a very short sarong that deliberately keeps her *not-so-innocent* parts uncovered, and a long lei, made from skinny leaves that match the wristlets on her arms and the head wreath, which is presently hung up and waiting for hair and makeup.

Another Goddess is the lion-headed Egyptian Goddess, Sekhmet, who led the Pharaohs into battle and who's breath apparently formed the desert. Her body paint is a sheer white, plunging X, that crosses just below her belly button with a gold brooch at the apex, then wraps wispily around her thighs. Under the sheer white she has a high waisted, golden thong, and two very prominent, fawn colored areolas. Her artist, who is a waif of a thing with a red bandana tied in her hair, and bright red lipstick, is currently working on the golden, gladiator sandals, that go all the way up her model's legs. The gold is repeated in the snake arm-cuffs at both biceps, and even from here, I can see the detail in the snake's scales. Paco had told me the headpiece is *something to behold,* and that Verna, the artist, is counting on it getting her the finale spot in the show.

The model who had been fighting with someone over the phone earlier, is the Japanese Goddess, Benzaiten. She has a very sexy version of an open Kimono, very short, and with two high slits in the sides.

The fact that Benzaiten rides a dragon is evidenced by the dragon scales that run along the insides of the model's legs. The front of her body paint looks very clean and sexy, but the back is almost morbid, with six painted arms on it. I can't remember everything Paco had said about them, but they hold a sword, a jewel, a bow, an arrow, a wheel, and a key. Her real arms are to be joined in prayer.

Her artist looks like he had a rough night, and takes a smoking break every forty minutes or so, then wafts the cancerous odor past us in his wake.

The male model whose body paint had really caught my eye is being painted as Hades, the Greek God of the underworld. His artist is Eliza, and from what Paco says, she's his biggest competition.

It turns out, the artists are vying for the show's finale, to be decided once all of us are finished. As far as I am concerned, Eliza has the finale in the bag. Her model, who is painted head to toe, is disturbing and grotesque. Every bone, muscle, and tendon has been darkly contoured and highlighted with a pasty white.

The paint was creepy enough, but once he put in the black contact lenses, he started to make me physically uncomfortable. Being the closest model to me, his dark supernatural appearance is near enough to practically absorb.

He looks freakish, and every time he looks over at me, it makes me feel like the devil is taking me in, and likes what he sees.

"Ok, I've done what I can down here, now I need your help," Paco, says as he drags a metal stool over, bunching up the tarp beneath it.

"What do you want me to do?" I ask, my concentration on Hades broken, as well as feeling completely stunned he would need my help at all.

"I need to do your contours," he lets that sink in, and then adds, "And if you can open up for me, I won't need to touch you as much."

I let his meaning marinate for a minute.

"Not that I mind touching you, it's just less invasive this way," he explains.

"Ok, sure," I say, pretending not to care. I really *shouldn't* care, because the more my crotch is painted, the less of my bare, intimately pink parts everyone will see. It's just the starting point that's really distressing. Starting out with unpainted and spread-open parts is intensely awkward, and on top of everything, the devil, Hades is staring at me with his black, soulless eyes.

I sit back and rest the edge of my ass on the cold metal stool. Then, in defiance maybe, I spread my legs to the coolness of the blowing fan. My lack of confidence in the matter is only evidenced by my tightly clamped jaw.

I find it less weird to stare back at Hades than to watch Paco get acquainted with my *contours*, so I grind my teeth together and peer right

216

back at the God of the underworld, while cold blasts of misting paint hit my warm center.

I feel like a plucked duck, hung in an Asian street market for perusal. Especially the way my legs are open to Paco and Hades *and* the fact that my unpainted breasts are commanding so much attention from the underworld.

Hades does not look away, not for a second, even when his penis starts to elongate and become rigid. When he reaches for it, Eliza slaps his hand away and says, "No way, Dude," which makes me snort on a stifled laugh.

Paco looks up at me with a questioning look. He follows my gaze, and then pivots around to face Hades, who now has his fingers laced behind his head while he continues to stare at me... sporting a raging boner.

Paco turns back to me, then adjusts his position, so his body blocks my Hustler shot from Hades.

"How about you put the robe back on until I decide what to do with those titties," he says as if suddenly realizing what a piece of meat I look like.

I glance around for the robe, but it has vanished, so I just accept that my boobs are going to draw some attention, especially framed in painted leather and buckles like they are.

If I'm honest though, it was kind of fun to tease Eliza's model, and it took my mind off Paco's own fixed stare. So after Paco's cock-block, I find myself sliding back into discomfort.

It's not just Paco's view that's uncomfortable, it's his *proximity*. If he stood up right now and wiped his mouth, it would not even be out of context.

"A little wider, Jessie."

I open wider, which feels almost impossible, but I do. "So, tell me about Macha's aspect of Mórrígan," I ask, as a distraction from the paint molecules coldly dusting my vagina lips.

"Sure, yeah, she is thought of as a prophetess who shows herself to those about to die. It's said that she appears to people while washing bloody clothes at the edge of a river. When she is approached, she tells the enquirer the bloody clothes are theirs."

"Nevermind, let's stick with Macha," I decide.

He laughs, "Can you spread wider?"

"Um, no," I answer honestly.

"Ok, I'll need to touch you. Tell me if you feel like I'm crossing the line though."

"Paco?"

"Yeah, Mama?"

"You crossed the line a loooong time ago."

He laughs, then touches me.

In the spirit of lecherous prodding, there is none, he simply adjusts my pieces and parts for the spray of the airbrush. You would think he was simply moving a lock of hair from off my shoulder.

Now that I'm not looking at Hades, and am paying attention to Paco, I can see that he is using his fingers to block my more tender bits from the paint. As he moves lower, toward my opening he puts his fingers against the inside of my inner lips, then explains, "If the paint gets on the slick part of your pussy, it will sting like a mother-fucker."

"Got it," I say, but in my head, all I can think is, *his fingers are touching my vagina, his fingers are touching my vagina, his fingers are touching my vagina.*

***

By now, everyone except me is finished, and back in their robes having hair and makeup done. My makeup artist sits on the fan, looking bored and wondering out loud if the hair she brought is going to be too bright.

"No one told me your hair was such a dark red. I mean, Paco, you said Goddess Macha...and like...RED."

"Lilly, for fuck sake, mix it all together," Paco says, completely unconcerned. "I mean, look at my sketches, there are different levels of red in her hair. This is not a crisis, Lilly."

I ignore their banter, but I'm very much looking forward to getting back into my robe. At this point the sun is down, I'm cold, and the fan is blowing relentlessly as Paco sprays my chest. I'm glad he decided on some paint coverage, but in truth, it isn't much.

He has painted a mostly sheer, white top. What little coverage there is, is wide open and looks to be tied with loosely crisscrossing strips. Due to strategic battle rips, one side only covers the top half of my breast, leaving the nipple almost completely visible. The other areola is behind the sheer fabric paint but still makes a showy appearance through the filmy paint coverage.

Paco has also taken the liberty of enhancing, through the use of paint contouring, my endowments, as well as darkening my areolas.

With the exception of my enhanced breasts, I really do feel almost *dressed*. I think the act of covering my flesh colors with Macha's battle garb has absolutely played a role in not feeling entirely naked. Not to mention, there are so many dimensions and intricacies to Paco's work, that the final result is spectacular.

I actually look like I have on tall, slouchy boots and post-combat, albeit awfully sexy, warfare attire.

Paco airbrushed what he called a 'leg rig' on my thigh. Even painted, it looks like a holster for the multiple knives, and various bone handles it holds securely to my leg.

All of the strapping and buckles look absolutely authentic to worn, burnished leather. He also went a step further and painted forearm gauntlets, made of brown leather and the same rusty chain that unifies the entire outfit.

Paco has downplayed the whole red Goddess theme, but the red accents are peppered in. The thigh-high fishnets, the lacing on the arm gauntlets, the rivets up the side of my boots, as well as the blood splatter across my neck and sheathed knives on my thigh. However, the red accents happen to be the most notable in the region of my scarlet garters and crimson panty-wedgie, right along with my heavily contoured and accentuated, booty.

"Jessie, you look like you kick so much ass. I fucking love how this turned out." Then he turns to his makeup artist, "You ready, Lilly Mama?"

"I was born ready," she kicks her legs forward and hops off the fan while pulling a rat-tail comb from behind her ear.

She immediately starts sectioning the hair on the sides of my head, and I know from Paco's drawings, this is where I will have lines of braided cornrows.

"Ok Jessie, to remove the body art, you will need to re-activate the alcohol-based paint. You can use coconut oil, baby oil, or my personal favorite; cold cream."

"Well then, I'll just swing on by my grandma's house and see if she has any," I tease.

He smiles, "You really do look hot, are you happy with how you turned out?" his question sounds a little insecure, or maybe not insecure, maybe he is looking for confirmation that he really is *that* good. It reminds me that he is competing with the other artists for the finale.

"Are you kidding? I love how it turned out! It's amazing. Now, who gets the finale?" I ask. It sounds eager, like I want it to be me, but that could not be further from the truth. I want Paco to win, but I absolutely do not want it to be me, so my eagerness is not out of excitement for him, but to relax me if I hear he is not the winner.

"I don't know, but I'm gonna find out." He turns and struts toward the concession table, wallet chain swaying with the rhythm of his swagger.

***

By the time Paco finishes socializing and snacking, I have had about fifty pounds of bright red hair extensions sewn in, to co-mingle with my own, too dark and disappointing auburn locks. I have multiple rows of intricately braided hair, held tightly against my scalp on the sides, and at least two extra inches of height from the voluminous flowing tresses that fall to my waist. There are probably fifty small braids throughout, and one that rings my forehead like a fallen halo.

"I might want to add a jewel to your forehead, let's see how you look fully made up," Paco says before draining the last of his bottled water.

Eager to see if I'm right, I ask, "It's Hades right? The finale model?"

"Nope, I knew it wouldn't be one of the guys. With only two male models, we all agreed they should be interspersed. Even with that gi-nor-mous headdress on the Native American, Great Spirit."

"I bet it's the Hindu Goddess Kali, right? All blue and ferocious looking?" Lilly asks.

"Is she the one with the skull necklace, and the severed arm skirt?" I ask.

Lilly nods, confident in her choice.

"Nope, keep guessing," Paco says.

221

"Who is the Eskimo looking one? With the white fur?" I ask.

"That's the Inuit Goddess, Pinga, she escorts newly deceased souls to the upper world to be purified before being reincarnated," he says, as though proud of knowing such valuable information, then continues, "Incidentally, did you know that the Northern Lights were thought to be caused by holes in the upper world, allowing the lights from the Gods to slip through?"

"Duh, everyone knows that," Lilly says, teasing him. "Is she the finale?" she asks, as she dusts a fog of powder over my cheek.

"Nope."

"Shit, is it me?" I ask, and I can't hide the resignation in my voice.

"No, Mama. It should be though," Paco says, his voice tinged with disappointment. "You are second to last though, so that's good for me."

"I agree, it should be you," says a deep voice, that accompanies the disturbing Hades in his approach.

"Hi, my name is Tyler," he says as he extends his hand to me.

"I'm Jessie," I say as I accept his hand. I can't help but notice his swaying penis, painted like a bony appendage, thankfully flaccid for the moment.

"I'm sorry for my obscene display earlier. I didn't realize jerking off prior was a necessary prerequisite and not a simple suggestion," he smiles, and his perfect teeth undermine his sinister, outward appearance.

"Glad you liked the show," I say, with a smile of my own. Despite how it sounds, I'm not flirting because if this man walked up to me with no body paint on, and *sat on my lap*, I would still have no idea who he is. He could be a banker or a priest, the fact is, he is an outright, faceless stranger, and he is of no consequence to me.

"Anyway, I just wanted to say hello. Have a great show, and maybe we can connect later," he says, with another breezy smile before he turns and walks away.

Lilly stretches around me to watch him walk away, "Maybe he and I should connect later! Look at that ass!"

"I think he wants to eat that paint right off your contours, Mama," Paco interjects.

"He's the God of the underworld, Paco! *As if* I would ever let him eat me out," I say with stunned exaggeration.

"You're right. Someone send Eros over!" Paco shouts.

We all laugh, and I adjust the sash on my robe.

"Who did you guys decide on for the show's finale, Paco?" Lilly asks again.

"You're getting close, there are only a handful of Goddesses left, Ladies," Paco encourages.

"I can only think of that one all ripped apart, but she doesn't look that great…is it her?" I ask, but of all the models, her artist had the least amount of skill, and she certainly has the least amount of paint.

"Oh, you're thinking of Coyolxauhqui, the Aztec Goddess. Do you know the story behind her?" Paco asks as he withdraws a bottle of Jack Daniels from his supply cart.

"She was butchered by her brother, the God of war. He chopped her up, and flung chunks of her down Snake Mountain."

"How nice," I say as I watch Paco take a swig then pass the bottle to Lilly.

"Close your eyes, Jessie," Lilly says after a long sip, before handing it back to Paco.

"There is a large stone disk called The Great Coyolxauhqui Stone that commemorated her death with pictures of her body parts on it. It was excavated from the base of the Huitzilopochtli shrine, where humans were sacrificed and similarly flung down the steps. The stone served as a warning to enemies of the Aztecs, and the defeated warriors were marched past the stone on their way to be sacrificed, just like the Goddess Coyolxauhqui."

"That's a horrible story," I mumble, as Lilly packs eyeshadow onto my lids.

"Ok, ok, you guys haven't actually seen the finale model yet. She was painted by Morgan, who is either shy or standoffish, I haven't decided which. She keeps to herself, doesn't like her work scrutinized before it's finished, so she stays on the DL. Trust me, you will know her work when you see it. Almost all of us agreed, she gets the finale."

I hear Lilly take another swallow of Jack Daniels. Then she blows the whisper of Jack across my eyelid to help dry the liquid liner.

"Um, hello? I'm the one who has to walk naked down the runway. Shouldn't you give *me* a swig of that?"

"You need to go grab something to eat, and have some water, then you can have anything you want," Paco says with a grin.

***

I'm wiping mustard off my hands when I see the finale. She approaches the snack table like a consecrated hallucination. I swear she is back-lit by divine light and emoting the music of a cherubic choir, accompanied by harp song.

Everyone stops short, conversations cease, audible gulps can be heard, and then she speaks.

"Wow, everyone looks fantastic. This is going to be quite a show, right?" she beams, and she's as charming and sweet as she is beautiful.

The ferocious, blue model gives voice to what the rest of us are thinking. "You look fucking phenomenal! I can see why all the artists picked you."

"Aren't you sweet," she sings, "Any one of you all could be the finale, I just got lucky this time." The fact that she is humble about the whole thing endears her to me even more, but more than a few models still look at her like they've swallowed a fly.

I guess it makes sense that everyone wanted to be voted the best by all the artists, but I could not be more grateful it's not me. A little of the spotlight is fine for me, a little exhibitionistic charge, then done. I really don't want to garner more attention than I absolutely have to in order to surprise Silas.

I head back over to Paco and Lilly, who are each busy with their own tasks, but who chatter away like two excited chipmunks. Paco is going through digital images in the photo viewer of his camera and Lilly is touching up her lipstick in a lit-up, compact mirror.

"I just saw the showstopper," I announce.

Lilly raises her face from the mirror to glance around.

"Oshwn, African Goddess of beauty. Pretty great, isn't she?" Paco asks. "I would be happier if Morgan wasn't such a snob, but her ability is undeniable."

Paco hands me the bottle of liquor, then points to the locker key, still pinned to my robe. "Grab your heels, Mamacita, it's time for some portfolio pictures."

I take a really long drink from the bottle, then say, "K, I'll be right back."

***

Once I return with my shoes and then step into them, I ask, "How do you want me to pose?" then take another long swallow of smoldering whiskey.

"Just hit some poses, like when you go out there," he says, and I fill with anxiety. I didn't really think about what I would do *out there*. Of course, I will need to do something besides walk out, turn around, and walk back.

"Do this," Lilly commands, as she stands up, bends a knee, and cocks a hip, essentially forming the shape of an S with her body. Every angle of her body is exaggerated, yet it looks effortless. Then she brings one wrist behind her head, "boom," then both arms up, "boom," then both down, "boom," then she turns around and hits three more sexy poses without a second thought.

I bumble through some awkward poses while the two of them coach me every step of the way, then the motions become less amateurish. Eventually, Lilly throws in some more committed poses, a little more head thrown back, more stripper tease, and more pouty nymph.

The fact that I don't look or feel quite like myself is helpful, but still, some of the poses are raunchy, and I prefer my face not be in them, especially the bending forward ones, and the squatting down ones.

"Crap, the show starts in half an hour. I need to get back to the hotel and shower. Lilly, can you help her?

Lilly nods and gives him a thumbs up from behind the upturned bottle.

"And Jessie," he pauses, "Make me proud." The look on his face is hopeful, if not exactly confident, then he adds, "I'll see you out there."

When he turns to hustle away, and then jumps off the loading dock into the back alley, Lilly says, "Don't worry, Jessie, you got this," it's just the reassurance I need, but I reach for the bottle anyway.

Chapter Twenty Five

Showtime

There are stagehands getting us into position, powdering our faces, and fluffing our hair. There's also an excited hum to the room even though it's cold enough to chatter my jaw.

The loading dock is closed and locked tight, but the nighttime chill still manages to seep into the concrete space, reminding me the sun is down and debauchery is brewing.

"You look amazing," comes a voice from behind me, and it can be only one. The Grand finale, the stunning Goddess Oshun.

I turn, "Thanks, so do you," it sounds stupid, and like the understatement of the century, but it's the best I can manage with my heart pounding in my throat like it has traded places with my larynx.

Oshun's neck looks elongated by a stack of shimmering golden rings that rests across her shoulders and chest like a saddle. The same stacks of painted rings line her forearms. The rings are so realistic looking, I expect them to chime when she moves.

She is the only model to have bigger hair than mine, and hers glitters with the sheen of perfection. Her body paint looks like she is clad in nothing but jewels and golden chains. Against her dark skin, the golden airbrushing looks three dimensional and regal.

Though her appearance is sovereign and mighty, her demeanor is not at all haughty or high-born. In fact, she is warm and genuinely kind.

I'm really nervous, but I'm mostly excited to see the look on Silas' face. I feel a little like a bride who forgets to be nervous about everything just wondering if her groom will tear up when he sees her.

I had practiced posing with Lilly to the point that it feels pretty natural now, but we had also passed the bottle of Jack back and forth a few times, so I feel a little giddy and lubed up for the show.

Erik had promised to make sure Silas was in attendance, but I have no way of knowing where he will be. It would be easier if I saw him right away and could direct my movements toward him, but I also want to do a good job for Paco, who probably thinks I'm going to run down and back, covering myself the whole way. As if I could, I have Silas to impress, as well as everyone who has ever questioned his choice in me.

Each time the door opens to swallow another model, pushed out by the stagehand, I hear the booming music. There have been enough Goddesses ingested by the stage for me to realize each one has a different song.

As the line dwindles, my urge to pee intensifies as does the pounding in my throat, and all I can do is teeter on my high heels and try to take deep breaths.

"Don't be so nervous, you are going to blow everyone away, even if you do nothing but stand there," Oshun says, "Plus, I *promise* you will *not* feel naked, and the nervousness will absolutely *evaporate* the moment you step on the stage."

I fear she has a really inflated idea of my capabilities. I smile in response, but even that is overshadowed by the clamor from the crowd. It seems that Paco may have been right about Freya, and she seems to be working the hoard into a tizzy.

Each model's catwalk has a stronger effect on the masses, to the point where I'm not sure if the crowd is loosening up, or if the girls are upping their game. Either way, I'm second to last, and I'm already naked. Hopefully, backbends and handstands will not be required to keep with the momentum.

Fuck, it's almost my turn.

***

Facing the stage door, the unscrupulous need to pee is overwhelming, and I wonder if that compulsion will evaporate as well. Ironically, the stagehand passes me a bottle of water and says, "Here, take a sip."

After I wet my throat, it's only moments before she adjusts her earpiece and says, "It's showtime, Sweetheart," and hustles me through the door into the abyss.

At the moment, I'm still out of view behind the curtain, so it gives me a second to snap out of my stunned paralysis. When my song starts, it's upbeat but still heavy on the base, it reminds me of tattoo shop music or something the Pussycat Dolls would dance to. With the flavor of electronic, R&B in my ears, I take a deep breath and step into the spotlight.

My first pose is out of necessity because I'm startled by the intensity of the lights. I can't see anything except a mostly dark, horde of people, in shadow from the eclipse. The brightness eases as the spotlight tempers itself away from my retinas.

The roar of the crowd emboldens me to take a few more steps, then a few more. I pose again, but this time it's more fluid, like when Lilly did it. The crowd goes wild while I scan the room for a familiar head of sexy, disheveled hair.

There are hundreds of people here in the main room of the club, but for some reason, I feel like Silas will stand out. When he doesn't, I give myself over to the alcohol-induced buzz and the pumping music.

Every time I do anything besides walk, the crowd explodes, so I become a little more confident with each passing heartbeat, and get a little more daring in my movements. The natural progression of confidence and a faceless yet approving audience is that I start to walk less, and dance more.

I hope Paco is back and can see me, he doubted my ability to work the crowd, so he should see this. I raise both arms sexily above my head and slink my hips back and forth as I lower myself almost into a squat.

Lilly called this move the *stripper slink*. Then, I take it a step further and drop one knee to the stage, and slowly move my other knee to the side, opening myself up.

Simultaneously, as I open my airbrushed *contours* to the hoots and hollers of the masses, the spotlight moves from my face, and I'm able to make out the faces in the first few rows of the audience.

Namely, I've spread open my legs for Salinger, who is as wide-eyed and unblinking as a horned owl. I gasp and drop my other knee to the stage, but I'm still kneeling wide legged in front of my coworker. *Fuck!*

Now I'm frozen here, with my accentuated nipples swaying above Salinger's face. *Fuck! Fuck! Fuck!* He told me he was going to be in Las Vegas for this party!

I have to remove my, parading, never felt more naked, body from Salinger's immediate proximity, but I have to be coy about it because Silas is in the audience watching me right now.

I am instantly sober, instantly and vulnerably naked and Goddamnit to hell, I'm in the fucking spotlight.

The only thing I can think to do besides jump up and run is to flip over on my hands and knees, to crawl over to the other side of the runway. Which I do, in order to get my tits and vagina away from Salinger's hungry stare. In the process, I give him the uncensored view of my ass and naked core as I slink away.

The runway is not very wide, and I have not gained a whole lot by crawling away from Salinger, except that now, my new side of the stage explodes with a thunder of their own.

I rise up, still on my knees, but no longer bending over for Salinger. The view of my painted(ish) tits receive their own set of applause, so I arch my back and thrust my chest forward for lack of anything better to do. It would be a tame, pin-up pose if I were not completely naked. The fact that I have to salvage this atrocity *and* remain undaunted is a surprisingly ugly little twist.

This is the point where Silas pushes his way to the front, and I see his gorgeous face, lit up with understanding.

I'm flanked by Salinger's lustful gaze and Silas' frank recognition, and I'm just praying my song cuts off, and a giant hook yanks me off the stage.

I lean down to kiss Silas, knowing that the action again gives Salinger an eyeful, but I'm at once comforted by his easy touch.

Once Silas breaks the kiss, I stand up and finish my walk to the end of the runway and back. I'm able to hit a few more fluid poses, but by the time the music stops, I damn near dive off the stage through the exit curtain.

The audience had loved the show, but I'm shaking and near tears. Silas strides over to me from behind the door Oshun just vaporized through. The stagehands are all that's left backstage, so we are mostly alone.

"Holy shit, Jessie Hayes! When did you learn to do that?" Silas asks delightedly, before pulling me against him, apparently not at all worried about my head to toe paint.

I can't respond at first, I'm still trying to pull myself together from the fiery blaze I just crashed in.

"You are so fucking sexy! I can't believe you put it on blast like that!"

"That was a ridiculous spectacle, Silas! I'm so embarrassed," then the tears come.

He holds me against him, "Are you insane? That was the hottest thing I've ever seen," then he pulls back and looks into my face, "Wait, you're serious?"

"I just made a complete fool out of myself in front of everyone," I mumble, trying to keep the tears from washing away my eye makeup.

"I respectfully disagree, Pipes."

Then Paco and a woman swarm in.

"Fuck-an-a, Mamacita! I didn't think you had it in you!" Paco is beaming, and it looks sincere. "This is my wife, Valentina."

"Hi," I squeak.

"Wow, Jessie, what a show! You worked it like you were born to show off Paco's work!"

"Yes, Jessie, thank you," Paco adds.

What? He is thanking me?

"Thank you both for saying that, Jessie has a hard time with compliments sometimes," Silas explains.

"Are you ready to accompany me on the stage?" Paco asks as he extends his hand to me. The other models and artists are already beginning to line up.

"Wait, what? I have to go back out there?" I ask, and it almost sounds panicked.

"No, Chingona, you *get* to go back out," Paco says, while Silas laughs at his term of endearment for me. If memory serves, I think Paco just called me a Bad Ass.

Then Paco turns to Silas, "You take care of my Lady, and I'll take care of yours," then he takes my hand and whisks me away, back toward the stage entrance door where the models and artists are gathering.

Everyone is buzzing around, excited the pressure is off, except me. I feel like my performance was atrocious and an encore feels hugely inappropriate. Not to mention, I do feel absolutely naked. There is nothing quite like sexy Salinger's smoldering gaze to cut right through the painted disguise and force me to bare my soul, and my very, very naked body.

If I were not caught up in Paco's current, I'd be hiding from him, slathering cold cream all over me in search of a new disguise. But as fate would have it, here I am, about to do an epic walk of shame.

Paco holds my hand as we walk out in a double file line, in order of our performance. As each artist and model reach the end of the catwalk, they pause as the artist's name is announced along with the model's Goddess name, then her real name. *Great.*

There are varying levels of applause for each pair, but it does seem to build. Now it makes sense that the artists waited to vote on the order, because the body art ranges from very good to phenomenal.

As we walk the green mile, Paco beams a big, white-toothed smile, nodding and waving to his adoring fans.

I'm starting to feel better, basking in his obvious pride. I might even smile a little, though my nakedness makes me feel shy and bashful. I can distinctly feel every sway or jiggle of my breasts, but the more I try to still them with quieter movements, the more they seem to parade themselves.

When we get to the end of the runway for our turn in the spotlight, the audience erupts with applause and catcalls. Paco bows when his name is announced and kisses the back of my hand. Then he twirls me around when my name is, again causing a ripple of haughty movement to my illustrious breasts.

I feel like we stand here, with my exaggerated nipples and showy contours on display, at least twice as long as the others did while Paco revels in the adoration of his airbrushed masterpiece.

It takes everything I have, not to cover my nudity while I stand here. I can actually feel the heat from the lights on my skin, and it makes me feel ripe, and overexposed for the sea of faces before me.

I can't see Salinger, but I can feel him studying my body, committing it to memory, so I can never feel clothed in front of him again. Kind of like me watching his naked prowess as he fucked Bradley in the peep show room; so much finesse, so hard for me to forget about when I see him at work.

The stage is elevated, which makes me feel like the audience is parting my lips and looking up my vagina. The only recourse I have to break the lascivious stares is to keep moving, so I turn my back to the crowd and pose coyly while draping one arm across my chest and pouting over my shoulder. More whistles at my arched back, and pushed out booty, and then thankfully Paco takes my hand again. This time he leads me down the catwalk back toward obscurity, and self-preservation.

Chapter Twenty Six

Expo

Silas is despondent about me wanting to put clothes back on for the rest of the party, and I can't exactly explain that my sexy coworker is in attendance. Instead, I kiss him, then make a beeline directly toward the bar, dragging him behind me.

I would honestly be fine if it weren't for *Salinger*, who, if this were a movie or an erotic novel, I would already be having nightly threesomes with. Anyway, remaining naked is going to require a Herculean effort, or a whole lot of alcohol.

"Jessie, this is an exposition party, shouldn't you show off Paco's art?" then Silas smiles salaciously, "And your smoking hot bod?"

"I'm feeling kind of shy, Silas."

"You could have fooled me," he winks and then guides my chin in for a kiss.

A bartender I've never seen before asks Silas what he can get for us.

I break the kiss, and answer before Silas can even open his mouth, "We are going to need a few shots of Jack Daniels, and don't be shy about leaving the bottle."

The bartender grabs a new bottle and twists the top off before setting it in front of me, then he reaches for a stack of shot glasses, and lines them up.

Silas hasn't taken his eyes off me, but I hope he realizes I can't tip the bartender with anything but a paint smear.

"I was pretty sure you were up to something, but I never would have guessed I'd find you up there, strutting your shit like a professional," he says, as his eyes drift over my painted chest and strategically exposed nipples. "I thought Erik was going to have a psychotic break when I wasn't watching the show, now I know why."

"Cheers you two," the bartender slides our shots in front of us.

Silas automatically withdraws cash and deposits it on the bar before reaching for his shot glass.

"My girl doesn't mess around, looks like we're drinking whiskey tonight," he announces with a broad smile, then clinks my shot glass before we both swallow the liquid fire.

"So, what have I missed?" I ask, recovering a little too easily from the liquor.

"On the main stage, you only missed the Burlesque show at nine. You, of course, were present for the ten o'clock show, the eleven o'clock is Rope Bondage, twelve o'clock is fire, and one a.m is oil wrestling."

"Ooooh, I want to watch the fire one."

"I watched part of his run-through, it's very cool," Silas says as he reaches for his next shot, raising his eyebrows at me. He is leaning casually against the bar, his easiness is so sexy, it makes me want to grab him by the face and drag him into a playroom.

I pick up my shot then suck it down. It hardly even touches the inside of my mouth, but I don't care to spend the evening sober, not with Salinger prickling all around me like sexy static.

I'm sincerely hoping this is not the night Silas and Salinger meet, but it's my liver's problem now.

"Is it bad that I really don't care about the demonstrations? I mostly just want to undress you and smear my paint all over your naked body," I say, as I close in on him. I think my whiskey shots are coupling up and making babies in my stomach because I am really feeling giddy.

He straightens up and wraps a relaxed arm around the small of my back, tickling my flesh with each fingertip. "I'm looking very forward to messing up your paint. I think I'll start here," he says, as he nuzzles my neck and lightly licks my ear. Shivers run through me, but the goosebumps are restrained behind what feels like a layer of hairspray all over my body.

I start unbuttoning his white dress shirt just to feel his smooth chest against mine.

"Baby, I'd fuck you standing right here if I didn't want you to see a few demos... peruse the toys...maybe try some of them," he slides his thumb back and forth over my nipple, "And by then, it will be time for the fire show."

I groan with very little interest in seeing them, "What are some of the demos anyway?" I speak right against his ear and press into him to remind him I'm not wearing any clothes.

He keeps me inside his personal space, and murmurs right back into my own ear, "There are all sorts of suspension demonstrations, electrostimulation, some intriguing furniture," he breathes against my ear. "And that doesn't even touch on the toys... some of the very toys I plan to use on you tonight," his breath tickles against my ear canal.

"Well then, maybe we should go check them out."

***

As we make our way around the club, we see suspension techniques ranging from simple; boot cuffs, ankle cuffs, wrist gloves with buckles, all the way to elaborate; rope harnesses, ridiculous positions, and nontraditional materials including plastic wrap. There are examples of both men and women suspended all around, hung from ceiling brackets like offerings at a flea market.

One woman is hanging from a spreader bar, bent in half, with her wrists and ankles bound together and her legs spread open in a wide V, allowing an unfettered view of her shoddily groomed vagina.

Another is suspended with intricate ropes while lying face down, her arms wrenched up and back by two innocent looking thumb cuffs that contradict their true nature.

A man is suspended in a position that tugs on his wrapped penis if he eases the strain on his tippy toes. I can almost feel the Charley horse in his cramping calves, and I wonder how long he has to remain that way. As I ponder his dilemma, he lowers himself to stand on flat feet, and his penis stretches like Play-doh through a Fun-Factory.

Despite the wince on Silas' face and the visual of webbed, stretched-out penis, another suspended model captures my attention.

She is bound to a Saint Andrew's cross. She's not necessarily *suspended*, but she's confined so that her spread legs hover above a deeply angled rope. The half inch rope presses into her clit and attaches somewhere above like a raunchy zip line.

At first, I don't understand her beaded sweat and look of agitation, because she's pulled so tight on the cross, she can't even move against the rope.

"That's not sanitary, he should have used a barrier film," Silas states, like a disappointed sensei.

I look back at the writhing model, and Silas guides my questioning look toward the source of her persecution. There's a personal massager, with a fist-sized head tied to, and dangling from the rope. It incessantly vibrates the rope against the woman's slit. Even with the club music in the background, now that I see the vibrating machine, it's the loudest thing in the club.

Silas takes my hand and asks, "Ready to move on, or do you want to be strung up by a world-famous suspension artist?"

"I may be really buzzed right now, but there is zero chance of me getting strung up by anyone."

"Then, on to the toys," he smiles and leans in, then kisses me while both hands securely grip my ass.

"I'm kind of cold, I need to put something on before we peruse the *toys.*"

"How about this," he says as he finishes unbuttoning his shirt and opens it wide enough to pull the bottom out of his low slung pants. "I feel overdressed next to you anyway," he says as he helps me slide it up my arms.

Cloaked in warmth and the ambient smell of his soap, I feel like a shark that has just sensed a stringy, ringlet of blood, dissipating as it's released into the ocean. I want to circle him and pull him under, devour him and never surface again.

"Silas," I say, as I place both palms on his broad chest and walk him backward a few feet until he is up against the wall, "Must we deal with these tiresome formalities?" I ask with a quiet, yet exaggerated pout.

"I don't care about whips and floggers." I caress his package without a care for all the other people in the vicinity. Truth be told, I want to get out of these towering heels, get this paint washed off, and have sex with Silas until the break of early dawn.

He turns me around, and holds my back against him while he speaks into my ear, "Do you think whips and floggers are all I have to offer you?"

His shirt is gaping open on me, so I button a few buttons while I shimmy my ass against his stiffening cock. A few people take an immediate interest in what's about to happen.

He purrs against my ear, "So many fun things you have never experienced. Like the finger cage with double, spiked pinwheels that I can roll up your naked spine before I kiss my way up its trail," he pauses his whispered seduction long enough to kiss my ear.

"Then, there is a silk scarf, that when tied properly around the base of my cock, leaves a knot… to rub up against your beautiful clit while you ride me."

I groan, and more people lose focus in the suspension techniques before them to turn and look at us.

I want him to unzip his pants and slide into me right here, in front of everyone, but I know he won't. He's so big on anticipation at the club that there's no way he would take me here like a clumsy, rutting bull.

He slides his palm into the front of his former shirt to cup my breast, "So many fun ways to stimulate your sensitive nipples," he says, as he plucks at the hard peak.

I press into his erection, trying to coax him into more, but he is already holding me tightly against himself.

With one hand, he unbuttons the highest clasped button, and then the next. I'm facing the group of onlookers, so when Silas moves the unbuttoned shirt to my sides, exposing my breasts to them, it feels naughty and explicit even though I have some coverage from the paint.

My artfully undressed nipples are on pointed display while he fondles both of them and breathes gently into my ear.

When he releases one nipple to reach into his hip pocket, I lay my head back against him and groan. My impatience is partially because he stopped toying with my nipple, and partially because it's super hot being presented to the onlookers under his skilled hands.

It's not unusual in the club to see such displays, but I am not completely accustomed to exhibiting myself when they are close enough for me to see the color of their iris' and the stubble on their chins.

Once Silas finds what he was looking for, he gives my left nipple a tug, then dallies it with one finger until I almost cry out. Then he closes something cold and tight on it. It makes me gasp and look down.

He has placed two bean-sized, round magnets on either side of my protruding nipple. They pinch tightly, making my head swim. He repeats the ritual on my other side, and I find that the squeezing pressure is right on the edge of my pain threshold. It is intensely erotic, and with the magnets, my nipples feel as big and ripe as raspberries.

When I pinch my thighs together, squeezing my clit the best I can, Silas' laugh rumbles in my ear. And when I start to feel like I could orgasm right here, without another touch, he whispers, "I wanted to take them out of ice water, but my pocket will have to do."

"Silas," I whisper, then trail off.

He says playfully, "Now… how about we go have a look at the other toys?"

"Yes," I whisper. The truth is, if I were to stand here squeezing my legs together, with my nipples pinched between these metal balls for two more minutes, I would come right down my leg, for everyone to see.

***

With the magnetic balls safely back in Silas' pocket, we pass the electrostimulation displays at a decent clip. Silas knows I have no interest in them, so we hardly notice the smell of static in the air while we pass the *interactive* displays.

There are violet wands with every size and shape of glass electrodes, a rubber crescent wrench looking thing called the Flex Capacitor, an electro-drum device that could serve as a spiky paint roller, and an e-stim paddle. The participants all look dutifully engaged in the process, but it still doesn't have any sexual pull for me.

Maybe it stems back to when I was a kid and my brother dared me to touch a tiny yellow rope, strung along a neighbors back fence. The zap had flung my arm back and felt like it charred my palm. The pain had gone all the way up my arm and into my neck; it also shattered the dubious trust I had in Jonathan for months afterward. I'd like to say Jonathan felt bad about it, but he still laughs when he tells the story, so I'm guessing not.

"Ahhh, the beautiful Goddess, Macha, how kind of you to stop by my humble display," a pale man says, with a smile on his lips. His own dark red hair is in competition with his cheekbones as his best feature. "You are stunning, please, allow me to demonstrate."

His attractiveness makes me slow, and then stop to hear what he has to say. I close the shirt around me as if it will provide protection from any thin yellow cords. Silas remains next to me, curious himself as to how this will play out. He knows I'm not interested in electrical kink, but there is humor in his eyes anyway.

"Beautiful Macha, please, your hand," the man coaxes.

I extend my hand, palm up like I'm expecting to be paid. Actually, more like I'm expecting him to deposit a steaming dog shit onto my hand.

He pulls on vinyl gloves first, then slides his hands into soft white gloves. Each glove has a single snap at the wrist, which evidently are the leads to conduct the electricity. He plugs the power source in, then reaches to take my hand.

I close my eyes but still have to fight the urge to pull back.

He takes my hand gently, like he only wants to shake it, and then rolls it palm up. There is some tickling through my palm but not much, only enough to make me open my eyes and watch.

Next, he begins to massage my forearm, indifferent to the painted arm wrap and splattered fake blood. As soon as his other hand touches my arm, the sensation ratchets up from delicate tingle to vibrating pulse.

"It's not as bad as I thought," I smile at Silas.

"BAD? Not at all, my beauty. Electrosex is the pinnacle of sensation play. With its conductive energy leaving your body shivering, and aching with anticipation," the man says, almost affronted by my comment.

I notice the metal finger-tip claws that he has distressingly close to an e stim machine and the thought of scratching claws paired with erotic stimulation makes my tingling arm crawl with the aberration.

He adjusts the attached machine, sending the sensation back to a tingle as he continues to caress my arm. He nudges my rolled-up sleeves further and further up my arm with each bold advance.

"My dear, imagine me lightly caressing all the way up your arms, my fingers fluttering across your décolleté, then titillating movements as I caress down between your breasts," he says, his arctic blue eyes never leaving mine, and his voice almost enchanting.

"The anticipation of me skimming across your ridged nipples is so heavily desired in your dream state, but I resist. Then, I continue my sensual journey down to your, *ripe... little... clit*—"

"**Ok**, that's enough, Chief," Silas states as he breaks the spell, amusement perched on the curl of his lip.

"Thanks for the demonstration," I add with a giggle, as I turn away. Silas' reaction was completely different than the cracked jaw I would have expected, and for some reason, I find it funny. *Caress and titillate my girl while fucking her with your eyes, but leave her ripe little clit out of it.*

I'm still giggling while tucked against Silas' body as we walk away. I'm not sure if something is really funny, or if the joke is on Jack Daniels, but I can't seem to wipe the smile off my face or swallow the giggles.

"Changing your mind about e stim, are ya?" Silas jokes, through a broad smile, "Or do you find you're hungry for a ginger-snap?" he says, as he lets out his own bottled up laughter.

I personally hate when people refer to red-haired individuals as gingers, but that man was one sexxxxy ginger.

On our chuckling, drunken way to the toy exhibits, we encounter some scandalous, yet strangely compelling, kinky devices. First, there are several versions of forced orgasm towers, each with a willing participant strapped into submission, and some form of humming device chastising them.

There is something Silas calls a barrel horse, with a pink-cheeked man bent over it. He growls every time the flogger tastes his partially exposed ball sack, yet he doesn't close his unbound legs to prevent it. Silas shudders as we move along to the next demonstration.

A sign hanging from heavy, oversized chain links introduces the *Spanish Rider*. There are five of them, three in use. The individual devices are designed as a tower, with multiple options for binding the *rider*. For example, one woman is bound to the tower with her wrists secured high above her head, another with her hands at the base of her spine, and the last with her arms stretched out wide, in a crucifixion pose.

One uniting factor among all the women is that their legs are all spread widely apart, and bound tightly at their ankles. Each one is perched precariously on a blunt, triangular... saddle, which is pressed against their vaginas and not at all comfortable looking. However, all of the naked women seem lost in a slow, quiet ecstasy of their own. Each face reads pure euphoria, even, rapture.

"These creep me out," Silas shudders.

"Why? Do those women look creeped out to you?" I ask, just as the first one begins to keen and roll her head back and forth.

"They are devised from the French Chevalets, which were torture devices, and I imagine agonizingly painful."

On closer inspection, I see the empty triangular saddles each have four electrode plates. Once I see them, I know unequivocally that I will not be resting my naked vagina lips against plates with an electrical current running through them.

One of the men exhibiting the devices motions for me to step up to an empty tower. I can't even respond, I just slowly shake my head. It's at this exact moment that the keening rider, galloping toward orgasm, moans loudly then comes in violent, noisy bursts.

The man widens his eyes and shrugs his shoulders in an exaggerated motion like I'm crazy to miss out on the opportunity to light up my vaginal lips.

"Fuuuuuuck that," I whisper as I cling to Silas' bicep.

After a few steps, Silas says, "I want to show you this next one, I already ordered it."

"Does it require a source of electrical current? Or is it a medieval torture device?" I ask.

"Nope, it's a little trampoline, bouncy seat thing," he puts extra articulation on the words *bouncy seat*.

"How romantic," I tease.

We round the corner, and Silas says, "Here we go." The bouncy seat is a simple enough design, with rocking-horse style, pipe legs wide enough for a man to lie between, and two wide strips of elastic across the saddle of the thing.

The tone in this environment is more like an adult Romp-A-Room, or gymnastic party arena, with participants paired up all around the demonstration space. There are a myriad of different positions on display, but suffice it to say, the creative uses are endless.

Closest to us, is a couple with the man in a sitting position with his legs extended before him. The bouncy seat straddles his naked lap as the woman bounces above him. Were it not for the elastic saddle between them, she would merely look like she was sitting on his lap, bouncing with ease. His cock, easily sliding between the stretching strips of elastic.

"It reminds me of the whole yoga ball fiasco," I say, referencing a failed attempt at wheelbarrow sex and then a sloppy and unstable run at bouncy, yoga ball sex. For days the sight of the green yoga ball and handprint smears on the wall mirror in his building's gym made me snicker. Then, one day it was just gone, popped or otherwise violated, but erased nonetheless.

"This looks more stable…and versatile," he nods to another couple. This pair faces each other, with her calves draped over his shoulders while happily bouncing away.

"Awww, I think that one's my favorite," I flick my chin to point out a woman rocking above her lovers face while he eats her out.

Some male grunting, loud enough to distract from the peppy music, draws our attention to a woman lying tummy up on the bouncer. Her ankles serve as one man's earmuffs while he rails into her with her head dropped back, so she can deep throat another man. The men grunt and groan almost in unison, while her small breasts quiver from the force of the thrusting.

***

After finally making the rounds and ending up at the long-awaited toy section, I cringe at the site of a woman having a studded breast binder fastened to her body. She has a shiny ball gag in her mouth but doesn't appear to be in too much distress. I would be screaming RED. Just the thought of metal spikes against my tender nipples makes me turn too quickly and run smack into Silas.

He holds me against him and runs his hand up my backside, under the shirt. "He is able to control the bite of those. It's not as bad for her as it looks."

"Maybe I just needed some of your attention. I mean, look at this highly eroticized environment," I say, needlessly spelling out the fact that, around the ten-foot diameter demonstration platform, are a dozen people purchasing and using the items being displayed.

"You need some attention? What interests you here, hmmm? The glass Ben-Wa balls? How about the forced orgasm belt with the vibrator attached?" he spins me back around to have a look at the offerings while he moves all my hair in front of one shoulder and sucks my ear into his warm mouth.

There is a couple directly across from us, and for a split second, I think it's Salinger. I had all but forgotten he was here. The woman is doing a lap dance for him while he is seated on a stool behind her.

Is that him? No, his hair isn't that long. Is it?

Silas finds the buttons of the shirt again and releases them with a flick. As my shirt is falling open, I again get a glimpse of the man across from me while the woman leans forward, grinding her ass against his crotch. It might be him, with his normally perfect hair a bit mussed, but I still can't be sure.

On the platform between us, a woman with beautiful almond-shaped eyes and flawless skin lies back on her sheet of silky black hair. She is wearing nothing except strappy shoes that crisscross her legs all the way to her knees. She holds up a funny glove with different ridges and bumps on each finger, then slides it on her hand as she opens her legs.

While I'm still pondering if it really is Salinger under the lap dancer, Silas opens my shirt all the way.

I inhale sharply, as my painted nudity becomes visible and Salinger's eyes land on me. It's definitely him.

My naked body feels different displayed for him now. I don't know if it's because he has a woman on his lap, or because I'm good and drunk, but it's kind of hot how he watches me over his chic's shoulder. It's a deep, penetrating gaze, right over the top of the demonstrator on the platform.

I return his sultry gaze with no notice of the demonstrator's playful, ribbed glove or her dancing fingers.

Silas dribbles some oil or maybe lube across my breasts, evidently pilfered from the display cache. He rubs his hands over my stomach and chest. The now oily paint smears together, like a child's fingerpaint design, with all the colors melding into one, dark gray smear.

Then he uses the tails of my shirt to wipe the paint from my body. He reveals fresh, uncamouflaged skin while sullying the dress shirt beyond recognition.

My breasts jostle against the firm wipe down, and my nipples come radiantly to life with the lack of disguise and bold introduction to the open air.

Silas erases Paco's careful handiwork in a few sloppy moments, then dribbles the oil directly on my pelvic area. I can feel the oil curl around each carefully painted contour and tickle erotically into my slit.

As he gently wipes the paint from the creases between my legs, I can feel the bare skin pinken against the attention, as well as the lack of obscurity.

When Silas slides a stool between us, I don't hesitate to perch against it, and when he directs me to open my legs for his attentive hand, I don't look away from Salinger, not for a second.

Salinger tugs his woman's shirt off before yanking her bra into a belt and spinning her around. No longer accountable for his wayward stare, he keeps his eyes directed on the freshly wiped clean parts of my body.

When I flop my head back against Silas, he lowers a hand to my neck. He doesn't squeeze or even tighten his grip, but it's a show of force as he spreads my legs further apart.

I see Salinger's slow, deliberate grin as he signals his approval of my wide open thighs. The woman on stage, who I can see *peripherally*, has rolled to her stomach where she writhes against the bumpy-fingered glove.

When Silas advances his now similarly gloved hand between my legs, I gasp at the unfamiliar, studded plastic. He dallies a finger between my lips, warming it against my rawness, and moistening one digit of the glove. Then he drops his other hand to twiddle a very pretentious and highly responsive nipple.

Salinger, likewise toys with the set of tits on his lap. I'm watching his ministrations so intently; it makes me feel like it's *him* touching me.

To have both Silas and Salinger touching me at the same time would be absolute nirvana. Their hands caressing and adoring my body, both of their tongues anointing my flesh, their perfectly wielded cocks—harmonious in their skillful devotion to me. The fantasy calls a shiver up my spine and brings a mischievous smile to my lips.

As much as I would kill for a threesome with Silas and Salinger, I know with certainty this is the closest I will ever get. So I arch my back and thrust my chest forward to put on a show for Salinger, while simultaneously opening my mind to a very naughty and vivid imagination.

I'm feeling so turned on right now. The fact that Salinger can plainly see my unpainted, bare breasts and the pinkness of my core is driving me absolutely wild with temptation.

His stare is almost as physical as it is rabid, while he provokes my body with nothing more than a forbidden look. It's as if he's hypnotized by my open legs and exhibited clit. I can imagine his tongue against it.

I adjust myself on the stool and open my legs wider for Silas, as he tests each finger of the glove against my impossible wetness, bumping each uniquely clothed digit over my clitoris.

The glove fingers with bumps and spiral ridges, respectively, are too much, making me jerk each time they bounce over my highly sensitized nub. Silas determines the finger with small texture lines is the best when I'm this turned on, so he slides it repeatedly through my slit and thoughtfully against my showy button.

I watch as Salinger lifts the woman from his lap and begins to peel down her tight pants. Once she takes over removing her clothing, Salinger digs in his pocket then withdraws a rubber. The woman with Salinger can't believe her good fortune as she steps out of her clingy pants. But when she bends over naked in front of him, he hardly registers it as movement while he keeps his eyes locked on my forbidden landscape.

She gets on her knees in front of Salinger and releases his erection from battered jeans. He tells her *not yet* while his heavy cock sways back and forth. His lip curls into a wicked smile when he sees me looking at his naked tribute. He obviously recognizes our game of I'll show you mine if you show me yours, and his penis is all but saluting me.

Her mouth closes around Salinger's shaft, just as Silas begins to plunge one finger of the glove inside me. The walls of my vagina squeeze around his finger so I can feel each and every ridge in the texture. I adjust my footing, hooking one three inch heal around a rung of the stool and brace myself against Silas' body behind me.

Now that penetration has been introduced, Salinger boldly lifts her mouth from his dick, rolls on a condom and impales her while still turning her away from him. Watching her slide down his cock, then having glimpses of its crushing hardness each time she rises from his lap, is crazy sexy. Watching his ridged penis as it skewers repeatedly into her, is making me moan against the quickening advance of Silas' gloved finger.

Silas is kissing my neck, telling me how much he loves me, as I'm writhing against his ribbed finger. I'm also watching Salinger's cock vanish as it sinks into the willing vessel on his lap, then as it reappears in shiny glory.

When Silas uses the honeycombed thumb of the glove to rub my clit back and forth while still fingering me and stimulating my g-spot, I almost pee myself it feels so good. When I'm close to bursting, Silas withdraws his glistening finger, drags it up my body and taps it against my panting mouth.

Salinger stops his woman from bobbing, with two hands around her waist, and waits in agony to see what I'll do with the finger that's waiting at the threshold of my mouth.

"Show me what you want to do to me, Baby," Silas groans against my ear.

I extend my tongue and slap it against the bulbous head of the glove a few naughty times, then grab his wrist and suck his finger deep into my mouth. Simulating head on something like his finger is easy compared to the choking mouthful of a fully erect penis. It allows for some creative liberties, and I take advantage of that. Employing some porn star tactics, Salinger receives an eyeful of my oral skills, and judging by the fevered look on his face, he will extract them from his memory bank often, and at will.

"What are your thoughts regarding the toys you wanted nothing to do with?"

I slurp away from the tip of the glove, "I like them so far, but you are so busy fucking my mouth, that you've left my other parts lonely and abandoned," I pout.

"I haven't abandoned your other parts, Pipes, I'm simply slowing you down and building you toward a colossal orgasm," he explains, "Look, our moderator has not yet given in to *her* fuck glove, and you want to carry on ahead of her?"

It occurs to me that while I have been watching Salinger, Silas has been watching the platform, mimicking the demonstrator's techniques, and assuming I'm doing the same. I'm actually relieved to hear that, it's better than the alternative of Silas being aware of the little tête-à-tête between Salinger and me.

"The unfortunate thing about the glove is that I can't feel you against me, your pussy or your mouth."

I wrench my head further back so I'm looking into his face, "Well Silas, which one would you like to feel first?" I ask as I drop my hand behind me to stroke his penis.

"I think I should check to see if you are nice and wet first. If you happen to be," he guides my legs open again, sampling with his flesh and blood fingers this time, "I'll want you wrapped around my dick in pretty quick succession."

I finally look back to Salinger, he has slowed things down himself, but his eyes are still locked on me. When he licks his lips, to moisten them I think, I see his tongue move in slow motion, and I can't help but imagine him licking me, tasting me.

Silas opens me to Salinger, spreads my folds and slides his finger into my indecent display, never guessing the amount of fuel he is throwing on the fire.

He rolls my nipple as his thumb finds my clit. The arc of metaphorical electricity it causes is complete only when Salinger's gaze moves from my dilated core to my eyes. This is the point he begins fucking his woman in earnest. I watch while her face twists with abandon as he dials and tugs her bouncing nipples.

I feel impossibly wet, and the reality of Salinger watching it happen is the icing on the cake. Salinger makes a bold move and winks at me, making my heart flutter.

Silas comes around the stool, picks me up and deposits me cleanly onto the demonstration platform. I'm terrified he saw Salinger wink, but when he hooks his arms under my knees and buries his cock in me, I know he didn't see it.

Silas is alternating slow grinding movements, with deep penetrating thrusts. It distracts me from Salinger's broken eye contact, shattered like an icicle plunging from the eave.

I wanted to look him in the eyes as I came. I can't explain why, but I want to explode around Silas while Salinger is a part of it. I want to see Salinger come while watching me, to pump his seed into someone while wishing she was me.

Just thinking of Salinger's cum reminds me of my un-birth controlled state, and Silas' bare, pumping cock. "Si-las," I groan, as he slams into me. Salinger's new view is of the top of my head, and my jouncing tits.

"Yeah, Baby?" Silas asks, with his complete concentration on fucking me, and not talking during it. Sweat beads on his forehead and his face twists with something approaching delirium.

"Con-dom," I say, it comes out broken and put back together because of his unrestrained thrusts.

"I'll pull out," he chokes.

My breasts are unusually sensitive with the jouncing, so I bring my hands up to control their quaking.

"No," I hear from behind me. *Could Salinger be talking to me?*

I lay my arms back above my head, then hear, "That's right," then I *know* he's talking to me. Ballsy Salinger, he is going to get us caught.

In a somewhat less obvious attempt to contain the movement of my breasts, I begin to toy with my nipples, bumping my fingers against them.

A groan from behind me, "Aww yeahhhhh, JB… yeah, baby."

Then, I know he is coming, I can't see or hear him, but the energy in the room changes. It's like knowing the baby in your arms is finally asleep. It's just a shift in the voltage or something.

Silas' jaw clenches and I know he is waiting for me, but I'm not even close. I let go of one nipple and drop my fingers to my clitoris. Silas would be tending to it himself if he were not holding the bottom half of me up.

I have faked many an orgasm before, to simply get on with things, but never with Silas. Never. So I do something I'm not proud of. I picture Salinger's fingers on my clit and his mouth on my nipple, while Silas fucks me.

Chapter Twenty Seven

Aftermath

Recovering from a night of drinking is much harder than it used to be. I remember back in college, I would hardly skip a beat after a bender night. I would drink some water before bed and wake up fresh as a daisy for early classes. My freshly brewed coffee at hand while blithely typing lecture notes into my laptop.

Headaches never figured into my recovery day, and certainly not the delayed vomiting brought on by the previous night's antics. What is that all about anyway? Our livers take the alcohol in stride for approximately twelve hours, retaining every drop before giving up on trying to purge the madness? Then it shrugs with indifference while we choke on poetic justice the next day?

Last night after the club had been a blur. I have vague memories of a coconut oil rubdown then a murky bath, but none of it had been sexy. It was more like a loving parent tending to the child with diarrhea running down their leg.

Silas had done a passable job, but this morning I still wore last night's war paint behind my ears and in the crease beneath my left breast. Poor guy did his best. Of the two of us, he was better equipped to line up the Uber that ushered us home and order the pizza we ate with an unabashed fury. He had been pretty drunk too, he can just pull it off better than I can.

This morning, Silas doesn't even need sunglasses to open the fridge like I do. It's certainly a different road for us today; I'm in bed, tucked into a ball around the cramping abdomen that doesn't even feel like my own, and Silas is out for a run. He is bringing back bagels and coffee at least, but he prefers to sweat out his bodily toxins while I wrestle with mine, surrounded by oily, coconut scented sheets.

When Silas re-enters the room, I press my ear further into the pillow in hopes of fending off his good cheer and buffering the loudness of it.

"Pipes," he sounds parental and slightly disappointed, "I think you would feel better if you got up and moving."

"And I think, you're wrong," I roll over to face him, with my eyes squinting from the light, not the aggravation. He is sweaty and perfect, with his earbuds hanging out of the neck of his t-shirt and a coffee cup in each hand.

"Come shower with me so we can go pick up Ruby," he smiles then adds, "Then we can relax and watch movies all day." He puts both coffees on the dresser while I eye him skeptically.

"It's not only my hangover Silas, I have the most ridiculous cramps. It feels like my intestines will rupture if I straighten out my body," I crack a smile because I recognize how overly dramatic I sound.

"Well, there's no help for that. Looks like there's more bagels for me," he teases while he starts to tug the comforter off me. Then he gasps, "Oh shit, Jessie!"

"I know, the coconut oil greased up the sheets."

"No. Baby, something is wrong," he looks stricken.

Alarmed, I sit up and look for what he is talking about. It's blood. Not a ton, but enough to stain my thighs and smear the white sheets.

I jump up, mortified to have sullied his pristine bed. It's been so long since I've had a period, I forgot what a nuisance it can be. I don't even own any tampons.

"Nothing is wrong Silas, it's just my period."

"Are you sure? That's a lot of blood, and you said you felt like you were going to rupt—"

"Silas, it's my period. I didn't expect it yet, the doctor said it could take months, but stop looking so distressed. You have a daughter for goodness sake, you will have to teach her all about hers in a few years."

"Aghhh, I can't even—"

"How to insert a tampon…. How to tuck the string in," I giggle while heading for the bathroom.

Chapter Twenty Eight

Moment of Truth

"Silas, are you sure you're ready for this?" I ask, uncertain if I'm even ready for it. Getting pregnant is a monumental undertaking. Handing the baby over for someone else to raise is an anxiety-provoking, nearly impossible thing to do. And dating someone who isn't even the father is something beyond my most basic comprehension.

"Ready for what? To insert a rubbery cup of two other men's warm semen into my girlfriend's vagina?" he smiles, "Because, I think I can do a pretty decent job. I won't even spill any." He leans in to kiss me, as I sit on the edge of the bed, afraid to lie back.

I scoff at his ill-timed humor, "No, I mean, are you ready for this whole journey? I'm going to get fat, my ankles are going to swell, I'm going to get stretch marks…and start producing milk from my breasts." All my superficial arguments bubble to the surface, but they mask the biggest fears of all. The ones where I grow a baby in my body, love and nurture it for nine months and then try to go on with life while Corey and Devin settle in with their perfect little baby.

"Sweetie, I'm ready for this journey and all the ones that follow," he lowers himself to one knee, so he is not standing above me anymore.

"We can't turn back after this, the snowball will only gather speed and fortitude...it's going to drag us with it, Silas."

"This is completely your decision, Jessie. If you want to change your mind, I will support you. But if you still want to do this for them, I will hold your hair back while you vomit from morning sickness, I will rub your swollen ankles and feet, and massage cocoa butter into your stretch marks. We will watch the baby grow inside you and follow its progress with ultrasounds and countless doctors' appointments. And when he or she is born, we will cuddle and love that child no differently because of a legal custody document. And one day, when we are ready for a child of our own, I will hold your hair back while you vomit from morning sickness..." he is holding my hands between his while he soothes my last minute jitters. I'm so comforted by his whole demeanor that I hardly notice when he slides a ring down my finger.

"I told you I was ready for this journey with you, and I meant it. Now, I want to ask you to take a journey with me," he pauses, and my eyes well with tears.

"Jessie, you waltzed into my life and changed everything. The moment I met you, you had me under your spell. I used to think love was just a silly emotion and a baseless need, but I've come to understand love with you by my side. Now, I recognize it's more than just a simple emotion, or petty need. It's the feeling of transcendence—of knowing you are *exactly* where you belong."

A tear trickles down my cheek as I realize what he is doing. I'm dressed in nothing but a t-shirt, about to be impregnated with Corey and Devin's sperm, and Silas is on one knee, expressing so eloquently how we both feel.

"Never would I have dreamed I'd find the most perfect person to share that kind of love with, but here you are, teaching me what it's like to *be* loved as well as exemplifying the purest, most basic yearning I have ever had. Jessie, you are what I've always wanted in my life."

A choked sob escapes my lips, and I want to throw my arms around him, but I also want him to keep talking because his words sound like my soul's harmony.

"I want to be with you forever, Jessie. Will you marry me?"

Keep Reading for a Sneak Peek of Book 4 945 Cedar Avenue

Also by KC Decker:

Standalone Books

Little Dove

My name is Etta Freeman.

There is something special about me.

Not special in a good way, though, more like special in a way that will get me killed one day.

It's not something I talk about with anyone, but that doesn't stop me from trying to snare my neighbor in my devious web.

He is angsty and brooding and completely sexy in a scrappy, bloody knuckle kind of way.

I should also mention that he's a scheming, felonious drug dealer and I'm drawn to him like flies on shit.

The problem is, he doesn't yet know his role in my narrative, but he will fall in line.

They always do.

Trigger Warning: Little Dove contains content that some readers may find distressing.

Of Ash and Angels

* Silver Medal Winner of the
International Reader's Favorite Book Awards

Justin:

I've never had a therapist I didn't want to punch in the face. As a collective group, they all say there is no way around grief, only through it, but for me, grief has become who I am. The idea of shedding it is as ludicrous as stepping outside of my own skin.

The fact is, some things can break you. I mean, shatter your soul and cast it into the wind in a billion tiny pieces. To think you might one day be able to find all those infinite pieces of yourself, patch everything back together, and move on with life—well, I don't even need to dignify that with a response.

Norah:

A few months ago, I shaved off a hundred and eighty-five-pound parasite. Then, once I was rid of him, I wondered why I didn't stick it out because the dating world is treacherous these days. Turns out, so is unemployment.

I suppose, to offset all the swiping left and streaming marathons in my life, I should take this job. There is a massive problem with the position, though.

The problem's name is Justin Abernathy.

Gradation

Friends. Ride or die, right?
Always have your back.
Know all your dirty little secrets.
Love the shiny parts of you, and embrace the crappy ones.
Yeah? Well, I don't know about all that nonsense because my friends are a bunch of assholes.
They're taking over.
They're commandeering my love life.

They're constructing a dating profile for me, and it's bad…
Because I don't even have the *password* for it,
and I have to do *exactly* what they say.

Mercy

**INTERNATIONAL BOOK AWARDS FINALIST and
KIRKUS FEATURED REVIEW RECIPIENT!**

My parents abandoned me a decade ago to the walls of this institution.
They believed my troubled childhood mind was something sinister
instead of homegrown or explainable. The truth is that my condition is
complicated. It's messy and often misunderstood.

I've worn all types of labels over the years: Non-believer, pariah,
deranged, *orphan*... It's all in my file if you care to understand me better.
However, the label that implanted the deepest and garnered the most
attention is the one I wear, like a Scarlet Letter. It precedes me when I
enter a room and gets whispered about like a schoolyard crush.

Paranoid Schizophrenic.

Dr. Sutton has some lofty ideas about my condition and claims mental
illness is only one aspect of hundreds that make me who I am. Not one to
shy away from a challenge, he thinks he can help me. His confidence is
legendary, but I've carried this burden for a long time. Despite what he
thinks, I can't be fixed.

He doesn't realize I'm falling for him or that I have some lofty ideas of
my own. He should know better because people like me deserve a hero,
too.

The Jessie Hayes 4 Book Series
(Must be Read in Order)

1462 South Broadway (Book 1)
**Winner of the National Excellence*

in Romance Fiction Award)

It's said that a bird never has to doubt the stability of her branch because her trust is in her own wings.

I myself, am trying to grow some wings of my own, but I'm kind of mired in place right now.

My roommate fondly calls my situation *a rut* and seems to think he knows how I can climb out of it.

The problem with his solution is that he's stone-cold crazy.

There is no way in hell I'm going to a *sex club*.

A scorching, witty, and unexpectedly tender story about finding courage in the unlikeliest places—and discovering the kind of freedom that doesn't come from a stable branch, but from daring to fly.

720 Linden Street (Book 2)

My kinky introduction to BDSM has been less about dipping my toe and more about being tossed into the deep end…bound.

That simple fact has required me to make some pretty hefty leaps outside of my comfort zone.

Turns out, there is a whole lot more to the BDSM scene than I initially thought.
There's a staggering array of possibilities, all wide open for me to see and experience.

You see, my boyfriend owns a sex club.

And I have a lot to learn.

Trigger Warning: 720 Linden Street contains content that some readers may find distressing.

1700 Grant Street (Book 3)

Have you ever found yourself at a crossroads on your journey, with your entire future depending on tiny little decisions here and there?

Do you resist temptation and stick with your current choice? Or will you always wonder how life *could have been*?

When you get to this branching of your life's path, it's not enough to merely choose one direction. You must distance yourself from the rejected road. Because dancing between the two will slowly unravel you.

And it will start with your fickle heart.

945 Cedar Avenue (Book 4, Salinger's Story)

A wedding engagement is a joyous occasion, right?

Well, I suppose that depends on your perspective.

If you happen to be on the side of the path that branches to the left, when the love of your life chooses to go right, you may have a different opinion.

So, what do you do when someone else's choice annihilates the future you counted on?

The answer to that may depend on your membership status at a certain sex club.

Namely, 1462 South Broadway.

COMING SOON!

<u>The Space Between</u>

<u>Midnight Sun</u>

JOIN KC DECKER:

Mailing List: www.KCDeckerBooks.com

Instagram: www.instagram.com/author_kc_decker

X: www.X.com/KCDeckerBooks

Facebook: www.facebook.com/kc.decker.79

Bookbub: www.bookbub.com/profile/kc-decker

www.KCDeckerBooks.com

Dedication:

This book is dedicated to anyone who has ever struggled with their own demons. If Salinger, Jessie, or Devin's story resonates with you on a deeper level, I applaud you for your strength. Every character in this series has faced adversity to a certain extent—whether it be physical, emotional or societal but the message is the same. Mel Robbins said it best, "You have been assigned this mountain to show others it can be moved." So, if you have your own mountain—big or small...this book is for you.

—KC

Bonus Material
945 Cedar Avenue

Chapter One

Thinking

Damn, that girl has my heart. I cannot think of a more perfect woman than Jessie Hayes. She is *stacked* and that body torments me constantly. The fact that I've seen her naked on several occasions will be my complete undoing, I'm positive of it.

The first time I saw her perfect tits she was masturbating for her laptop camera. She had been broadcasting her arched back, straining nipples, and spread thighs for that numb nut, Silas. That's when I knew I had to have her, never mind company policy—I'd rather quit and live in poverty for the rest of my life than keep her off limits a second longer. Of course, that's when I told her that I loved her, a tiny detail that upon further reflection, I should have kept to myself.

She didn't tell me she loved me back, and she certainly didn't draw me in to her perfect nakedness for the fuck of the century. No, she started crying and shaking her head back and forth—as if the tears weren't soul annihilating enough. Suffice it to say that was not the reaction I was looking for. But the image of her with her fingers in her panties and her body wrenched back over some pillows, so her tits *flaunted* themselves at me, will be forever etched in my memory. More like burned into my memory, to surface at the most inopportune times imaginable. I can literally not even look at the woman without picturing her topless, and all the things I have done to her in my alone time would shock a high budget porn star.

That little showdown in the hotel room with Jessie and her dime piece of a body had me on the brink of needing to nut under my desk before any sort of a meeting with her. And that lasted for *months*. Her body is only part of the package though. She is really smart, and I have never met anyone with a personality like hers. She's like a dude, in that, she is funny and you can joke around with her. But she's also deep, and tuned in on an emotional level that is just the right amount for me.

She was an extreme emotional support for me after my tours in Baghdad, and she didn't even know ten percent of what I had gone through. She didn't push me like my, now ex-wife had. Jessie made herself a constant, quiet presence that held me up from the inside, like an emotional scaffolding. She knew it was bad, and that I was tormented beyond reason. She would sit with me in my dark house for hours at a time and do nothing but hold my hand. It sounds crazy, but I had drawn strength from her—not enough to function, but enough to go on.

I knew I loved her way back then. I also knew I didn't love my wife with anything near the intensity I felt for Jessie. My wife did me a favor cheating on me while I was away serving our country *and* when I was back stateside while my body healed from the rigors of war.

I was laid up for months recovering from the injuries I suffered at the insurgent's hands. The roadside IED had ripped through me and claimed the lives of seven of the best men I have ever known. I will *never* be the same, and sometimes I still wake up screaming, trying in vain to warn them.

It's crazy that my mind has pieced memories together for me that I couldn't possibly remember. Like the ringing stillness. There had been a moment of absolute silence when everything was still, right before the blast. It felt like entire minutes of realization, but with the slow-motion inability to move or call out. Just the static filled passage of time as it clicked by.

The reality is, there was no warning. No moment of stillness. No realization of what was about to happen. Griggs and McCarty had been arguing about whether or not getting a handy from another woman constituted cheating on your spouse. Then, in a flash, all I knew was searing pain and the rank smell of antiseptic. It felt like I was in a Full Nelson hold with a cement truck on my back. I can still smell the hospital sheets when I think about them. They smelled like hot, powdered ash, and my face was against them for weeks before I was stable enough to be transported back to the United States.

The USMC had shipped back an empty vessel, and Jessie gave me hope for the future. Hope that someday the agony of loss would let up its grip, if only a little.

When I caught my wife in our bed with another man, I was almost grateful. I couldn't stand to be around her anymore. The things the woman ranked as a level red threat were as trivial as fingerprints on the stainless steel fridge. I couldn't begin to unburden myself by sharing what a person sounds like when their lower leg has been blown off. Or how you can taste the metallic tang of your Lieutenant's blood as you shove gauze into the wound in his chest.

I couldn't do it anymore. I probably pushed her away with my emptiness and raw despair, but I couldn't understand why I had lived when my brothers had died. It's like I was spared so I could live to tell the tale. Except I couldn't tell it, it burned my mouth and tasted like ash. It also left an almost unbearable pressure on my back where skin grafts were healing, and muscles had been stitched back together. The ordeal overseas succeeded in vaporizing everything I used to care about. Everything except Jessie. She was my beacon in the storm, directing me safely back to shore.

She is the most beautiful woman I have ever seen, she is caring, she's fucking hilarious, and that *hair*. Her hair is a dark red that is so striking my dick swells just thinking about my fingers entwined in it. The amazing thing is, she has absolutely no idea how appealing she is to men. She never developed the pretentiousness normally doled out among the pretty people. Jessie isn't high maintenance like the women I tend to draw the attention of, she is down to earth and just as self-deprecating as the rest of us.

The fact that I work very closely with her is a blessing and a curse, today it's a curse. She is wearing a tight black skirt that hits right above her knees and some heels with a strap around the ankles that accentuate her legs and remind me of a pin-up girl. I would say her top is inconsequential in its mossy greenness, but because I know what's beneath, with remarkable clarity, no top is truly inconsequential.

I have been struggling for a few months now, ever since the exposition party at 1462. That night marks one of the other times I have seen her naked. Not completely naked, well yes, completely naked, but she was painted like a warrior. Another image seared into my brain for all time. I swear she saw me from the stage and looked me right in the eyes before she slinked down in front of me and spread her legs open.

The stage had been about waist height, so when she parted her legs and presented herself to me, I seriously considered burying my face and never coming up for air. The fact that she was covered with body paint did little to conceal her body from all the hungry eyes on her. For one thing, even if the paint *had* been clothes, they would have been very skimpy. If anything, the paint called attention to her tits and ass, never mind her delectable, open, and begging pussy.

Pretty sure she had been teasing me, I was surprised to see the look of horror on her face and her instantaneous roll onto her hands and knees to crawl away from my thirsty stare. But then she had slunk away from me sensually slow and all the while waving her bare crotch, even the unpainted parts, right at me.

My cock was responding to her display like it's practically conditioned to do. That is until that fucker, Silas popped up. She planted a kiss on him that I felt on my own lips, as well as in my slackening dick.

After the Goddess show, I was as confused as ever by her mixed signals. I swear she keeps me on the hook just in case Silas punks out. What she doesn't know, however, is that I'm no consolation prize. I have way too much pride and self-respect to play second fiddle to another man. Nope, once Silas is out of the picture, she is going to have to work for me.

It will happen soon enough, I know her too well. Once, she broke up with a great guy because he wore loafers. Another time, because the dude got up from his couch to fix the flipped up blinds—she was just certain he was too OCD for her. Seriously, it doesn't take much. An eye goober, the mispronunciation of "supposedly," a car that smells like cat pee…really, I could go on forever.

I already mentioned that I told her, I love her, but she doesn't have to know I would drink her dirty bath water. I just need to be patient. I'm going to let her get all the ridiculousness with Silas out of her system, and then she can challenge herself a little with me. That way, she can actually pine for something that stands a chance of working.

Silas is on borrowed time. He has already *literally* sexually assaulted her, leaving Jessie saddled with anxiety at best, PTSD at worst. Then there were those surveillance photos to further destroy the trust between them. I could actually buy a drink for whoever hatched that plan. Anyway, his time has to be just about up, the breakdown of trust in a relationship is the hardest to bounce back from.

Apparently he gold medals in the sex department. Everyone talks about him like he is some sort of *sexual leviathan* or something, but I haven't seen anything all that impressive from him yet. I've watched him fuck her three times now, one she knew about, two she did not.

Now, before you start thinking I'm some kind of pervert lurking in the bushes, let me be clear, 1462 is an expansive bounty of sexuality. Sex and nudity drip from the ceiling like an interior sprinkler system. There are private rooms that cater to every fetish you can imagine, and even some you've never even heard of. However, the entire first floor is very, very public, and the club events are what legends are made of.

One such event was flashlight night, where the club was pitch-ass dark except for flashlights. A girl I hook up with at the club sometimes, Bradley, wanted me to attend the party with her. Now, Bradley had no idea I knew Jessie, but she was intrigued by the fact that the owner, *The Almighty, Silas*, was fucking in the public part of the club. She evidently had heard about his sexual prowess and wanted to observe what all the fuss was about.

When Bradley and I made our way over, Jessie was lying on an inclined liberator cushion with her hips at the top and her ass hanging over the peak of the liberator. Her knees were spread, and Silas was eating her out. Most of the flashlights were trained on her tits and her open thighs, but I wanted to see her face when she got off. So I waited, mesmerized by her writhing, naked body until she started to moan. When I shined the flashlight on her face as she came, I thought to myself, someday it will be me that makes her strain her head back and groan like that.

When Silas fucked her, it was pretty straightforward. No bells and whistles. Not to mention, the quick glimpse of his cock I saw proved he was no Dirk Diggler. I would say he's definitely bigger than average, but I've got more girth on him hands down. Her quaking tits were what I was most impressed with, so much so, that I missed her face when she came the second time. I imagine the blood had been pooling in her head the way her hips were raised, and I've wondered since if that had any bearing on the strength of her orgasm.

I never took her for the showy type, but to be fair; in that dark environment she was basically obscured. Not her body, mind you, but her person—Jessie Hayes was concealed pretty well. Not like the third time I saw her getting fucked, that was full Jessie, and I'll get to that, but first I'll explain the second time I watched her having sex with that douche bag.

She and Silas were in the mock interrogation room. There is a two-way mirror, but they really had no way of knowing if anyone was watching. It's not like the Peep Show rooms where as soon as someone locks the door to the booth, a red light turns on, so the performers know where to direct the show. I've fucked Bradley in there so many times I don't even care if people can see my scar anymore. It used to bother me a lot, but not anymore. I've performed in the Peep Show area when only one red light was on, and I've been in there when every single one of them was lit. Needless to say, Bradley *is* the showy type.

Anyway, back to the interrogation room. Jessie was handcuffed with her hands behind her back while she blew Silas. All I could see at first was his stupid ass, but when he moved, I saw her shirt was open, and her delicious tits were out and proud. There had been a few of us watching the scene from the other side of the mirror at first, but the rest got bored from the lame role play and left.

Eventually, with Silas sitting in the chair facing me and Jessie's cuffed wrists behind his neck, things picked up again because Jessie was taking control. She faced him, straddling his lap while Silas raised her skirt so that it only covered the top of her ass cheeks. She wasn't wearing panties, and I was straining so hard to see between her legs I was probably fogging up the glass.

They were only about seven or eight feet away from me, and she had her ass popped out as Silas sucked on her nipples. The thing was, while Silas was caressing her ass, he would gently spread her for me—well, for anyone that happened to be watching but as luck would have it, it was just me. My dick was so hard having that view of her that I almost left to find Bradley before they even had sex. Once she did finally lower herself down his shaft, it didn't take long. I was pretty disappointed in his stamina if you want to know the truth.

All of that nudity from Jessie, and witnessing all of that sex *still* doesn't even come close to the exposition party a few months ago. She was naked at that point in the evening because Silas had wiped most of the warrior paint off her tits and from between her legs. This time was different though because this time she *knew* I was watching. Besides knowing I was watching, she *one hundred percent* performed for me.

She looked me in the eyes the whole time Silas toyed with her body, and she held her legs open to me the entire time. When she sucked his finger, she licked and savored it like it was a dick, while staring right at me. When Silas turned her and deposited her onto the toy demonstration platform, she was disappointed to break eye contact and kept stealing glances back at me. She didn't even seem like she was enjoying it when he fucked her.

The exposition party was just another indication for me that Silas' time with her is limited. She wanted me that night, I could feel it.

Work the following week was intensely awkward because she shyly stayed in her office with the door closed. If she had questions or needed me for something work-related, she texted me instead of walking into my office like she normally would have. As time went on, the work atmosphere normalized again, and thanks to my keen ability to ignore the obvious, she seems back to the normal JB.

I feel like it's important for me to stay the course with Jessie. I know how she feels about me, and I know she is torn, but I will never accept the divided attention of a woman, I deserve better than that. I never want to have to convince her I am the better catch. If she never comes to that on her own, I can accept that. What I can't accept is dishonoring myself by trying to push her into choosing me. I could have easily had her the night I picked her up from the margarita bar, but I want no part of her breakup, and I'll not try to sway her.

Women are not a problem for me. I can get ass anytime I want it, but I won't settle down with the wrong woman again. I also never want to wonder if my girl is thinking about another man, and if Jessie doesn't end things with Silas all on her own, I would always wonder.

End of Chapter One

945 Cedar Avenue

www.ingramcontent.com/pod-product-compliance
Lightning Source LLC
Chambersburg PA
CBHW030237200626
46816CB00002BA/398